OUTCAST

RUTHLESS PARADISE BOOK 1

LEXI RAY

OUTCAST

Copyright © 2022 Lexi Ray

All rights reserved. No part of this publication may be reproduced, distributed, or transmitted in any form or by any means, including photocopying, recording, or other electronic or mechanical methods, without the prior written permission of the publisher, except in the case of brief quotations embodied in critical reviews and certain other noncommercial uses permitted by copyright law.

This is a work of fiction. Similarities to real people, places, or events are entirely coincidental.

Editor: Tracy Liebchen

❦ Created with Vellum

PLAYLIST

555—Jimmy Eat World
Something Beautiful (feat. Masked Wolf)—Tom Walker, Masked Wolf
7 Billion—OBB
psychofreak (feat. WILLOW)—Camila Cabello, WILLOW
The W. A. N. D.—The Flaming Lips
Cooped Up (with Roddy Ricch)—Post Malone, Roddy Ricch
Left Hand Free—alt-J
Worth It for the Feeling—Rebecca Black
Something Good Can Work - The Twelves Remix—Two Door Cinema Club, The Twelves
Love Like Ours (feat. Tarrus Riley)—Estelle, Tarrus Riley
Spend Your Life—ELKI
Adore You—Harry Styles
Pizza Guy—Touch Sensitive
Wrecked—Imagine Dragons

You can find the playlist on Spotify

PROLOGUE
CALLIE

When a hundred elite students flew to Zion Island in the middle of the Atlantic for spring break, they didn't know that while they were chugging expensive booze and dancing, the world had exploded into a nuclear war.

While they dove off their fancy yachts and floated in infinity pools, the powerful military nations showered each other with warheads.

While they snorted drugs in their paradise cribs and fucked each other's brains out, millions were wiped off the face of the earth.

The sound of the world turning into a scorching cemetery was drowned by the techno music that blasted across the paradise beaches of Zion.

Then the cellphones started dinging with messages and calls but stopped abruptly. Social media went silent. And when the signal dropped completely, they knew something was wrong.

But by then, there was no way to reach home.

Many of them didn't have a home anymore.

Nor did they have families.

I still think that they were lucky. In the way you are lucky when you don't have to watch the world turn to dust.

Or see scorched bodies scattered across the landscape of rubble.

Or hear your loved ones wail.

Or watch them die…

Two years have passed since the Change. Yeah, there is irony in the word that carries with it despair and horror and signifies the turning point when the almighty proved that they can do anything for power. While they compared their dicks, they spat out warheads, wiping out city after city.

It will take decades to repair the damage and a lifetime to heal the scars.

The bombing stopped a long time ago, but the real enemy is the fallout. It's a silent invisible monster that claims thousands every day.

And then there is Zion.

Untouched.

Self-sustaining.

It's my only hope for a normal life.

It's where Abby, the only person I have left who is dear to me is.

And I am one of the few lucky ones to join the paradise.

1

CALLIE

"Zion is like going back in time," the young tattooed captain says before we zip up the hazmat suits and put the masks and respirators on.

If going back in time means to a world before the nuclear war, respirators, or fallout, it's a good thing. Even the pandemic years before sounds like child's play compared to this.

Leaving mainland is surreal, considering the world is in lockdown.

We file through the door that leads outside to the Yellow Zone—the coastal part farther away from the big cities. Yet, the protective equipment is still in place.

"The islanders are sensitive," the captain explains and winks as we go out onto the docks and load onto a large speedboat.

I am curious.

Anxious.

Petrified.

I will have to face Archer Crone.

I can't stop thinking of what is to come.

Three hours later, I still stand at the taffrail on the deck and stare at the horizon through the fogged plastic shield that covers my face. I want to tear off the respirator that makes my face all sweaty and breathing shallow, but I can deal with this for a chance to leave the mainland.

We are zipping off the coast of Georgia, which is now the most southern point of the states, since Florida is underwater, when the captain motions to us with the big glove of his hazmat suit.

Two years since the Change and the coastal areas are still flooded, deserted, and quarantined. Except the military ports. Public access is denied except to those who can buy their way in or out.

Though there is nowhere to go.

Borders are closed.

So is the rest of the world that survived. They don't want us. No one wants us anymore. The land of the free is now a prison.

Except for Zion Island. It's an exception in every sense.

There are seven of us, the lucky winners. All in protective suits. Shuffling toward the stern of the boat where a man hoses us down with decontamination solution. They take this seriously, it seems.

"Off!" He waves the familiar signal.

I struggle with the zipper under my chin that will let me out of this gray monstrosity. By the time I take off my face shield and respirator, Katura Ortiz next to me has already pushed the suit down her legs and kicked it off to the side.

"Damn! Finally!" She exhales loudly, lifts her head to the sky, and inhales deeply.

We've been acquainted for only three days since the orientation, and already I feel like she's become the closest person to a friend.

"*Ka-too-rah*," she introduced herself back on mainland days ago.

"Can I call you Kat?" I smiled.

"If you are family or a close friend." She cocked her arrogant brow at me.

Her bronze body is lean with muscles. The black tank top hugs her torso beautifully. Her cargo pants are full of pockets. I know she has a knife hidden in one of them, among other things that are not allowed—there will be a thorough search at the arrival to the island.

Katura shakes her thick dark hair, braided halfway along her scalp and loosely cascading down to her mid-back. She smoothes it, rips off the protective plastic from her backpack, and makes her way back to the deck.

I struggle to get the protective suit off me and inhale deeply.

The sea breeze feels liberating. This is perhaps the first time in a while when I can breathe without having the fear of radiation. But then, what do I know?

The sea-gulls ka-kaw in the sky as if nothing changed in two years since the war.

The ocean smells salty. Waves crash against the hull of the motorboat that speeds toward the horizon, to the only place that might be the actual change.

The water is deep blue-gray, shades darker than the

stormy sky. The wind blasts into my face, but I smile. The open sea makes the bad memories go away. If only for a short while.

I watch everyone getting rid of their suits. They glance around, smiles chasing each other.

They know it too.

This is our ride to freedom. To the place that escaped the war that destroyed half of the world. The Western world, that is. But that's semantics. Because the developing world and the surviving nations want nothing to do with us anymore. Or yet. Even the developing world is better than the Western countries that crumbled like houses of cards. Cities leveled to the ground. Radiation killing the survivors. The rest struggling to get back to semi-normal. Though nothing is normal.

Except for Zion. Right.

My heart beats fast in anticipation.

I struggle with my black hoodie that feels too hot. Everything seems too hot. The temperatures are hotter than usual in May.

Usual.

That has become a strange word. But in two years, the strangest things become usual—internment, martial law, food rations, drastic climate change, tsunamis, protective gear, gas masks.

Death...

I have no one. It's a tragedy that, combined with millions of others, became a statistic.

You don't dwell on the loss, you feel lucky you survived.

Or so they keep telling you at the weekly communal therapy.

I finally tear off my hoodie, tie it around my hips, and walk up to Katura, who laughs as she talks to the captain.

She is a gorgeous creature. Puerto Rican father. Ukrainian mother. Built like Wonder Woman. With the attitude of Commando.

I wish I had as much strength as her. At nineteen, she is an Amazon—an expert in first aid, weapons, and martial arts. I clung to her for the last three days we spent at the Transfer Center. She seems like she has her shit together. And I, three years her senior, still feel like the world doesn't make sense or has a purpose.

Katura talks to everyone—she is the social type.

"Hey, babe, hold this." Katura tosses her backpack at me and smiles at the tattooed captain with dark hair, beard, and a charming smile, who leads her away, grinning, down to the captain's cabin.

Ugh.

Those two have been rubbing together ever since the Transfer Center.

A scrawny guy with glasses, an Elon Musk meme shirt, and cargo pants comes over to stand next to me as we both stare at the ocean in silence. He is around my age. They say barely anyone over their mid-twenties is chosen to go to Zion.

The geeky-looking guy pushes the center of his glasses onto his nose with his forefinger and smiles awkwardly at me.

"Are you excited?" He looks around like he was born in a Minecraft world and nature is alien to him.

I wonder what he got selected for. Everyone has to have good looks and a talent or a skill. At least, that was what the network hustlers said. Zion doesn't choose just anyone.

I smirk at the thought. It's a frat-sorority world all over again. But can you blame them?

"What's your card?" I ask the guy instead.

"IT."

Of course.

They can overlook your appearance if you have skills like that. With a failed banking system and disrupted communication, IT is more valuable than food. They say Zion has its own satellite tower and data center.

"We are lucky, you know," he says when I don't answer.

The ones who still have families left are the lucky ones.

I am so over these conversations.

I shift the backpack onto my shoulder—the only thing we were allowed to bring with us—then grab Katura's and head toward the cabin. Whatever Katura is up to—talking, smoking pot—I'd rather be with her.

I walk down the steps, inhaling the smell of salt and damp leather and decontamination spray, and halt.

"Fuck… Yeah…" The grunts are male.

"Harder, babe…" That one is Katura's, and it makes my insides twist with unease.

I take another slow step down and am about to round the corner when I see Katura's knees, wide spread, and a white muscular ass and hips thrusting between them.

Gross.

I scramble up the stairs and almost fall out onto the deck.

My heart is pounding, and I feel my face catching on fire. I have no choice but to come back and stand next to the scrawny guy who is chatting to several others.

Five minutes later, Katura strolls out onto the deck, shamelessly fixing her tank top straps, a satisfied half-smile on her face.

"What up, babe?" she throws at me.

A lighter in her hand clicks, and she lights a joint, then exhales tastefully, and the smell of weed laces the salty air.

God, she is beautiful, untamed, and so wild in the worst and best ways possible.

The boat hits a large wave and slams into the water, sending most of us scrambling while Katura remains almost unmoved, her stance wide, a joint between her fingers.

The captain comes out. His eyes, blazing as if he is looking for treasure, find Katura, and he comes over.

That's the thing about Katura. She can fuck a random dude, and he will cling to her as if she promised the world to him. That's her invisible power. I feel it too. It's in the way she talks, acts, and in her no-fucks-given attitude.

The captain reaches around her to take the joint out of her fingers.

"Care to share?" His grin matches Katura's as he takes a deep drag, not taking his eyes off her, and passes it back to her, his hand possessively on her waist.

I look away, wondering if my gaze has too much envy. I wish I was like her—screwed any boy I wanted, fought anyone who dared look at me the wrong way, completely content on my own.

But I'm not. I feel forever lost after losing my family. Like I don't belong anywhere.

Katura's nonchalance is magnetic. She takes everything she wants from this life.

"You never know when the world ends, babe," she said back in the center and laughed. Her laughter was so liberating that, for a moment, the trip to the island felt like a vacation.

It's not. I should know better. Considering the circumstances and the person in charge.

Right now, I can't stop thinking about the captain's bare ass between Katura's legs. I don't even have a boyfriend. Haven't had one since…

Right.

The Block Party four years ago.

"Fuck." The captain loudly exhales a cloud of smoke. "The weather is shit. We are riding straight into a storm. But the Chancellor is impatient. So buckle up, Dorothy!"

He slaps Katura on the ass and takes over the helm from his deckhand.

And here is the reminder.

The Chancellor.

Ugh. My heart starts hammering in my chest at the mention.

That's what they call him on the island.

Archer Crone.

A fortunate son.

Former university star quarterback.

A handsome devil.

My ex-boyfriend.

Yeah…

He is the one I will have to bow to in order to finally find Abby, my only surviving cousin.

Sounds easy enough.

That is if Archer doesn't use everything he's got against me. I am the girl who got drunk one awful night during a Block Party four years ago and slept with his best friend. The girl he unleashed his wrath on. The girl who ran as far away as possible, switching universities and burning all bridges.

Dammit. This might have been a bad idea, but the risk is worth it.

I grip the railing tighter. That all seems like an eternity ago. Four years, to be exact. I haven't seen him or talked to him. But now it's time. I need to find Abby.

I've practiced the speech I will give Archer a hundred times in my head. After all, what happened four years ago wasn't my fault. That night was hazy. And waking up in Kai Droga's room was a nightmare come true. What followed was another nightmare, and another, and a never-ending reminder that one night can turn your life into hell.

Until two years later.

And the Change.

Hell has many shades. Many faces.

Kai Droga's beautiful face that I once wanted to kiss has become a nightmare and a bitter reminder of drunken mistakes.

"Nervous, babe?" Katura stares around at the ocean.

The water is rough. The boat swerves and jerks to one side, then another, hitting the choppy water as it speeds toward the final destination.

Only an hour left, I think.

Katura seems unconcerned about the weather and the sky that is turning the color of boiling tar ahead of us. She always talks like she's got it all figured out and knows exactly where the world is going to be on any given day.

The boat slams yet into another rough wave, and salty water sprays us head to toe. The temperature is dropping too. I nervously look up at the sky.

"Hey, golden angel, cheer up." Katura gives me a backward nod.

I don't even know why she likes me or acts like my big sister. She runs her fingers through my blond hair that is being whipped out in all directions by the violent winds. For a moment, I wonder if she wants to take me down to the captain's cabin too.

"Soon we will be in paradise," she says with a smile.

And suddenly, a rumble of thunder cracks across the sky.

"Life vests!" the captain shouts.

My heart starts pounding.

The deckhand starts throwing orange vests in our direction, and we all tumble onto our knees as the boat jerks violently to the side.

The boat slows down.

The captain curses.

It gets darker too rapidly.

And then the rain starts pouring so fast and with such

force that we are soaked in seconds before all of us manage to pile into the captain's cabin. We scramble on the floor, rocking side to side as the deafening sound of the rain and the crashing waves against the fiberglass drown the shouts of the crew members.

My heart is violently slamming in my chest.

This is not good.

I gape at Katura, whose eyes are sparkling viciously as if she were born into a storm.

"We'll be fine, babe, just keep close to me," she says.

I nod, thinking that if I stick close to her, I might make it to wherever we end up.

She pats her pockets. "Shit. I don't have another joint."

I want to laugh at her casualness when she exhales in disappointment.

Then a roar comes from the outside.

"Hold o-o-o-n!"

And Katura says the words that make my insides turn icy-cold.

"Are you a good swimmer?"

I am not.

I feel dizzy.

That's when the boat slams against something hard and sends us all flying.

2

CALLIE

It's a disaster.

We are tossed and slam into each other like sacks of potatoes.

And then there is water.

So much water...

"Grab the life ring!" Katura shouts as the waves smash against the boat that is suddenly tilted.

We are on the deck, crouching, sliding, being pounded by waves.

I can't see because of the water splashing into my face.

There are screams, roars, and deafening thunder.

A massive wave crashes over our heads and sends us plastered to the floor.

I am sliding.

Someone grabs me and shoves something hard into my chest—a life ring.

"Grab it and don't let go!" Katura shouts.

And then we are thrown overboard by another powerful wave.

I am not good with water. Not a good swimmer. Not having the ground under my feet when the storm is raging around sends me into a panic that is blinding and deafening. More than the water that is suddenly all around me.

I choke. Cough. I am tossed in the water like a rag doll.

But I don't let go of the life ring. My arms are wrapped around it. Some heavy weight is pulling it in a different direction.

Katura.

I can't see much.

Water.

Splashes.

Wind.

More splashes.

Giant waves.

Salty water in my mouth, nose, and ears. Choking and drowning me.

It's never-ending.

It lasts for so long that I feel like I am in some creepy purgatory.

It's dark. I don't even know if it's the storm or the night that fell suddenly. All I know is that I need to hold on to that hard ring in my hands. Katura is next to it. If we end up in hell—it's the two of us. I don't want to be alone. Definitely not in hell.

I slam into something hard with my back and almost suffocate from the impact.

It's like the wildest rollercoaster gone off the rails.

I thrash like mad.

Coughing.

Choking.

More salty water.

I close my eyes and think that this is it—I will die on the way to paradise.

My feet slam against something hard, searing me with sharp pain.

I want to make it.

Somewhere. Anywhere!

There is always that instinct to live that kicks in during the worst moments.

Then there is something hard under my feet.

"Hold on!" It's Katura again, her voice God-like in the darkness. "Don't let go of the ring!"

We are tossed around by the waves, the tide of it suddenly stronger than before but rhythmical. Pulling and pushing. Wave. After wave.

There is solid ground under my feet again.

I am blind from water and rain.

I am choking and nauseous and dizzy from all the swallowed water.

But I am being pulled forward, crashed by a wave, then dragged back by the tide and pulled forward again.

"Come on!" Katura shouts next to me. "Walk!"

And I realize that the solid ground under my feet *is* land.

We've reached the land!

I try to see where we are, but it's dark. The rain is a hazy wall around us. Another wave pushes me forward, but the water around subsides as I finally crawl out of the water and collapse on the hard surface.

Land.

There is a shout from somewhere. Not Katura's.

And then there *is* Katura. "Help! Over here!"

There is an echo of voices ahead.

But I can't think.

Darkness is all around it. It's noisy and salty.

I laugh, my forehead touching the wet sand, water dripping off me as I hug the ground, ready to break down into tears.

Strong hands pull me up.

"Can you walk?"

I can't even stand.

I am being lifted off the ground.

I am in someone's arms.

I don't care.

Take me somewhere dry and safe.

"I am fine. Fine!" Katura's voice echoes through the rain.

It's pouring. Pitch-black. But there are flickers of light—flashlights? And whoever is carrying me—he can carry me to paradise or hell as long as it's dry and I can breathe.

"There is another one!" the person carrying me shouts.

A man.

The voice is strangely familiar, echoing with the memories.

I must be hallucinating.

There are more shouts as I am being carried somewhere.

I smile.

We are here.

I press my shaking hands to the rain-soaked chest.

The rain lashes mercifully, but there are voices, people, land.

My head bobs as I try to rub my eyes and cough, fighting the burning sensation in my chest and nose.

There is light.

Light!

"There are three of them," the voice says.

So familiar.

I know it.

I finally wipe my face and eyes and look up at the man who still holds me in his arms as he steps into a dimly lit room.

Fate is strange.

It's weird.

Unpredictable.

Cruel.

Right now, it sends a blow so hard that I think I died and ended up in some screwed up dream.

Because I know the face in front of me.

He…

The sight of him is like a silent slap.

I am confused, lost, and shocked.

Can't be…

The eyes that stare back at me are as confused. And as shocked. And dark. Probing. Hypnotic. Overwhelming.

Four years later, and I still feel too much gazing in those eyes—a jolt of excitement, anger, hurt.

Shame…

I thought that the worst would be meeting Archer Crone.

But the worst is in front of me.

The man who ruined me four years ago.

Who took my innocence and turned my life into hell.

Who is a constant reminder of past mistakes.

The boy I never wanted to see again.

Kai Droga.

3

KAI

I can't fucking believe it.

This is not fucking happening to me.

My insides turn into a knot at the sight of her.

Callie Mays.

It's deja vu. And I can't work out the feelings that turn inside me like a ball of snakes.

It's pouring outside. Three of us were on a night watch when we heard the shouts and saw the shadows in the water.

Three girls.

Two life rings.

Life vests.

We haven't seen any new faces besides the town Savages and Divide patrol on this side of the island in months.

I picked up the one who couldn't walk.

And it's *her*...

If nightmares could come to life, this was it.

The last time Callie Mays was in my life, I lost my scholarship, wrestling career, and my best friend. The chain of events that followed turned me into a monster—a guy with tattoos that start at the neck and cover a large part of his body down to his ankles. They cover skin so scorched with second-degree burns that, four years later, I still shiver at the memories every time I take a shower and run my hands down the etched skin. Half-smooth with transplanted skin. Half-ridged with the ugly twisted scars.

Ink covers it all but not the memories.

Monsters are real. Especially when you see one in the mirror.

I stare at the girl, who I still hold in my arms, and am paralyzed with the memories. They flicker in my mind like fire sparks. The Block Party and a chain of events that brought me to this fucking island.

Blood pounds in my ears.

Bo stomps into the Common Lounge and halts, studying the three girls. "Fuuuck…"

I hear his voice and I don't. Because I can't stop staring at her and she at me.

The low words coming from the others don't quite reach my mind.

"Fuck, man. Like we need this."

"The boat crashed. There were ten of us."

"Only three are here."

"We should take them to the Divide. Right now."

"They are Archer's property."

"It's dark. Not tonight."

And I am still frozen to the ground.

I can't process this mess.

This wet blond hair plastered to the face that I dreamed of and had nightmares about.

These blue eyes.

This gaze that destroyed everything I knew and loved.

She stares at me with the same shock and horror.

And then her gaze changes into panic and what looks like hatred.

So does mine.

In sync.

Her hands start pushing at my chest, and I drop her out of my arms so abruptly that she stumbles onto the wooden floor. She cowers slowly toward the other two, who sit on the floor, shivering and smoothing their hair, staring at everyone gathered around.

I look away. It's me, Bo, Owen, Guff, Jeok, and Kristen.

Maddy, barefoot and wearing a loose summer dress, darts in and halts, smoothing her wet hair with her palms and gaping at the girls.

"Whoa." She stares with a foolish grin on her lips like Jesus just arrived.

The dim light in the lounge makes it even more surreal.

This is a bombshell.

Nightmare before Christmas.

A bad joke.

Her.

I want to tell Bo to get her the fuck off this side of the island. But then on the other side of the Divide is the Chancellor. Archer fucking Crone. Why am I not surprised that he finally brought her here?

This gotta be a bigger trick than the Change itself.

The three girls get rid of the life vests but sit on the floor in puddles, staring up at us.

"They will stay till morning," Bo says. He clicks the lighter and lights a joint. "Then we'll decide."

"Wait. Decided what?" Jeok asks, fists on his waist. "They don't belong here."

"Wait." It's the pretty girl talking, the one with the bronze-toned skin and braided hair. "We are on Zion, aren't we?"

She has her elbows planted on her raised knees as she stares around. This one is fearless. I can tell. She is too relaxed like she just came back from a mud run.

Callie sits with her head down, wipes her nose with the back of her hand, then glances up at me. And as soon as our eyes meet, she glances away, and my heart beats like a war drum.

Fuck...

"Yeah," Bo echoes as he leans on the doorway, smoking slowly. "On the wrong side of it."

He runs his fingers through his long dark dreads and spits out a piece of tobacco.

I hear muffled voices from outside, and several more people peek in, then gape with the same astonishment as they start crowding the Common Lounge. There are low straw-filled mattresses around and a table, but the three girls sit on the floor like they are prisoners.

I try to process my feelings and can't. I feel hatred at what happened four years ago, at Callie being a coward back then. And I feel the familiar jolt of excitement that I always felt looking at her. Like she was a little star winking at me from the sky.

This is fucked up.

I try not to look at her, but I want to study her, to see what changed. Because I haven't seen her in four years—not a single post from her social media.

She hasn't changed. Even drenched and miserable, she looks like she always did—perfect despite her messy blond hair.

But I have.

I am wearing jeans and a t-shirt that hide most of my ink but not nearly enough.

I see Callie's gaze drift along my tattoos—knuckles, arms, then up to my neck.

Yeah, petal, that's new. Take a good fucking look.

Anger starts simmering in me like hot tar. That familiar poison inside me is back.

I know these stares too fucking well.

Her eyes, wide with shock, meet mine and dart away.

I smirk, walk up to Bo, and take the joint out of his fingers. I take a deep drag, knowing perfectly well that I can't get high enough to come to terms with what is happening.

Jeok huffs and puffs. I can't blame him. When the fight on the Westside happened two years ago, his friend got killed. He is the last person who wants to get on Crone's radar.

"We don't have room for them," he snaps.

But Bo won't hear of it. That's why he was elected the leader of the Eastside.

"They will stay here tonight. Let's bring sheets and a change of clothes."

Maddy blurts out, "I got it," and runs out. Good, willing Maddy. The girl is golden.

I pass the joint back to Bo and stomp out of the Common Lounge.

It seems like we've been inside for only a minute, but the time was lost because it's drizzling outside. The storm is calming. By morning, this place will be the same sunny paradise as it is ten months out of the year.

I inhale deeply and run my fingers through my rain-soaked hair, the world suddenly dizzy and surreal.

The air is damp. The waves crashing at the shore are not nearly as violent.

The night is dark. But I can't help seeing *her* face, knowing *she* is right there, ten feet away from me, inside that lit room.

"What's up, man?" Bo's low voice behind me makes me shake my head.

"Nothing."

Liar.

I wish I never saw her face again.

But what do you fucking know?

Fate is a sneaky bitch. It reaches its claws at me two years after the Change.

Hundreds of miles away from the mainland.

On an island that is secluded and off-limits to the outsiders.

With the program that allows seven arrivals every four months.

Odds—one in a thousand.
And her.
On the wrong side of the island.
Because of some stupid storm.
Kill the weatherman.

4
CALLIE

It's windy outside. The girl who introduced herself as Maddy brings us clothes and kicks the rest of the people out of the room. Some glare at us, others smile and stare in disbelief as they file out of the room, leaving just the three of us and the girl.

It's some type of a cabana with a tarp wrapped around it on three sides. There is no door, and I see glimpses of the lamps as they disperse into the darkness.

"Bo said we will have a meeting tomorrow and discuss what happens next," Maddy explains.

She has brown hair loosely tied into a bun on top of her head. Soft features. Big lips. Soothing low voice and a heavy tan.

I like her already. She studies the three of us with care and too-obvious curiosity. She is eager to help, and there is a motherly feel in her gestures, like she is in charge here.

Katura strips in seconds and changes into a pair of blue shorts and a black t-shirt.

"We need to be on the Westside," she says business-like and flops onto one of the mattresses that are our beds for the night. She acts like a travel agent messed up her schedule, and she expects it to be fixed any minute. She looks up at Maddy. "You have a joint?"

Maddy studies her curiously for a moment, then smiles but without much cheerfulness when she says, "Get some sleep. I'll see you tomorrow."

It's only me, Katura, and another girl, short and skinny and with a scared gaze.

"What about the rest from the boat?" I ask meekly, in hopes that someone knows what happened to them.

The question hangs in the air unanswered, and I have a nasty feeling in the pit of my stomach at the thought that we might be the only survivors.

I am queasy and exhausted. Everything sounds muffled. There is water in my ears, and the inside of my nose burns from inhaled salty water. Salt is on my lips and in my hair. It coats my dry skin.

A guy brings us water in tin sports bottles with a logo that says, *Pura Vida. Welcome to paradise*, and I drink until the water starts trickling down my chin.

"Owen will be outside all night, so if you need anything, ask him," says Maddy.

"Why is he outside?" Katura snorts.

"For protection."

"From who?"

But Maddy doesn't answer, smiles warmly at me and the other girl, and walks out.

There is much to be learned about this island.

The third girl is tiny and the same age as me. Dani—I remember her name from the Transfer Center. She is too quiet and looks like she's been holding back tears for some time. She sits motionless in the center of the room and stares down at the floor.

"What a clusterfuck," Katura says, exhaling loudly. "We are lucky we survived."

Her words sink in as I finally rise from the floor, my body like jelly. I nudge Dani to get up and walk her to one of the mattresses. I will share the second one with Katura. I pick another pair of shorts and a t-shirt and hand it to the girl, then change out of my wet clothes, my every muscle aching.

Lucky, indeed.

The events of the past hour are a nightmare. But it all takes a backstage as I can't stop thinking about Kai Droga.

How did this happen?

When the light is off, I crawl onto the mattress with Katura and lie down, staring at the dark ceiling and listening for the sounds from the outside.

The splashes of the waves against the shore.

The strange birds in the distance.

The muffled sound of someone shifting in his seat, probably that guy, Owen. And a faint glow as if from a cell phone.

Cell phones don't work here, do they?

And *him*.

The image of Kai is right in front of me. But it's not the Kai from four years ago. Yes, the tanned face with a sharp outline of his jaw, the dominant but hostile gaze, and the smoldering black eyes belong to the boy I know.

But the rest of his body…

His neck is tattooed. So are his arms, the ink covering every inch and disappearing under the sleeves of his t-shirt.

When did he get tattoos?

He is the same but different. He was always strong and muscular from wrestling practice, a head taller than me. But now he is chiseled with muscles that strain his shirt, which makes him look even taller and larger. I've never imagined Kai Droga inked. He was a wrestler, clean and charming, a starboy heading for the nationals.

Now he looks like a bad-ass biker.

And his eyes…

I never forgot his gaze.

It used to be so intense and warm. He was the good one out of the bunch of privileged boys who ran the Deene University campus. The only one who wasn't filthy rich or had influential parents. My first true crush. The *only* one ever, in fact. I liked to think that he liked me too.

Until the night of the Block Party. When I suddenly was so drunk. When everything was dizzy and slow, and he led me to his room and took my virginity without my consent.

Or with.

That's the problem.

That night was a blank. I don't remember anything until the morning.

I will never forget the horrible feeling starting in the pit of my stomach that morning when I knew that things would only get worse. Much worse.

I wake up in someone's bed, covered by a blanket that bears the trace of Kai's cologne—the smell that I love so much. The scent that belongs to my boyfriend's best friend.

I don't remember getting here. Let alone anything that happened.

Shit.

I pull the blanket aside, and—

No-no-no-no-no.

I am wearing nothing but my panties.

And that horrible feeling in my stomach grows stronger, making me wanna vomit.

My head is a glass jar full of metal beads. My mouth is dry. I feel queasy. And sick.

Shit.

Did it *happen?*

I don't remember anything, let alone the act itself.

It was supposed to be special. And sweet. And with Archer, maybe.

I look around and see the pictures on the wall.

Kai Droga.

No-no-no.

I close my eyes and try to swallow the nasty bile that is rising in my throat.

I scramble out of bed and grab my clothes from the chair. Dress. Bra. Sticky. Covered in puke.

Oh, God, no.

I pull all of it on, cringing at the sour smell and fighting the urge to vomit, grab my shoes, and tiptoe to the door.

There is silence outside. There is silence in the hallway as I creep toward the staircase. Down to the ground floor. The muffled sound of a TV comes from somewhere. Music drifts out of someone's room. I reach the ground floor and look around to figure out where the front door is.

I round the corner and almost bump into a guy with spiky hair, wearing only shorts, a can in his hand. One of Archer's friends.

Crap.

His face splits into a shocked grin. "Aaaaaaaaw shiiiiiit, guys!" he almost screams.

I feel my face catch on fire. I scramble past him, focusing on the front door.

And that's when another guy blocks my path.

And more of them start walking out from all corners, a dozen of them.

All cheering, giggling, booing.

"Is that what Kai was hiding in his room?"

Someone cackles.

Fear sweeps through me so strongly that my knees almost buckle.

I will never forget those twenty feet to the front door of the fraternity house as a dozen guys start whistling and clapping.

A walk of shame is never easy.

Neither is cyber-bullying, memes, nasty texts, threats from Archer that same day, and my car spray-painted with the bright yellow "SLUT" across it.

That was the day I ran, switched schools, and never came back to Deene University. Nor did I ever talk to anyone. Except Abby, of course. My life was months of hell until people I knew at Deene forgot about me and found other entertainment.

I've never seen or talked to Kai since. Or Archer. *Especially* Archer. I've never told anyone what happened that night.

And now Kai is like a heavy blow from the past.

Except this time, when our eyes met, his were blazing with so much hate that it made my stomach turn.

I should be the one hating him for what he did to me. But that was before the Change. Before I lost my entire family, just like many others. Before the fallout and the ruined country, barred from the rest of the world, became the new reality.

Exhausted, I let my eyelids droop.

I just want to wake up in a place that doesn't remind me of the traumas of the past.

But the only image that floats across my mind is *his* face. The last thought that flickers in my head before I fall into a deep sleep is, *What are the odds…*

5

KAI

There is no way I can sleep now. Not till tomorrow. Not till *she* is out of my sight.

I need a stiff drink. A joint. Blow would be better. Loud music would be great. Someone to fuck would be a bonus. But these are reserved for special occasions. They require tokens, and those are rare on this side of Zion.

Nevertheless, this night is special all right.

So I stomp toward the workshop.

It's my domain.

It's the place that reminds me of dad's garage and everything he taught me.

It's the place where I can't hear the ocean. In the moments of peace, I like to pretend that we are not in this tropical prison. That our families are not dead. That we can go on with our lives, however fucked up.

"Fucked up" has shades. You learn it after two years of doctors and plastic surgeons and physical therapy and psychologists. You think you went through hell. Only to go to the island to take revenge on the guy who turned your life into hell, because you needed to kill this monster called hate, and find out that hell is the Change.

Yeah, the irony. You thought life was fucked up until the world you knew ended.

"Bro, wait up!" Bo's voice is behind me, and in a moment, he catches up and walks right beside me. "Wanna tell me what's up?"

I open the door to the workshop too forcefully and flip the switch of the lamp, wired to the solar panel.

The light illuminates a small room, thirty by thirty feet. Wooden walls are covered with hanging tools. Crates are stacked in all corners and are loaded with materials, ammo, and homemade guns.

Yeah. One year you are a star wrestler, heading to the nationals. The next, you help your dad build cars. And then you make guns from wood, metal barrels, and ball bearings because you live on a fucked-up island and need to protect yourself and hopefully—*hopefully*, though it's been only hope for two years now—get out of this fucking place.

"Bro, you are angry. I can tell." Bo follows me inside and takes a seat in a wicker chair by a desk.

It's quiet. I like quiet. It turns off dark thoughts. Not many come here except Ty and Bo, who occasionally help me with making weapons. It's a long process—getting the necessary stuff bit by bit from the town, exchanging it for the pot that we grow and tokens.

I open one of the drawers and pull out a bottle of local rum.

"Whoa. A special night or something?" Bo's arms cross over his chest, feet crossed at the ankles. "Care to share?"

Ever since I came to this island, Bo, who was the manager of the resort on the Westside, was another person who hated Archer Crone. We have that in common. Bo is good at listening, navigating, mediating, and planning. Hence, once we left the Westside, he was elected the leader.

"Nothing to share." I pour rum into glasses and pass one to Bo. "I know one of the girls. We used to go to Deene together."

I don't feel like talking. And Bo doesn't ask questions, only stares at me.

His skin is almost coal-black from the sun exposure. We ran out of sunblock a year ago, and now use coconut oil that doesn't work nearly as well. His thick curly hair is tangled into dozens of dreadlocks and gathered by a tie at the back of his head. His eyes are almost chalk-white against his black skin. And so fucking prying that I want to tell him everything.

Just not tonight.

Bo is nothing like the polo shirt and Movado wearing pristinely dressed luxury resort manager that he was when I got to Zion. It's like his entire personality switched since the Change and Crone taking over the Westside. He is in his early thirties, built like a Spartan. Two years after the Change, his smooth business-like behavior changed into a Rasta meets Black Panther.

Bo is like a brother to me. He would understand everything. But I want to be alone right now. I want to process what happened and how to keep my cool.

The door whispers, and Ty pokes his blond head in.

"Br-r-ru-u-uh," he stretches.

I shake my head and blink away. "Don't. Not now."

Ty used to be in Archer's crew. He knows my and Callie's story. He knows better than to ask questions now and promptly disappears.

I pull a hand-rolled cigarette out of a pack, light it, and inhale deeply. The tobacco hisses as it burns. Its scorching heat seeps into my lungs.

Better.

I take a swig of the strong evil-smelling rum that we get in town, and it rips my throat.

Better still.

"We didn't quite get along, that girl and I," I finally say and fall back into a wicker armchair, tilting my head back against the headrest and closing my eyes.

"Wanna talk?" Bo asks.

I shake my head.

I hear him stand up, down his drink, and set the cup down.

"Yeah, tomorrow is gonna be one hell of a day. Communal meeting after breakfast. Get some sleep."

But when the door closes behind him, the last thing I think about is sleep.

Callie Mays, the golden girl, is on Zion.

Fifty feet away from here.

In the Common Lounge.

I take another drag and chug the entire drink, then pour myself another one.

It's crazy what our minds can do.

Mine spins like a rollercoaster with the images from the past that fuck me up more than booze or pot.

The Block Party, the biggest in years.

Callie's slender body, moving on that low podium to the sounds of her favorite Doja Cat song. Her cute blue string dress, floating around her curves. Her hips swinging. Her luminous blue eyes flicking here and there, but mostly at me. Rosy lips curling into a cute smile.

There is always that smile. She never smiles like this at Crone. Only at me. And blushes.

Holy hell, how she blushes when I am around!

Then there is Jules, rubbing on me like a cat in heat, though I can't take my eyes off Callie.

And there is Crone.

He's already gotten blown in his Maserati by some cheerleader, but he wants more. Always wants more. Her. And he doesn't feel like playing the hard game.

"I'm gonna fuck her tonight," he announces so casually as if Callie is another one of the girls who drop their panties at his command.

He grins and waves at her when she smiles at him, dancing on that podium—so innocent, so naive it makes my hands curl into fists.

I flex my fingers at the memory and take another gulp of rum.

And then there is drunk *Callie.*

And me, carrying her to the frat house to my room.

Undressing her…

I exhale at the memories.

There will always be that image of her dancing.

Followed by the dark ones.

That morning wasn't supposed to go that way.

But how was I supposed to know when the effect of roofies or whatever was in her drink would wear off? Because she wasn't drunk—she was high the night before. How was I to know that she would leave my room on her own in the house full of hungover frat boys?

No fucking calculation could've prevented that.

I am in the kitchen, drinking a beer and trying to figure out how to tell Crone I brought his girl home because she was too drunk to walk.

That's when the cheers come from the hallway.

I crane my neck, and my heart falls.

Callie.

Fuck.

Her blue eyes are full of panic as she skirts the wall toward the front door.

Fuck!

I freeze, knowing that's it. I fucked up.

Ty slaps me on my back. "Well done, bro."

"That's not what you think." I want to punch every single one of those fuckers. Except it's too late.

"Whatever it is, bro. You always wanted her. Good for you. But Archer will kill you."

And Crone almost does.

The rumors spread like wildfire across the campus. "Callie Mays in Kai Droga's room."

My phone starts dinging with messages.

One of them is from Crone.

"I'll fucking destroy you, Droga."

I tried to forgive myself for what I'd done. I should've left Callie at that party, right? Should've let Crone have what was his. He was my best friend. A girl should never come between best friends.

I exhale again. Because the rest is history tattooed on my monstrous skin.

Yeah. It's crazy what our minds can do.

Because as soon as I take another swig of rum and close my eyes, here she is again.

Callie Mays.

Petal.

Swinging her hips to Doja Cat and smiling like the next day our lives won't turn to fucking hell.

6

CALLIE

I don't know what time it is when I wake up. I hear soft voices outside the cabana, and then they are gone. But what is more unusual is the wild cacophony of birds. It's like waking up in a parrot zoo.

Katura is fast asleep next to me. The girl can sleep through a war.

The room is sunken in the soft morning light. Thirty by thirty feet. Simple. Two mattresses. Low Asian-style couches like in the chill-out lounges. The low wooden platform in the middle is littered with books, magazines, an ashtray and dirty cups. White translucent curtains hang all around, shifting in the slight breeze. It could be a fancy lounge at some resort if it didn't look so rundown.

I get up from the mattress and pad across the sandy floor toward the opening to the outside.

Wow!

The lounge, shaded by palm trees, is only fifty or so feet away from the water. Birds of all kinds chirp like mad in flower shrubs and trees. And the view in front of me is like a postcard.

The waves lap softly at the shore. I fight the feeling of suspicion. You start being suspicious of anything when you live during fallout. Unless you have a radiation detector at hands.

But they said this island is untouched.

A miracle, really.

After seeing desolation, miles of familiar places turned into no man's land, destruction, law-abiding citizens turn into marauders, mile-long lines for food donation, and abandoned towns and ruins, this place is truly a paradise.

Just wow.

I can't help but stare at the azure waters with cyan patches and sprinkles of darker brownish weed floating closer to shore. It's so calm that the storm the day before seems like something out of my nightmares.

I walk from under the shade created by the trees onto the beach.

The beach is less than a mile-long stretch of sugary-white sand and beyond—majestic blue infinity.

Along the beach are a number of bungalows—some are tiki huts, others are makeshift patched up cabins. A larger, open-sided cabana with a coconut-palm-branches roof over wooden beams, raised wooden floor and long tables and rows of benches must be the dining area.

Hammocks are strung here and there between the palm trees and plumerias. A guy snores in one of them, his tatted hand hanging down almost to the ground.

The beach is surrounded by the green jungle. Palm trees

duck almost to the ground onto the white sand, snaking toward the water. On either side of the beach and just some distance ahead rocks are peaking out of the water, and the sound of the crashing waves is louder there.

When I narrow my eyes, I see more details. Specifically, the beams, many of them, sticking out of the water in symmetrical rows. And it dawns on me—this *was* once a resort.

I walk toward the water, feeling the warm sand under my feet. It must be just past dawn. The sun is barely above the horizon, and there is pleasant coolness in the air, licking at my skin.

I inhale deeply.

God, it's been a while. After the Change, you learn to breathe carefully, which is ridiculous, because radiation finds you anywhere, regardless of whether you are wearing a respirator or a protective suit.

To my right, just a distance away, there are several girls in the Sun Salutation pose. It almost looks like a tropical yoga retreat.

I step up to the water and smile when the first wave rustles to my feet. I wiggle my toes in the wet sand and wait for the next wave.

My heart clenches, my eyes burning with tears.

This is so perfect that what happened to the rest of the world seems utterly unfair. Maybe I am still not myself.

My body is sore.

My muscles ache.

My head is still heavy from all the swallowed water the night before.

My hair is a messy bird's nest.

My skin is prickly with dried salt water.

I need a shower.

Something to eat.

My backpack that is gone.

I stand on a random beach wearing someone else's clothes at the mercy of the fate that brought me here. And I want to drop to my knees and weep. I wish I'd die right here and now so I could remember this world as beautiful as the sight before me.

A gull cries out over my head, then lands not far from me and cocks its head as if I am an intruder.

"Hey," I say softly.

My chest shakes as I try to suppress a sob. I don't have a single friend in this world, except Abby on the other side. And I do feel like an intruder on this island. But there is nowhere else to go.

"Hey," I hear behind me and turn to see Maddy walking up to me.

Her smile is endearing, but it fades as she notices my tears and nods, looking away.

She comes to stand next to me and studies the horizon as if she doesn't see this beauty every day of her life.

"Welcome to Zion."

7

MADDY

I LIKE THIS GIRL. BLONDE. PRETTY. SAD BLUE EYES FULL OF tears.

Is she crying?

Jeez.

I sigh as I stand next to her.

The view gets old, no matter what they say.

Not a single day after the Change feels like luck.

Sure, we haven't seen the destruction with our own eyes. But many of us lost it all just like everyone else. We didn't have to hide in bomb shelters, join search parties through rubbles, or live through looting, riots, and martial law. We didn't get tagged like cattle by the level of radiation exposure.

But the pretty island turned vicious over the span of several weeks.

First, it was mourning. Our cell phones stopped working. The only way to connect was through the data center on the island. It was our tie to the world, controlled by

Archer Crone. And even when we learned the news and had the confirmed deaths, we didn't believe it.

How could you?

The world went into lockdown almost instantly. Borders closed. International air and ground traffic stopped. Only several months later, when Archer resumed the full connection with the mainland and, despite data centers destroyed all over the world, the internet was restored, we all tried to get in contact with the survivors. Most of the survivors had a clear message, "Please, don't come. It's hell."

Those who wanted to leave were allowed to. Never to come back.

But what would you do in a country that has martial law? Where the coastlines are completely destroyed and contaminated? Where only thirty-fifty percent of the land is livable?

Some of us weren't given a choice. That was part of the fight that broke out on the Westside.

Back then, we didn't know that the island would turn into hell, and the one in charge would be Archer, the Chancellor, as he declared himself.

Because he could.

Because his loyal dogs ruled everything.

Because his daddy bought every resort on the island, East and West, several years before the Change.

Why? Because he is the Secretary of Defense. Surprise, surprise. You can connect the dots.

And just like that, Archer became the king of the island. With servants, a tight circle of followers, minions, and his goons. Smart, too. He controlled the tower and the data center. He had access to the mainland. He had boats that went back and forth, bringing the necessary goods. He became the king, the mafia don, the owner, the slave-master, the pimp, the executioner, and the master of fate. You name it—that was Archer Crone. And if you weren't willing to lick his boots—well, you ended up on the Eastside.

Twenty-one of us.

We were lucky he let us reside in the secluded resort. We had the basics. Sleeping accommodation. A small supply of dry goods. A garden in the back. Two boats.

We lost some of it during the last storm as well as the wooden deck and overwater bungalows. We learned pretty quickly how to handle the garden, the greenhouse, the chicken coops, and the fruit trees.

You learn anything when you are hungry. Including fishing and using about anything as food.

Still. It's not paradise. Not when you have zero knowledge of what's happening beyond its borders, having to meet in secret with those from the Westside to find out. Not when you have to grow pot to sell to the town on the Northside in exchange for tokens that will buy you meat, cereal, coffee, booze, tobacco, and used clothes.

You learn.

You survive.

You realize that self-sufficiency is hard fucking work.

Then you find out that seclusion does not always mean safe. And when the thugs from the town attack one night, you lose a friend, and then another friend, a girl, Olivia, whose fate becomes much worse than those who died during the bombings. Her name is said quietly and with the awful memories of what humans can do to each other when stripped of basic human values.

You make a little cemetery in the jungle and hope that it doesn't grow.

You carry on. You are twenty. You want to call your relatives and ask why you should even bother surviving. You want to hear their voices. You want someone stronger, older, and wiser to tell you it's gonna be alright. You want to sit one full day without having to think about what chores are on the list and whose night shift it is. And you push away the thought that maybe your relatives are not all dead, despite seeing their names in the released government records of the deceased.

Thanksgiving comes. No one looks at each other. You charge your phone—that useless brick—because it carries memories. So you sit all evening and flip through the pictures. Over. And over. And over. Though the dear faces start feeling like they belong to someone else's life.

Then a hurricane comes and wipes out half of the structures and almost the entire supply of food for the next month. One of your friends breaks down and wanders off into the night, only for his body to wash up ashore a week later.

The cemetery acquires another grave.

But you carry on.

Because that's what you've learned to do.

Paradise is a great word. It lacks responsibility. Because responsibility is a burden that makes you grow up too fast.

This is not paradise. This is survival. Coping. Waiting it

out. With a grim thought—there might not be anything in the future to look forward to.

Sure, we have good days. We are a family. We learned to share and take care of each other. There are occasional parties and booze and music from before the Change because, unlike the Westside, we don't have internet access. These are the moments when we forget that we have no one but each other. And we laugh. And sing. And drink. And kiss. And fuck. In those moments, we truly feel lucky.

But such moments are one in a hundred. When you wake up the next day, the azure waters and the luscious jungles with the bright parrots are still there—it's Groundhog Day all over again.

I don't tell the blondie all of that. She will find out. As we walk along the beach, she asks questions, and I answer some of them.

She seems like a nice girl. Another survivor, Dani, looked like she was mute last night. And the third one—Katura—is a bad-ass bitch who thinks she has her shit together and is too confident for her own good. I gotta give it to her, it's good for survival. There are plenty of such girls on the Westside, who will do anything to please the Chancellor. Katura might just fit right in.

I explain to Callie "the village," as we call our little settlement, and how things work around here. Somehow, I want her to stay. The Westside will break her—I can tell. The selected winners don't know what they signed up for.

When we come back to the village, the air is already thick with smoke and the smell of food.

The other two girls sit at one of the tables in the dining

area and talk to several curious people. Katura, the cocky one, is eating an orange, spitting the seeds onto the ground. She has a story, that one.

Bob Marley trickles through the air.

"Music? How?" Callie stares, surprised.

I chuckle. "We are not all back to basics. There are solar panels everywhere. That's how we get electricity. It used to be a high-tech new-age resort. We charge our phones and speakers and lamps. There are generators. Phones can be used for Bluetooth messaging and stuff."

There is a splash on the shore. We turn to see the boat pull in. The boys jump out and unload the coolers, which look heavy, and we all cheer.

"That means they had a good catch," I explain to Callie. "We eat a lot of fish. Plenty is out there. And it's free. Corn flour is dirt cheap, too."

But Callie doesn't hear me as she stares at the boys, who are goofing around on the beach. The sun is still too low, and they are shirtless and barefoot.

It's Kai, Owen, and Ty. They are always together, and they are the best at it. I smile as Owen pushes Kai, who stumbles and rolls onto the ground, then jumps up and tackles Owen, both rolling on the ground, shouting and laughing.

As I turn back to Callie, I notice her gaze—it's the same intensity as the night before. Her eyes are narrowed but unblinking at the boys in the distance. One in particular.

I saw it last night. And it's much too obvious—she and Kai know each other.

8

KAI

As we carry the coolers toward the dining area and kitchen, I give Ty another warning glare.

"Keep your mouth shut," I say. "This will only work against her if you say something to others. I'll handle it with Bo. He should know."

Ty was all never-ending comments during the fishing trip.

It's a shock to him, too.

He was part of our crew back at Deene. And when I was finally out of the hospital, I transferred to online courses but kept in touch with several. Including Ty. He still hung out with Crone and the gang, but since the shit went down on the Westside after the Change, he has been one of the Outcasts. That's what we call ourselves, jokingly or not.

He knows Callie, who disappeared off the face of the earth after that Block Party.

"What are the odds?" he murmurs again as we bring the coolers into the kitchen.

"Shut it," I snap.

I am tired of hearing this phrase, but it's a fact.

I am wearing only my board shorts and am too aware of myself, of my inked body.

And of every voice around.

I want to hear hers.

It brings back memories.

But I don't want to look around openly.

So I take my time in the kitchen that is open into the dining room so I can see everything.

"I'll sort out the coolers," I tell Ty and Owen, and they don't argue, because they are starving, and breakfast is already being served.

Ethan whistles as he surveys the catch. "You are on the roll," he says.

He is our cook and in charge of the pantry and produce. Tall, skinny, long hair, and a goatee. He and Maddy are also in charge of the inventory.

I start sorting and unloading the fish into a sink. Now and then my eyes scan the two long dining tables, searching for Callie.

And then I see her.

She sits at one of the tables facing me, and I don't realize that I stall as I study her, absorbing her looks.

She looks exactly the same. Except her blond hair is not flat-ironed but frizzy and a mess. Someone's t-shirt is too loose on her, and she looks more relaxed, unlike the pristine perfect Callie from Deene.

As if sensing my gaze, she raises her eyes and meets

mine across the dining room, and my heart starts pounding like mad.

I look away and make enough noise to make it look like I am busy.

I can sense her gaze on me, and it makes my body tense like an iron rod. My skin blisters at the realization of her gaze.

I take a rag and start wiping the coolers, my eyes focused on my inked hand, black knuckles, and fingers.

I look like some gang member. But hey, that's better than looking like something just chewed you up.

The humming of everyone's low chatter is interrupted by loud laughter. It's Ty. Our fucking sunshine. He is making new friends. And it's nice to hear laughter. It's nice to have "guests."

"Hello, Kai."

The voice makes blood shoot to my head.

It's hers.

The sound of it right behind me makes me shiver.

I turn around slowly. I am on my knees with a fucking rag like a cleaning boy. But I straighten my shoulders and conjure the most indifferent demeanor as I give her a backward nod.

"Long time," I say, holding her gaze.

It's hypnotizing like it's always been. The memories flash like a lightning bolt between us.

God, she is gorgeous.

I wanted her off this island as soon as I recognized her face. I want to hate her for what happened four years ago.

But there is another feeling trickling like a stream of

water through the desert cracks. That feeling that made my heart pound like mad in my chest back at Deene every time our eyes met. That made me scan her social pictures for hours at a time. That same feeling that made me jerk off at the thought of her more often than a fucking porn addict.

That feeling is back.

And I hate myself for it.

I realize we stare at each other for too long, and I drop my gaze and carry on with the coolers.

She doesn't say anything else and is being called over to the table.

Gone.

Good.

I exhale in relief like I've been holding my breath for the longest time.

Bo gathers everyone. My ears are turning into locators, trying to catch every word.

The sun is getting higher, and the heat is rising. Sweat gathers on my forehead. I am sticky. The sand scratches my knees. But the only thing I feel is—

Anticipation.

Yeah, it's fucked up.

It brings me back to that day after the Block Party when I saw her in the hallway for the last time in my life. The day we should've talked but never did. The day when I frantically texted and called her, and she never answered. The day that could've fixed the night before but instead ruined both our lives.

And that fucked-up anticipation is back because I want to talk to her. I hate myself for that too. There is too much hate, and it has nowhere to go but into that fucking rag that I scrub the cooler with like I'm trying to murder it.

Everyone gathers around one table. A collection of swimwear and shabby dresses and shorts, arms crossed at the chests, eyes darting around in excitement.

There will be voting.

Everyone is agitated. For the first time in months, there are new people around. They might be extra mouths to feed. They might be a liability. But they are something new on this side of the island that is drowning in fucking boredom and monotony.

More than anything, everyone wants to know what happened over there, on the mainland. These three lived through it. We are all desperate to know it from someone first-hand, as opposed to the videos and streaming news that Crone aired on the big screens, and the death toll lists that we studied for days and days after the Change, finding the names we knew so well.

Bo tells the girls about the Westside. He used to be a manager and a businessman. He knows how to lay down the facts.

"It's not a free ride," he explains, his hands clasped on the table in front of him, the three arrivals across from him. Everyone is crowded around like he is preaching. "You have to work for everything you get. Just like here. Archer Crone doesn't bring fresh blood just for fun, although that's a big part of it."

God, I love Bo's diplomacy. He should be a president or some shit.

"Here is the thing," he goes on. "There are over a

hundred people on that side. And there is no law except the Chancellor and his team. With a hierarchy of power where guns have the final say. Let it sink in for a moment."

I glance at Callie.

She sits with her head down. I can only imagine what thoughts run through her head. She used to go out with Crone. But after what happened, Crone's bullying went too far. He is not a man who forgives easily. I feel unease thinking about what he will do to her. I wonder if she realized that when she decided to come here. Why the fuck did she even come?

Katura is the one asking questions.

Feisty, that one. A natural leader. Hispanic or something of the sort, pretty, confident. That one has teeth. But something is missing, and I'm trying to figure it out. She is not like the rest of us—the ones who lost something with the Change. She is too businesslike, like she is on a mission. She enjoys every moment of the day like she has no baggage. And she keeps asking and asking about the Westside like she is gathering an intel.

Odd.

Eventually, all questions are answered. The Bob Marley playlist died a long time ago.

I'm the only one who is not at the table.

"So here it is," Bo says. "My suggestion is that you stay here for several days, talk to others, and figure out what you want to do. If you decide to go to the Westside, several of us will take you there. The shortcut takes about six hours across the hills and the jungle. We don't have ATVs or Quads to drive you. There is a chance that Archer Crone is looking for you. It poses certain risks"—he looks around the crowd—"that we are all aware of. So just to make sure the majority welcomes you here and gives you a chance, we will vote."

Bo—such a fucking mediator. He doesn't want anger or unnecessary fighting. So of course, he is doing it in the best tradition of democracy. He is also doing it to find out who has a problem with his decision so he can talk it over with them.

We are all careful these days. After Johnny broke down that one night after the hurricane and walked off only for his body to wash ashore later, the term "mental health" is more often on Bo's tongue.

"All right! Who is for letting our guests stay for several days before we make the final decision?"

He raises his hand and looks around as hands start shooting up in the air. Almost all of them, except for a few, including Jeok, who purses his lips. But after a second of hesitation, they join, too.

Everyone looks at each other with smiles and nods. And so do the three arrivals.

"Hey, you!" Bo's voice is loud, and I tense as I look up. His chin ticks at me. Everyone stares. *She* stares, I know it, though I don't look at her. "You are part of this, you know."

Bo's eyes on me are too intense. The fucker knows what he is doing.

I raise my hand reluctantly for a brief second and turn my gaze to Ty. He is grinning, staring at me.

Fucking fool.

I want to throw him into the ocean.

"Then it's set!" Bo rises from the bench, and everyone around loosens up. "You are staying until we have another meeting and discuss further arrangements. Maddy will show you around and explain what we do here and how we do it."

I keep wiping the coolers that have been wiped several times already when I see Ty's big bare feet approaching.

"You gonna scrub holes in those coolers or what?"

The fool is grinning, and I throw a rag at him, making him duck with a mocking laughter.

"Dude, you are low-key obsessing, I can tell," he says.

"Fuck off."

But despite how much I want to smack the hell out of him, he is right. There is that one feeling poking at my heart like a sparrow searching for seeds of hope—relief.

9

CALLIE

I want to talk to Kai.

I never thought I would, but here on the island, four years after what happened to us, I feel like he is one of the few people I know well. Or did until the Block Party.

He's changed so much that the only thing familiar about him is his face. From his neck down are the tattoos that cover most of his body down to his feet. It's shocking and mesmerizing. His hair is longer, past his ears, dark and messy and wet.

Kai was never a bad boy. Maybe, a bit dark. Quieter than the rest of Archer's obnoxious crew. An underdog among the sharks, but independent, not giving a shit whether he fit in or not.

But he's changed. There is no sweetness in him. His piercing dark eyes lack usual kindness. There's hate in them. His movements are jerky like he wants to rip things apart.

I can't stop looking. He takes my breath away.

I watch him the entire time Bo is talking and see him glance up at me. But as soon as our eyes meet, he looks away.

I want him to look at me. I want to talk. I want to finally sort out the why and what of that night. I want him to look me in the eyes and admit what he did. It was all his doing. And he has no right to glare at me like he does.

Yeah, I heard about his falling out with Archer. About the transfer to online classes. You reap what you sow. And then the accident. I don't know the details, but it sounded bad. I just never knew *how* bad until Abby told me almost a year later.

Kai rakes his fingers through his hair, and it's so sexy that, for a moment, I forget how much I hated him all these years.

The meeting is over. Maddy and Ty are leading me, Katura, and Dani toward the bungalow we will be staying in.

Ty is smiling as always. The boy with the heart. The Golden Retriever. Six feet of lean body. A wide grin. A golden tan that makes his blond shoulder-length hair stand out even more. He is like an Abercrombie&Fitch poster boy.

He elbows me as we walk.

"I never expected to see you here," he says. "How've you been?"

I shrug. With all that happened in the world, it's easier to talk about Deene than life.

"I mean." He shakes his head. "Considering."

"Yeah," I echo. "It's been rough, you know."

It's too early to ask questions. About his family and all.

OUTCAST

We will eventually. Though I am surprised that Ty is on this side of the island and not with Archer's crew. Maybe it's better that I am here, though I desperately want to see Abby.

I finally manage a smile. "You look great."

He laughs. "Well, considering."

I love his laughter. It's contagious. Always has been.

Palm fronds mixed with the sand prickle my feet, but it feels good. So does the ocean breeze and open space that is cheerful and not dusty and full of destruction.

The sun is relentless, and I fight the feeling of trying to skip to the shade. I'll get used to it.

It's surreal.

So are the next several hours.

Maddy gives us spare clothes and bikinis.

"You'll find that a bikini will become your second skin." She smiles. Everyone is super-nice and smily. "We get the necessities in town with tokens."

There are tokens instead of money on the island. Makes sense.

There is coconut oil.

"We make it ourselves, actually. It's a natural sunblock. Well, to a degree. You'll find out soon enough that you don't care about tan lines anymore."

The fresh water comes from the springs.

"There are several waterfalls on the island. We wash clothes there. We'll take you to one of them in the next few days."

Every bungalow has a shower and bathroom, but most of the pipes were damaged by the last hurricane. So they use the outside bathrooms and the shower that is in the back, close to the jungle, with the four chest-high bamboo screens for privacy.

Next, Maddy points out the bungalows.

There is a greenhouse where they dry and process pot that they grow to trade things with the town.

There is the Common Lounge, the large draped room where we spent last night. The swimming pool behind it is dried out and the poles of the cabanas are naked off fabrics. There are several tiki hut structures.

An open-plan kitchen with fancy stainless steel, granite tops, and a kitchen island, is covered with a layer of salt. And an open cabana, a dining room with two ten-foot-long tables.

Maddy explains the chores and who does what. There are schedules for cleaning and shifts written in chalk on the community board in the dining area. It's like a hippie farm.

Katura studies everything with interest. Dani with absent calmness.

I take it all in. It feels like some strange dream. An alternate reality.

And the only reminder that it's not is Kai.

10

KATURA

Alright.

I need to figure things out.

There is a reason we ended up here, and it might just be for the best.

I follow Maddy as she explains how their little communal living arrangement works, but I am more interested in what went down with the Westside.

Bo is the leader here. He is a magnificent creature, and I should stay close to him. He looks like a polished Rasta guy with his almost waist-long dreads gathered at the back of his head. But his manners are too thought-out, practiced, and precise. He seems like he has his shit together, and the way he reasons is just like my father. He is older, too, in his thirties. So he is not one of the spring-breakers. But he is too dominating and organized to be one of the island staff.

Maddy is the one in charge of pretty much everything. She can be useful. She is the mother, the sister, the godmother, the counselor—that type.

Kristen fucks her way through the Eastside. That one likes fun. She eyed me at breakfast with competitive curiosity.

Ty is the sunshine. Blond, tanned, perfect surfer's body, smiley attitude, all jokes and winks. And a talker. I should ask more questions. He'll spill all the gossip.

Ty, Kai, and Owen always stick together. Jeok, the Asian kid, occasionally hangs with them.

The rest—I will find out more about them.

By the time we are finished with our tour and are led into a bungalow that the three of us will have to share, I'm in a great mood.

"The boys will fix the cabin in the afternoon. It's been damaged by the storm, but it will do for now," Maddy explains.

And soon, it's time for lunch.

It's buffet-style. The two or three dishes are cooked and put in big bowls that everyone helps themselves out of. No fancy dishes. It's some type of fish ceviche with corn empanadas or pancakes or whatever they call it. They eat a lot of fish, which is fine by me. I can eat pretty much anything.

Every table has a bowl with fruit. Oranges, bananas, mangos, coconuts. Maddy explains that they get a lot of fruit. Nothing is wasted. They make juices and smoothies as much as they can. They press coconuts to make oil.

This weirdly reminds me of survivor camp trips my dad and I used to take. Except, exotic fruit sounds better than acorns or wild berries.

I study the crew as everyone eats and jokes. It's

refreshing—as if the pristine white beach and the emerald jungle are a natural mood enhancement.

Except for Dani. The girl is sulking like she has a bee up her ass.

And Callie. She is smiling now—a good sign. But her eyes dart to that boy who found us on the beach last night.

Kai.

He is a walking piece of art. A gang member at first sight, but he doesn't have that rough-around-the-edges attitude. It's in his face that, when relaxed, is pleasant and friendly. In the way he moves, calm and confident, with no snappiness, except when Callie is around.

Yeah, Callie. There is a story there. Why does he keep glaring at her like she poisoned his fucking food?

After lunch, everyone washes the dishes in buckets of water, then wipes them clean. It's a commune. I smile as I follow the rest.

And then I stroll to the beach.

The sun is relentless, the hot sand scorching my feet. The water is refreshing, and I want to take a dip.

I scan the horizon as I toss the sandals Maddy gave me, strip down to my new bikini, and step into the water. It's warm. It feels like back in Thailand on Koh Samui where Dad and I flew now and then.

I dive underwater, cut the waves, come up for air, and shake my hair.

There are rocks on each side of the beach, and more of them protrude from the water in the distance. The water is beautiful, like one of those Maldives pictures. I dive right into the wave, glide underwater for some time, then rise to the surface past the first break.

It feels fantastic! The end of the world has its perks.

I swim farther away from the shore, though Maddy said to watch out for rocks.

Screw that. You don't try—you don't learn.

I study the water surface.

That's why there is no major port here. No access. I remember the map. This side of the island is rocky. They have a big motor boat and a small fishing one. I guess they know how to navigate them around the rocky patches.

Maddy said there is a dirt road that goes north along the coast and reaches the town and the one that goes south, curving to the Westside. The Westside has ATVs, guns, and cameras. They have everything.

This side? It's like that old movie *The Beach* with that guy, DiCaprio, who used to be hot several decades ago. His young version in the movie reminds me of Ty.

Except this side of the island is on borrowed time. I'm not even sure why the Chancellor let them stay. Everything has a reason.

I don't need a vehicle to get around. It's a six-hour hike across the Divide to the other side. And if two or three days are enough to find out everything I need, I am out of here and off to the Westside.

This feels like paradise, but I didn't come here for a vacation.

I have a job to do.

11

CALLIE

It's easy to get used to the good life when nothing reminds you of the destruction.

Zion is a different world. The Change seems like some dark distant nightmare.

The island is beautiful. The sun sets behind the green hills that look like Hawaii or New Zealand, and the ocean acquires a pinkish-orange hue. It's like liquid metal.

Everything calms at dusk, and the center of life is the dining room, which smells of smoke and food. Everyone piles in for food, conversation, and laughter. Even a simple fish fry with salad tastes heavenly.

Dani is quiet as Ty makes her a plate and fusses over her.

Katura is chatting with Zach and Jeok, smiling as she tells a joke, and the guys roar with laughter. Katura is good with guys. And conversation. And finding her way into any company. She wears shorts and a loose surfer tank. Her body is gorgeous, lean with muscles. Barefoot, she looks even more like an Amazon.

I wear a t-shirt and shorts. My shoulders and face are already slightly burned, the skin tingling and scratchy with sweat and salt.

It's easy to get used to the good life when nothing reminds you of the past.

But my past is here.

He is tattooed head to toe, and no matter how much I try to keep my eyes on the plate as I sit between Maddy and Katura, I glance up at him.

He never smiles. Barely talks. But the bitterness burning between us is almost tangible.

And then the darkness falls. The solar lanterns light the area that becomes a small happy world. The dining room is cleaned up, and everyone drags chairs and blankets toward the Common Lounge, where a stone fire pit on the sand is lit. The bonfire illuminates almost two dozen people who settle around it.

"Where is Bo?" I ask. Because the only people missing are Bo and Kai.

"Probably, the workshop. Kai doesn't like fires. Especially bonfires," Ty explains, flicking a glance at me as he and Maddy arrange a row of cups on the sand and open jugs of brown liquid.

The accident. I nod. I remember the story.

"He hardly ever comes for these. But here you go." Ty nods somewhere into the distance, and I see Kai and Bo emerging out of the darkness, walking in our direction.

My heart is a treacherous whore, because, despite the

bitterness, it starts pounding in Kai's presence like there is a secret switch that he flips.

"Try this." Ty pours us glasses from a big jug, and Katura and I take a sip.

"Oh!" Katura smacks her lips. "Homemade beer?"

"Yeah." Ty smiles. "We buy it from town. It's dirt cheap."

I nod toward the jug that has the *Pura Vida* logo. "So this place used to be a resort."

"Yeah. One of those new-concept self-sustainable ones. Tons of solar panels. But a lot got destroyed by the hurricane a year ago."

Katura leans back in her chair, feet crossed at the ankle. "How often do storms happen?"

Ty sits down on the sand next to Dani's chair and pushes his blond hair back. "Every several months. Small ones. The hurricane season starts in June. That's when occasionally it hits big."

"June?" Katura cocks an eyebrow.

"Yeah. Soon."

"Hmm." Katura tilts her head. "What are the chances of this entire village being wiped out just like those overwater bungalows?" She nods at the bare beams sticking out of the water at the shore.

Ty only stares at her as he takes a gulp of beer.

You don't need to be a meteorologist or an expert to know that a big hit can destroy this place. And people.

As if to distract us, Owen asks about the Change and how it started.

"New York City was first," Katura says, and everyone at

the bonfire goes quiet.

Some of them are curious about us. Others are suspicious. But many of them came over now and then during the day and asked random questions about the mainland. They are hungry for information. Nostalgic, perhaps. They all lost something or someone.

"The impact wasn't that devastating in terms of damage," Katura carries on like an expert, "but the electrical grid and the bridges were destroyed. Imagine seventeen million people trapped in several square miles, with no sanitation or running water. Within a week, the city turned into a cesspool. It was a sanitary catastrophe. No access to medication. Looting started. Riots. Murders. All the good stuff. New York was the first one. And then the Citadel, Chicago, Atlanta, then the counties in Nevada and Virginia—the largest data centers."

"What does that mean?" Maddy asks.

"The towers—radio, cell, satellite—are only functional when the cables that connect them are not damaged. And that came next. But the real power—internet and stuff—are in data centers."

"Oh…"

"And then came the biggest infrastructures for collateral damage, ports, military. You get the picture."

What they don't imagine is not even the fallout that came next, but what lawlessness and abundance of weapons turn some people into. The scum of the earth can hide away their entire lives waiting for this moment and then crawl out. The demented minds go wild with violence. It's hard to imagine that good neighbors you've known all your life can turn into monsters who do unspeakable things to others. Humanity has many faces. The ugliest and darkest ones might never see the light of day. But when they do…

I close my eyes, remembering the screams of women when our neighborhood got raided by thugs with guns once.

"Australia is the new power now," Katura concludes. "But it's off-limits to pretty much the entire world."

Heads nod.

"What's with the Westside war?" Katura asks, suddenly changing the topic. She is always prying.

"We had a falling out," Ty explains.

Bo sits with a cup in his hand, quietly staring into the bonfire.

Kai is next to him but a little back, in the shadow, turned sideways to the fire as if it pains him to face it. He smokes a cigarette, holding it between his ring and middle finger. I can see his thumb tapping the end of it again and again. Is he nervous? I wonder why he came here at all. If he hates it so much.

"How bad is the falling out if you had to move all the way here?" Katura insists.

Everyone goes quiet.

Maddy clears her throat. "Let's just say, Archer held all the cards. He wasn't nice about it. A fight broke out. The Savages from the town attacked. Several people died. And the rules Archer announced afterward weren't to everyone's liking. Besides, he controlled the boats and didn't let some of us leave. So, yeah…"

I can tell by Katura's face she is not nearly satisfied with the story. It would be better to ask Maddy. In private. It's the first day, and I feel that not everything on this island is as pretty and hippy-happy as it seems.

You can tell by the occasional empty stares.

By the silence that falls awkwardly at random times and random words.

By the night watch—and not to watch out for Archer's crew but someone else.

By the winces at the mention of the town.

There are dark stories here. Deaths.

No place is paradise when people die at the hands of their own.

12

CALLIE

Everyone cheers up when Ty brings a speaker and turns on the music. Or it might be the local beer, sourish and bitter. It does the job.

I don't remember the last time I drank. I haven't drunk much since the Block Party. When one of the important moments of your life is a blank, you are aware of keeping things present. When that blank holds a dark secret, even more so.

But I drink anyway. It helps me relax. Slowly, it stops my body from being as tense as an iron rod in the presence of Kai Droga. He is like a mythical creature—the power that emanates from him makes me too self-aware.

The music is from before the Change. It breathes with memories and good times. It makes everyone relax, sink into their chairs or onto the sand.

Guff and Santino hang out at the hammocks strung between the palm trees.

The party divides into little camps.

Owen hugs his girl to him and they make out.

It's as if the war never happened. This could pass off as a college party. Or a camping trip. Burning Man decompression fest.

It almost makes me happy for a moment.

And then Doja Cat comes up on the speaker.

"Oooooh, snap! Guess who's crazy about this song?" Ty grins at Kai, who glares back at him like he is about to murder him.

It's *that* song. My heart lunges in my chest.

Ty snaps his finger at Owen. "Duuuude," they say in sync in a goofy stoned kinda way. "Put on that Doja tune," they both mimic in theatrically dumb voices and break out in laughter.

I sit frozen on the spot. This is *my* song.

"Maaaan." Owen chuckles and looks at me, then Katura. "Every time Kai is drunk or high, it's this song. On repeat."

"Shut it," Kai snarls from his seat.

I swallow hard, my heart thudding I my chest. It's *my* song.

"Seriously," Ty carries on. "It's Kai's obsession."

"Shut the fuck up. Dude!" Kai snaps and shakes his head, turning away to face the dark ocean.

Everyone goes quiet.

"Sensitive, aren't we?" Ty murmurs. He is already quite drunk. "It's just a song, dude."

But it's not. It's the last song I ever danced to. On that stupid podium. At the Block Party. For *him*, though he doesn't know it.

I stare at Kai, but he won't look at me.

The memories fall through me like a waterfall. Suddenly, it's hard to breathe. I take a gulp of the beer, trying to drown the awkwardness.

Bo starts another conversation. He is the mediator. And in a minute, everyone is talking, and Ty is joking around, and Zach throws his flip flop at Maddy, who tosses it back at him.

But the song is so familiar yet full of so many memories that I want it to stop. I want to rip the speaker off that table and toss it in the ocean.

I sit, transfixed. I must be tipsy, because the conversations fade in and out.

Rebelution comes on.

Again, I raise my eyes to Kai across the bonfire, and he is staring at me.

I don't look away, ready for his hate and am willing to give mine to him.

But there is no hate.

The flames of the bonfire flicker in the air between us. A current passes between us. It's strong. We don't look away like it's a duel. The flickers of the fire dance in Kai's eyes, leap off his tattoos, and pierce me straight to the heart that dances like mad.

He is like a God or a Devil, I am not sure which one. That night after the Block Party, that devilish gorgeous body was taking mine. And I don't freaking remember.

What I read in his eyes echoes inside me. I feel my heart clench. It's so tight, it's hard to breathe.

I bite my lip, trying to hold back tears. Because I know we both were at fault. I always wanted him, flirted with him that night, despite Archer by my side and Julie by his. I danced for him. And he was watching openly. We were two people lost in that intimate moment with hundreds around us.

But more than anything, there is one thing I admit. Again and again. No matter how much I lie, once in a while, I face the truth in my mind. It only happens when I get tipsy, which is very rare. But when alcohol hums in my veins and my mind drifts back to that semester at Deene, I know one truth.

Kai Droga was my first crush.

My secret obsession.

But he was taken. And I succumbed to Archer.

That night, I wanted to be with Kai. Except I wish I remembered. I wish he'd *made sure* I remembered. I wish I was his girlfriend. I wish it wasn't a mistake. I wish my boyfriend wasn't cocky, arrogant, vengeful Archer Crone, the king of Deene. I wish Kai and I hadn't taken such a heavy blow.

That's certainly more than one truth.

They all hurt the same.

The fire crackles, sending dozens of sparkles like fireflies into the dark air.

I finally peel my eyes off Kai and stare at the bonfire. The heat from it, me being so close, burns my face. It might be the sunburn. Or booze. Or memories.

Loud laughter snaps me back to reality.

"All right, kids, I am off." Bo rises from his chair, and so do half of the others.

When they leave, it's Kai, Zach, Ty, Katura, Maddy, Ya-

Ya, Kristen, and a couple other people I don't know yet who stay by the bonfire.

It's quiet. Peaceful. Reggae hums through the air, the sound of it lacing with the purring of the ocean.

Everyone is tipsy. Especially Katura. She acts like she's been friends with everyone for years.

It's only a matter of time until Kristen raises her mug in the air and says, "Well, we do occasionally have fun on this island. So cheers to that! Love conquers all!"

Zach pulls her by her waist and onto his lap. "Oh, yeah? You are in the mood for some fun tonight?"

She slaps him off playfully.

"Kristen"—Maddy points to her with her mug—"used to date Archer Crone from the Westside."

"Oh!" Katura's drunk eyes light up with interest.

But my heart skips a bit. I don't want these conversations. And I keep my eyes down, praying that Ty or Kai don't say anything about me.

"So what are you doing here then?" Katura asks cockily.

Kristen slaps Zach's insistent hands off one more time and shifts onto her chair. "Better boys here." She giggles.

"Hell, yeah," Zach says, not taking his eyes off her.

"We have naked parties if you are into it." Kristen looks seductively at Katura, and I have a feeling that with her, anything or anyone goes.

Katura cheers with her cup. "Sign me up!"

The boys cheer. And I don't like that.

"Maddy joins in occasionally. We all take care of each other here." Kristen's drunk gaze shifts to me and doesn't go away.

Katura snorts when she notices. "Count her out."

"Oooh." Kristen pouts her lips. "Shy or morally repressed?"

"Callie is not into guys," Katura says.

"Oh-ho-ho!" Zach grins at me.

"Since when?" Ty cocks an eyebrow at me.

I roll my eyes.

"Since the guy who ruined it for her," Katura interjects.

"Stop," I tell Katura.

I told her my story about the night of the Block Party. No names. No details. It was during those two days at the Transfer Center when we shared some things. Silly chatter. Girl talk. Katura is good about making others talk when she is so straightforward herself.

"It's ok, it happens," says Kristen. "The first one is a test-drive."

"Yeah." Now Katura is staring at me, all beer-sparkly eyes and a half-smile. She grows cockier by the minute. Mouthy, too. "Her first guy was when she was spiked. She doesn't remember a thing. She hasn't dated anyone since."

"Kat!" I snap, but it's too late. And my stomach turns at the words.

"Oh, man," Kristen whispers. "Tough luck."

I am mad. My face is on fire because Ty and Kai know what she is talking about.

I try not to look. But when I glance at Ty in that awkward silence that follows, he is suddenly too serious and flicks a glance at me from under his eyebrows, then takes a gulp of beer and stares back at the fire.

I really, really try not to look at Kai. The conversation

resumes, but my heart is beating fast. Blood is pounding in my ears. I am angry, and embarrassed, and upset. And I finally glance at Kai.

He is staring at me like he wants to murder me. I know that if I don't look away, I will cry.

So I rise from my seat as calmly as I possibly can, set the cup down, and without saying anything, start walking away into the darkness.

"Hey, girl, what's up?" Kristen's voice chases me. "Come back!"

Fuck you.

I don't listen. If I say something, my voice will break.

It's dark, but I sort of know where I am going, and I stomp through the darkness, faster and faster, toward the dim solar light that hangs on the door to the bungalow that's assigned to us.

Someone's footsteps follow.

They are loud and approaching fast.

I am at the door when I turn around and see Kai storming toward me, like a fucking devil, his eyes blazing.

I want to tell him to chill it when he pushes me with his broad chest against the door and puts his hands on each side of my face.

"Oh, yeah?" His voice is like an animal growl.

This is hate.

This is evil.

His eyes are narrowed and shooting poison. He lowers his face to mine and hisses, "Is that what you tell people, petal?"

13

CALLIE

I don't understand.

He is mad.

Why?

I should be the one who is mad.

"Tell people?" I murmur, but anger is rising in me like a tide. "First of all," I say louder, getting my courage back. "I don't tell anything to anyone. I only told Katura a short version." Anger is getting stronger, and now the feeling of hatred is coming back. My chest is rising and falling, almost touching his. "Number two," I hiss, trying to sound brave, though his large frame pressing onto me is distracting, intimidating, and arousing at once. "That night was all your doing. You were running around with Archer's crew and becoming just like him, weren't you?"

Kai laughs mockingly. There is malice in that laughter and in his eyes that come back to mine and glare when his laughter stops abruptly.

He is scary-looking—something I've never see in him before. Yet his closeness is intoxicating, charged with macular energy. No cologne, but he smells of salt, and damp clothes, and sand, and sea breeze, and tobacco.

He is still caving me, so close to me. *Too* close. His face inches from mine. One of his dark strands almost touches my skin.

He shakes his head. "I saved you that night, Callie."

Oh, that's precious. I frown in surprise, because he doesn't make sense.

"You were drunk," he says, his words laced with hate. "Probably high. It was probably your precious boyfriend who spiked your drink." His voice is low and dangerous, like a growl. "Your best friend was so drunk that she told me to leave you on the sidewalk to sober up. You don't remember, do you?"

I don't. But that's not what I am asking about.

"And yes, I brought you to my room." Every word is a snarl. "Because no one else gave a shit about you. And then everything else followed."

Are you kidding me?

"Everything else?" I snort in shock at his casualness.

"Yeah," he growls. "I wanted to protect you. But the next day, you just had to leave my fucking room, didn't you? Walk out into the hallway full of frat boys."

I still can't believe he is skipping the most important part.

The *worst* part.

"What about the night?" My heart starts beating like

mad because this is the first time I've confronted him. The anger and hurt have been pinned up in me for a long time.

"What about it?" He frowns.

"The fact that you took your best friend's girl and brought her home."

Do I need to spell it out for him?

His gaze darkens. His lips curl into that nasty smirk. "Archer would have fucking sodomized you if I didn't get you away from him."

Something turns in my stomach at the words.

It's confusing.

Because he avoids the obvious.

"Your boyfriend was a dick." His expression is savage and spiteful. His face is so close to mine that his warm breath grazes my skin. "Because he fucked girls and disposed of them, passed them off to others. And that's what his plan for you that night was. You were next. Everyone was already talking about it. But no. Callie was clueless, yeah? You were dancing that night like you were the queen of the world. And Archer was already telling everyone how he would have his way with you. *Girlfriend*." He snorts. "He was going to fuck you and dump you."

Harsh.

His words are a revelation and a blow.

But he still avoids the obvious.

"So you did it instead," I say quieter.

Finally.

It's out.

Anger and hurt are swirling so powerfully inside me

that I want to wipe this island off the face of the earth. With Kai. And Archer. And all the memories of the past.

But Kai's face changes. And it's not what I expected.

He shakes his head, frowning. "What?"

"So *you* did it instead," I say quieter, afraid of my own words. "Took advantage of me that night."

I want to sound confident, but the words are the most embarrassing confession.

Suddenly, Kai pushes off the wall and rakes both hands through his hair. His eyes widen. There is shock on his face, and I don't understand it.

"Are you fucking kidding me?" he whispers, gaping at me. "Are you. Fucking. Kidding me, Callie?"

I swallow hard. His beautiful eyes glare at me with an almost murderous intent.

"But..." I want to say something, but the words get stuck in my mouth.

His reaction is not what it should be. I've thought about this for so long. I expected fury, submission, or guilt on his face. But not this.

His chest is rising heavily. "Are you for real right now?"

"But you did, didn't you?" I whisper.

My world is shifting. It's sliding sideways, doubt pulling the ground from under my feet.

"You think I *raped* you?"

The word is like a razor slicing through my heart. It's quiet coming out of his mouth but deafening. I stare at him, and I can't breathe.

"I woke up naked," I explain, barely audibly.

It's my only argument.

Kai slowly descends onto me. Like a predator finally trapping his prey. He is so close that I am squeezed between the door and his broad chest hard as concrete.

"I brought you to my room," he says in a hiss that seems louder than a scream. We stare at each other with the hate from all the memories and clashes like an invisible grenade between us. "You threw up all over yourself. So, yeah, Callie, I undressed you. Because I didn't want you to sleep in your own puke. And I went to sleep in Trevor's room."

And I am free-falling.

How can it be?

How could I be so mistaken?

It's a roller-coaster that makes my vertigo go nuts. My throat closes.

I want to scream and cry at the same time. But I am dumbfounded. And weak. If I wasn't pinned against the door, I would've slid down to the floor. Because the world as I know it is crumbling once again. And my memories do with it.

Kai cups my face, and for a moment, at the feel of his touch, my body trembles with anticipation, because I think he might kiss me. The thought is brief and out of place and illogical.

But his grip is too strong, almost hurting me. And there is a tremor in it. I can feel it.

He brings his face so close to me that our lips almost touch.

"I can't believe your pretty little head made up such fucking trash," he hisses. "I didn't fucking touch you that night. There, petal." He pulls away, letting his hands slip off. "Now get the fuck off this side of the island and go to Archer."

He whips around, and in a moment, his footsteps crunch against the sand into the dark.

I am so shocked that I close my eyes, cover my face with my hands, and stand still for a while, my head tilted against the door.

Nothing happened that night…

The world suddenly goes too quiet, my heartbeat the loudest noise. My entire body is a pulse. My eyes burn. I want to whimper but hold my breath so I don't sound pathetic.

My mind is a whirlwind.

I am a virgin.

That thought alone is strange. You think your first time is a rite into proper adulthood. And here I am. Twenty-two. Hating the world and men. And myself with it.

And there is Kai Droga. He called me petal because I liked to draw flowers. He only did that occasionally when we were alone and laughed when he did so.

And then I turned him into a monster in my head, blamed him for an atrocious thing that never happened, and for everything that went wrong with my life afterward.

I can't even imagine what he feels right now, because the story conjured in my mind is a lie. A lie that even I have a hard time processing.

And I can't.

I need to be somewhere else.

With someone.

With loud music or others' voice.

I push off the door and walk back to the bonfire.

Everyone is still there and cheer when I approach.

"Where is Kai?" Ty asks.

But I grab the cup out of Katura's hand and chug it.

"Whoa, tiger, slow down!" She laughs drunkenly.

I pass the cup to Ty. "Another one."

He smirks with suspicion but obeys, exchanging glances with Katura.

I chug the next one too, wiping the bitter liquid that drips down my chin.

I haven't been drunk since the Block Party four years ago. And tonight seems like a good night to repeat yesterday's mistakes.

I want to go swimming and drown. To sneak to the other side and potentially get shot. The world is shit, but my false memories are even shittier, because I thought that the guy I had a crush on took advantage of me when he, in fact, saved me from regrets.

If I told Abby, she would have laughed at me, then said, "Should've answered his calls that day."

Ha!

And here's the truth. Kai did call and text me that day. But there was already too much going on, and I thought it was all his fault. So I ghosted him, and everyone else, and got the hell out of Dodge, burning all the bridges behind me.

I want to talk to someone. But there is no one except Abby, and she is on the Westside. I feel lonely and tricked and disgusted with myself. Tears burn my eyes, and I ask Ty for another drink.

Many of us don't have families anymore, and here I am, moping about one night of my life.

I want to talk to Kai. And I don't. Because now I don't know how to look him in the eyes.

I want to get drunk, except this time, I want to fall asleep and never wake up.

14

KAI

I am so mad, I can't think straight.

I stomp to the beach and walk straight into the water, dive into the rising tide and hold my breath as long as I can. I don't care that I might hit the underwater rock. It would be a fucking relief.

But the water is too warm. Too quiet. And I want it rough.

I want a storm.

Freezing cold.

Fucking snow and blasting winds instead of this tropical cage.

The emotions rip me apart from the inside. I scream underwater, then burst out to the surface and choke like a madman, flopping my arms around, spitting out salty water.

A strong wave puts me under, and I fight my way to the surface, coughing and choking, the swallowed water making me dizzy.

I crawl out onto the shore and, without looking in the direction of the bonfire and laughter that comes from there, walk toward the workshop.

The nights on the island are dark.

But my thoughts are even darker.

I am a fucking monster, ain't I? That's what she thought. Oh, the irony.

We are not born monsters. We become them, often pushed by others.

A week after the fire, Julie shows up at the hospital. I can't care less about her. Long before that Block Party, I fucked her once and went down on her out of pity. She fucked half of the football team but had a thing for me. And the Block Party—well, the only reason I was with her was because Crone had already roped Callie in.

And here is Julie, in the hospital, a week after the accident, looking at me and my bandaged body with tears, her bright pink mouth contorted in an ugly cry. And I get it, sort of. It's hard to look at a mummy.

"I can't do this, Kai, I'm sorry," she whimpers.

"Jules."

"I can't."

She called me emotionally unavailable before.

So fuck her.

She was the one stalking me for months. And now, when I most need someone to talk to, she leaves. Just like many others. And goes back to Crone's crew.

And that's how you slowly start turning from the monster on the outside with red blistered skin that takes forever to heal to a monster on the inside, who doesn't trust people.

My anger is still there. I am dripping with salt water. The wet sand is prickly under my feet as I step onto the wooden floor of the workshop and turn on the light. I toss my wet shirt onto the floor. I am so mad that I want to smoke and drink and fuck and break someone's face at the same time.

A rapist.

The word echoes in my head, and I can't believe that Callie would ever think that of me.

I light a cigarette and inhale deeply. The smoke burns my lungs, and I take another drag. And another. And another. It suppresses the tears or whatever burns my eyes, and instead clenches my jaw, teeth grinding—a man's reflex not to cry.

When the cigarette is gone, I light another, then take out the bottle of rum, twist off the cap with my thumb, and take a gulp straight from the bottle.

I take one of the handmade guns from a crate and stare at it. I want to shoot it. I've done it many times. I want to imagine Crone's face as I point the gun at it.

Fuuuuuuck!

I only came to this island, to the town up north, alone, because Qi Shan, who I still talked to occasionally, got into my head about Crone's big spring break bash, and that I should teach the fucker a lesson and sabotage the resort. Qi Shan had a beef with Crone at that time. But guess what?

I wanted to sneak into one of Crone's parties and beat

the fucking hell out of him or drown him. I didn't have a plan. I wanted revenge. I took that long-ass trip to get here, full of quiet rage and spite. Didn't accomplish a fucking thing. Lost my family behind. Found Qi Shan rubbing shoulders with Crone again. Yeah, that fucking traitor.

And then the news about the Change hit. Bombings. Cities destroyed. Borders closed. Any means of transportation stopped.

I feel like because of Crone, I lost everything. I could've been with my father and sister. Dead like them. But it doesn't matter. Because I would be rid of this fucking guilt that's eating me up.

And now *her*.

Four years.

And all these years she thought I was a monster.

Fuck you, Callie!

I sit in the chair and close my eyes.

How stupid was I?

I thought if we talked, there would be closure.

Healing.

I hate that fucking word.

First, the doctors after the fire used it over and over again. Burns over fifty percent of your body come with a lot of motherfucking healing.

Then there was the shrink. And it was healing again but with a different flavor.

Then the tattooist. Because tattooing over scars is prone to infection. And, oh, do I know the cost of it.

I heard that word so often in my life back then that it

made me mad, made me go to the gym and lash out at the punching bags, bruising my knuckles to a pulp so I had to skip the gym until my knuckles...healed.

Yeah.

Fuck!

I exhale and sit with my eyes closed for the longest time. And just when I think I am finally calm, there is a knock at the door.

I don't answer, but the door opens anyway.

And here she is.

Miss Flower.

Un-fucking-believable.

I want her to disappear, and I want to hear her talk. I want to throw her out, and I want to fuck her madly and split her in half with my cock so that she knows how it feels the next morning after being fucked.

"Hey, Kai." Her voice is low and seductive but out of place.

She smiles at me, walks in, and right away stumbles and grabs the wall, giggling.

She is drunk.

Fuck me if it's not deja vu again.

"I wanna talk," she says and walks slowly toward me.

I want to be angry. I want to laugh at this shitshow. But I stare at her without a word.

She sways like a dandelion in the wind. Her gaze is unfocused. She licks her lips again and again.

Oh, hell. Help me God.

She will not remember this tomorrow, because her eyes

are narrowed and she slurs and walks funny. We already know that her memory is Criss fucking Angel, conjuring some unbelievable shit.

"I want…" she says and looks around, lost.

I get up and kick the chair toward her. "Sit," I snap, because she will fall if she doesn't. And because I could never turn her down. Not then. Not now.

I am so fucking stupid about this girl. And so mad.

"I haven' drank since tha' Block Party, you know," she says, swallowing words.

"But you did tonight. Imagine that," I murmur and lean with my ass onto the desk, watching her with sardonic amusement.

"Kai," she says, sits down slowly, and looks at me. She hunches, her hands clasped between her knees. And fuck me if she is not the image of pure beauty and innocence. Even drunk.

Innocence, yeah.

What a fucking surprise.

"Kai," she says again, and I can tell that she has a hard time focusing.

I love the way she says my name. I want to be mad, but I am more disappointed that she is drunk. And I still feel like my insides shake at what she accused me of. More than anything—she is here, on the island, in my workshop—how is this not a fucking miracle? My mind is a mess. My head tries to rationalize things, but my body senses Callie several feet away and says, "Fuck everything. Come to me, baby girl."

"I'm sorry," she says, staring at the floor. "For wha' I thought. For wha' I assum…" Her words trail off. "For wha' happen' t'us."

To us…

Yeah, petal, it's a shame. But you have no idea.

I wonder if she knows about the fire.

I want to have this conversation, but she is way too drunk.

And the next thing I know, she covers her mouth with her hand, murmurs, "Oh, God," and stumbles to the door.

I dart after her and catch her from behind right before she falls off the porch. I hold her when she bends over and showers the sand next to the door with her vomit.

Jesus…

My arm is around her waist. I pick up her blond hair with the other hand and hold it as she vomits again and again.

"Fuck, petal," I murmur with anger and pity.

This is ridiculous.

We've been here before.

In exactly.

The same.

Situation.

When she is done throwing up and tries to stand straight, she can't. Her eyes are drooping, and so is her head. I wipe her mouth with my palm and wipe my palm on my shorts.

"Fuck, petal. What the fuck," I snap, holding her in my arms as she leans onto my bare chest and slumps in my arms.

"I'm sorry," she murmurs, her forehead pressing against my chest.

She is on a fast train to blackout.

I don't want to be close to her. Or touch her. Like she is a disease—bad mojo that is contagious. Because something fucked up will happen again.

I am the victim, if you think about it. I got it the hard way. Ruined career. Lost friendships. Scars. Tattoos. Because one night I found myself exactly where I am now.

And what do I do?

The same thing as years ago.

"Come on, petal."

I bring my arm under her knees, pick her up in my arms, and carry her toward her bungalow. I stumble in the dark, almost fall, curse, and carry on. Because despite how awful this shit is, the blondie with the luminous blue eyes, who is almost unconscious in my arms, is the most precious cargo I've ever carried. Never mind the consequences. Because the day I met her, my stupid ass heart decided that it would latch onto her and not let go.

And here were are.

Just my fucking luck.

Callie mumbles something, and her hands slide to my chest. They touch my scars.

My.

Fucking.

Scars.

I can't stand it, and I grind my teeth.

I bring her to her empty room and lay her gently on one of the beds, then turn and walk out.

It feels like my life is going in circles.
I go to the chair where Guff sits on night guard.
"I'll take your shift tonight," I say.
Because there is no chance of me sleeping.

15

CALLIE

"Babe, where did you go last night?" Katura asks at breakfast.

"I got drunk," I answer quietly so that no one hears. "Went to walk around and ran into Kai. He brought me back."

"Sure." Katura nods, digging into her grits with scrambled eggs.

My head is splitting. I got so drunk that I barely remember what I said when I went to talk to Kai. But I do remember throwing up and him carrying me to my bungalow.

Jesus. I embarrassed myself again. More importantly, I feel like I did exactly what I had four years ago—lost control and ended up with my face down.

And Kai took care of it.

I search for him around the beach as we eat breakfast. I want to find him and apologize, but he is nowhere to be seen.

Ty is trying to make small talk with Dani. She never says much, nor does she say anything when I ask her about the mainland. No family—surprise-surprise. But there is something else. And there is Ty, smiling and chatting her up. He clearly likes her.

It's our third day here, and I already feel like we are blending in. Shorts. Tank tops. Bikinis underneath. I have two. The one I am wearing is lime green with strawberries. It makes me smile and feel guilty. The tropical island has that effect when you know what the rest of the world looks like.

Maddy, Kristen, Ya-Ya, Katura, Dani, and I go to the garden, where we help weed and collect vegetables. The lunch is a salad with everything possible mixed into it.

"We buy protein powder from town. It helps to substitute for the lack of meat. Meat is expensive," Maddy explains. She is the one who talks most of the time. The rest of the girls just study us.

"Are there wild animals on the island?" Katura asks.

Ya-Ya, who looks like the queen of hip-hop with her big afro twisted into a large bun on top of her head, snorts. "What, you gonna run around like Katniss?" She rolls her eyes at Katura, who ignores her.

Maddy smiles. "We are not *that* efficient here."

No sign of Kai. I ask Ty about him. He shrugs.

"Check the workshop," he says.

"What's the workshop?" Katura is curious.

And when we finish washing dishes, Ty takes me, Dani, and Katura for another tour.

We walk toward a large shed that's separated from all the structures by a patch of palm trees.

"It used to be a utility building," Ty explains. "We use it to build things, make repairs. Kai is great with his hands. We all learned to be. Jeok takes care of the solar panels and wiring. Guff is in charge of any construction. We also make weapons."

"Weapons," Katura echoes, her eyes lighting up with curiosity.

"Yeah." Ty smiles. "Ask Kai. That's his hobby. He'll tell you all about it. Ladies…" Ty bows gracefully as he opens the shed door to let us in.

It's dim inside, and it takes me a moment to adjust my eyesight after walking in from the bright sun outside. And when I do, there he is.

Kai sits on a stool next to a desk and sands a piece of wood.

He is shirtless, with his back to us, his tattoos rippling from the movement, smoke curling in the air around him.

Dave Mathew's Band trickles softly from a speaker. It's one of his favorite. He likes rock music. He likes building things. His dad was a handyman who also used to repair and build cars and remodel houses and taught Kai all sorts of things since childhood.

I know all that because I used to be obsessed with trying to find out everything I could about Kai. He was an outlier. From a middle-class family. Scholarship to Deene because he was a wrestling prodigy.

That was what got him into Archer's circle. Archer

always gathered the best around him. Usually, the richest too.

Kai was not. He drove an old sports bike instead of an Audi or a Porsche like the rest. Archer, of course, drove his favorite Aston Martin Vulcan. Kai wore expensive clothes, provided by sponsors, but didn't have the gadgets or a fancy crib in California or a condo in Manhattan.

But here is the thing about Kai—he never tried to fit in, didn't ask for company, didn't seek attention. If something wasn't up to his taste, he let you know. He came into Archer's circle effortlessly, didn't chase the elite gang, didn't follow the stupid trends, and more often did things on his own instead of following the wind.

I think that was why he and Archer became so close. Archer, who was used to others' ass-kissing and bowing in his presence, found something in Kai that couldn't be bought or traded for favors—honesty and unbiased friendship. Something hard to come by in the world of wealth and fame.

Until a girl came between them.

And here I am.

My heart flutters at the sight of Kai as we walk through the dim workshop closer to him.

Ty whistles at him.

"What up, bro," Kai says without turning and tosses the wooden piece onto the desk. When he finally turns, he freezes, his eyes squinting at me, cigarette hanging off his mouth, smoke curling around his face.

Shit.

It always feels like my mere presence irritates him.

OUTCAST

Katura gives a low surprised whistle as she looks around.

"Came to give our guests a little tour," Ty says and starts explaining the shelves, the crates that are full of homemade guns and all sorts of weapons. He shows us the generators and explains solar panels.

Katura asks more questions. Ty answers, smiling at Dani as if she were the one asking. Dani looks like she couldn't care less.

And I keep glancing at Kai.

He is mesmerizing. Dangerous. Gorgeous.

Hostile.

He cleans up the desk, then stabs the cigarette in a tin jar, walks past me without meeting my gaze, and leaves the shop.

I should leave him alone. But if there is a good time to apologize, it would be now. Yesterday, actually, but I was too drunk. Four years ago, maybe, but I was too young, petrified, and embarrassed.

So I do the one thing that feels right—I turn and leave the shed, intending to finally sort things out with Kai.

16

KAI

I've avoided her so far today, having meals after everyone is done, keeping my head low at the workshop, trying to stay in my zone, with my music in my head.

But she follows, her footsteps fast approaching me from behind.

"Kai," she calls out, but I don't stop.

She follows still.

She is fucking sticky.

Like the island sand that gets into your every pore.

Like the salt that coats your skin and makes your hair coarse.

Like the parrots that chirp and screech in the mornings, and when you don't hear them, they peck at your garden, ruining the work you've done for so long.

There is no avoiding her now. Suddenly, this village is too small. Everywhere I turn, I see her.

I stomp toward the beach, not really sure where to go to get away from Callie.

Last night made me angry like never before. I sat till dawn thinking about the last four years that were a fucked-up chain of events that followed that one night. When she is close to me, I can't think of anything else but her.

"Kai, wait!" She catches up with me right as I step onto the open beach and head for the boat.

If I jump into the ocean, will she follow too?

She is not a good swimmer. I know that. She'd almost drowned at the lake when she was fifteen. It's a miracle she is one of the few who survived the boat crash.

I feel her hand wrap around my forearm, and I jerk it away, glaring at her, but not stopping.

And those eyes.

Fuck me tender.

They are sober, and there is no anger in them but rather apology.

Still, I keep walking, barefoot, along the scorching sand, though I don't care because after two years, our feet are calloused and hardened.

"Can we talk?"

I whip around abruptly, and she almost slams into me.

"About?" I meet her gaze that is hesitant now, as if she is not sure it's a good idea. "Exactly," I snap, turn, and keep walking.

"Kai, please." She grabs me by my forearm, and I whip around, jerking my arm away from her.

"Don't touch me," I warn in a whisper.

"Are these all scars…?" She reaches with her hand toward my chest, but I catch her by her wrist just in time.

"They are none of your business," I hiss. "Do. Not.

Touch me. Understand?"

I whip around and go straight for the boat.

But the little blonde is on a mission now.

"About last night. And before. Let's talk," she pleads.

"You already apologized last night. I guess you don't remember. Case closed, petal."

I am bitter. And I use that nickname that I gave her a long time again. And, oh, does it feel good to use something that meant a lot back then.

I approach the boat that is tied to a beam of the old pier, undo the rope, and jump in. But before I push off the beam with my foot, Callie hops right in and sits on her haunches, staring at me.

What's her fucking deal?

"I am coming with you," she says, suddenly so sure.

I want to laugh because she is not a good swimmer, she doesn't have a life vest on, and she has no clue where I am going.

Suddenly, I have an idea. It's the anger in me that ticks my mind with an evil thought.

She is about to say something when I jerk the motor switch and the sound of it drowns everything else.

Slowly, I stir the boat along the familiar path, veering among the rocks scattered around and protruding out of the water here and there. The day is beautiful, but my anger makes everything around darker.

Callie thinks she can say sorry for what she thought, sorry for what happened to us.

Oh, petal, brace yourself.

I am about to show you exactly what you did years ago.

17

CALLIE

I don't know where we are going. The boat is loud. I don't want to say anything, because the words will get lost.

I slide onto the bench and grip the edge of it. I don't like being out in the water without a vest. The wind whips my hair around, onto my face, and I let it because I am afraid to let go of the bench.

I stare at Kai, who holds the helm and stares up ahead, ignoring me. His jaw is set. Sunlight falls on his arms, catching the etched outline of his skin.

Scars. Rough skin as if it were carved by dozens of blades.

Still, he is brutally gorgeous. Like a villain out of a book. I can stare at him forever.

If only he wasn't mad at me.

He's never been vicious like this.

Four years.

An accident.

Tattoos.

That sharp hostile gaze.

I remember the story Abby told me. A fire. Second-degree burns over most of his body.

How?

When did that happen?

The only distraction from my nerves is studying his tattoos. His board shorts hang on his hips and come down to his knees, his legs decorated with the vines of ink that stop at the ankles.

The boat veers onto the open water, turns north, and zooms along the coastline that turns rockier, then speeds up, bumping at the waves.

My heart lunges in my chest, the images of the boat crash piercing me with arrows of anxiety. The boat slows down after several minutes as it starts approaching the coast and the dark opening in the rocks.

We are going toward a cave. For a brief second, I wonder if Kai is going to take me to a secluded place, kill me, and leave my body to the sharks.

When the boat slows down and throttles into the dark opening, I gape around.

We are inside a cave, a large dim space. The ceilings are about twenty feet tall, forty in some places, the stone all around us intimidating and suffocating. It would be darker here if it weren't for the openings between the rocks up ahead that you can't see. The light beams through in some strange trajectory, illuminating the caverns with a soft, almost magical, glow.

Kai turns off the motor, then pulls a lever, and the boat stops, wobbling softly.

Silence falls around us. It's like a vacuum. You can't hear the ocean from here. It's frightening and exciting at the same time.

Slowly, Kai turns to me, and my heart thuds in my chest.

His gaze is cold and something devilish. That same knife-like sharp expression that I saw last night curls his lips in an angry smirk.

"You think your sorry is good enough?" he asks.

The harshness in his words sounds hollow, echoing off the walls.

I don't answer and don't look away. Whatever he has to say, I'll listen.

It's too quiet inside the caverns. Dim. Surreal. I am not sure I like it. The water laps quietly at the small patches of rocks that form the endings on the sides. More dark passageways lead somewhere deeper into the caverns.

One could disappear here, never to be found.

An unpleasant feeling starts in the pit of my stomach as I watch Kai walk to the stern of the boat. In a second, he pushes off and dives into the water, sending the boat rocking.

I grip the seat tighter and stare at the circles in the water, searching the area around where Kai's head will pop up.

One second.

Five.

Ten.

It doesn't.

My heart starts beating faster.

No-no-no-no.

I get up, frantically looking around, turning, searching

and searching for him. Too much time has passed, but there is no sight of him.

"Kai," I say quietly, my stomach turning.

"Kai," I repeat louder, my voice echoing through the empty cavern.

My heart starts hammering.

He can't hold his breath underwater that long, can he?

Is this a punishment?

Is it supposed to be a joke?

What if it's some screwed-up revenge that he's been plotting all these years to make me regret what I did for the rest of my life?

What if it's an accident?

"Kai!" I shout, his name bouncing off the walls, the boat rocking under my feet as I spin around, my eyes searching the water.

My heart is beating so fast that it's hard to breathe. Bile is rising in my chest, and I want to throw up. I am so scared.

What if he is gone?

The feeling comes back—that same feeling when I worked with my aunt in Alaska, helping her at her food stand at a local fair during spring break when the news of the Change came.

That same feeling that makes the world spin around.

That nasty feeling that makes you wanna throw up, and you do when you find out that the major cities were bombed, and your parents were in one of them. You have that hope that they were not there, but you know perfectly well that they were.

And they are gone…

The news comes on the TV stations, however, few are streaming.

It's on the radio.

It echoes with the cell phone signal that one day goes dead. So does Wi-Fi.

It's in the news that there are few survivors in the big cities.

And your hometown doesn't exist anymore.

The memories and the feelings take me by storm. They bounce off the rocks around and above me that start closing down, suffocating me.

Panic spins the world around, simmers in the pit of my stomach, and I am free falling.

"Kai!" I scream.

But the scream only triples the panic that rises to a high pitch in my head.

"Kaaaaaaai!" I scream again at the top of my voice, my vocal cords ripping.

The view gets blurry as my eyes well up with tears.

I am panting.

My chest is rising.

The walls are closing in.

My entire body starts shaking.

I hear the voice.

Somewhere.

It seems like it's all around me.

"How does it feel, Callie?"

I whip around, trying to find the source.

And I see a blurry silhouette.

I wipe my eyes with my palm and stare at Kai as he stands on one of the rock landings about thirty feet away. Just staring at me. Like he just appeared there from nowhere.

"This is how I felt four years ago," he says.

His words are quiet, but the sound of them is intensified by the echo of the hollow cave.

"When you disappeared," he goes on, but his voice floats in and out because blood pounds in my ears. "When we should've talked about what happened. But you left me to deal with the consequences."

Tears start rolling down my eyes.

It's not fair.

He is not fair.

The panic is still there.

His words slice my heart like a razor.

But he is here.

Alive.

And more than the profound feeling of loss and horror that comes with it, I feel relief.

"That's how it feels," he goes on. "When the person you tried to be good to leaves you behind."

I try to stop crying, but the tears keep coming, rolling down my cheeks.

That's the thing with traumas. Anything—a sound, a word—can trigger the dark memories on the most peaceful day and in the most cheerful moment and descend on you like an exploded volcano.

My chest shakes with sobs.

I feel so weak and guilty and scared.

Panic overwhelms me again.

My knees buckle, and I sink onto the floor of the boat.

I can't hold it any longer. I break down and cry.

I wail. Loudly. Shamelessly. Not caring that I look like a psycho who is sobbing on the floor of the boat.

Because grief is like a monster under your bed. It can stay hidden for a long time. You know it's there. You think you have it at bay. But then, one day, you wake up and hear the noise, because it decides to come out. No matter how strong you think you've become, you panic when it crawls out, stands straight, and looms over you with its monstrous form. It suffocates you, presses down on you, and makes everything else disappear but the blackness. Deep. Scary. Drowning.

I sob hysterically, sitting on my knees, my hands over my face. I rock back and forth, trying to get rid of the feeling that the world is smothering me.

I hear the splash of the water, feel the boat rock heavily, and Kai sits down on the bench.

Get a grip, I tell myself.

But I can't. I wipe my eyes and face, see Kai's feet on the floor right in front of me, but I don't want to raise my eyes. Tears are still streaming. I still shake with sobs.

I'm too hurt. And I just broke down in front of the boy who once meant so much and is now punishing me for that.

"Petal…"

His voice is soft, but I don't lift my face. I wipe my palms on my thighs and try to suppress the little sobs that are like hiccups, shaking my body.

It's too quiet. The soft lapping of the water against the

hull and the rock walls echoes with the subsiding storm inside me.

"Callie, look at me," he says.

I shake my head.

I can't.

I don't want to.

But then I feel him move. And he comes down on his knees in front of me and sits back on his heels.

His hands cup my face and tilt it up.

The worst are not the words that he said. Or how they make me feel. The worst is his gaze, full of that same hurt that just ripped me into pieces. There is no anger in his eyes, but the myriad of emotions in them burns the air between us. He looks scared just as I am.

"It's all right," he says. "I'm here."

I don't know if he realizes what he just did, but my stupid tears just keep coming.

"What happened four years ago wasn't my fault," he says quietly. "What followed the day after could've been avoided, but it's not your fault either." I purse my lips, desperately trying to stop crying. "You were my weakness, petal." The words hit like a sucker punch, and my chest shakes in a sob. If he wasn't holding my face in his palms, I would've looked away, because this is unbearable. "We didn't deserve what happened."

I nod.

He leans over and kisses me on the forehead.

And I can't hold back anymore and start sobbing and crying again.

Kai doesn't pull away. He presses his lips to my head, and wraps his arms around me, pulling me closer to him.

"I'm sorry for what I just did, petal. I am a fucking asshole. I know."

I don't know where to touch him so he doesn't get angry at me. I want to wrap my arms around him but he might pull away. He is sensitive. And I don't want him to go. I don't want him to be mad at me.

I shake, trying to stop sobbing.

"Shhhh," he says.

"W-will you f-forgive me," I stutter as I speak, "f-for the worst of me that c-came out after that night?"

I mean the awful thoughts.

I mean being a coward.

I mean running away instead of dealing with things like an adult.

"Hey, look at me." His finger goes under my chin, tilting my wet face up so that I can see his eyes. His body shakes with a soft chuckle. "If that's the worst of you, petal, then you are not that bad."

Petal.

I chuckle through tears.

We are so broken.

So fucked up.

And we are finally making amends. At least, I hope so.

Two people torn apart by a misunderstanding and finally coming to peace in the ruins of the world.

In a dim cave.

Hugging on the floor of the boat.

This is change.

18

KAI

I AM NOT SURE WHAT HAPPENED IN THE CAVE.

I wanted to give Callie a little scare, knowing her fright of water. I wanted to teach her a lesson, which was shitty of me in the first place.

But when I saw her screaming and breaking down in that boat, I went into full panic mode.

I shouldn't have done it. We should have sat down and talked like she asked.

But that's what bitterness and hatred do—turn you into a monster, right?

And then she is in my arms. I don't even care that I am pressing her to my scars. Those scars are the harsh consequences. We have them deep inside. But mine are on the outside, too. Being called a monster behind your back slowly makes you one. But that moment when I saw her screaming my name and collapsing in that boat made my heart hammer in panic like it had never done before.

My stupid. Dirty. Broken. Fucking. Heart.

Still beating.

And still beating hard for Callie Mays.

Fuck. Me.

I hold her crying in my arms, and I feel too much. Anger. Regret. Guilt. Rage. Hurt. And something else that makes my heart beat like mad. Because she is in my arms.

Finally.

I shake, because she is the closest she's ever been. The past comes down onto me like a waterfall. What I felt. How much I wanted her. How much I despised her for running away like a coward.

This moment wipes away the years of hurt, the years between the day after the Block Party and now.

It's the moment that shows that I am not as strong as I thought, and my feelings for her aren't as weak as I believed.

Dammit, Callie.

We finally break apart, not looking at each other.

I start the boat and slowly motor it out of the cave.

The sun is low over the island, but it seems too bright. It feels like I've been holding my breath for four years and just now exhaled.

"There are life vests under that seat," I tell Callie, finally looking at her.

She sniffles, meeting my gaze.

Fuck, this girl is beautiful even with her face red and swollen from crying. Her blue eyes are even more luminous and sparkly with tears. The memory of how she felt in my arms makes my body want to wrap around her again.

"Will you save me if I start drowning?" she asks, chuckling and looking away.

I smile. And the sun seems to wink at me.

"Petal, that sounds easier than saving you from Archer Crone."

We both smile and stare at the blue water that is calm and shimmering in the sun. The words bring back the memories, but they are not as hurtful anymore. As if a weight has been lifted off my chest.

Maybe we can be friends now.

She asks me to kill the motor, and when I sit on the bench across from her, she asks me about my family.

My dad. Lilly, my younger sister. Both gone.

So is her family.

We chat. And chat. And chat. Like the cave episode didn't happen. Like we came out of some time warp that erased the horrible void between us.

We avoid talking about the Block Party like it's a still a forbidden topic. We talk about the siblings we lost and the Change. She tells me about the world out there. I tell her about the island.

"You are lucky," she says.

I shake my head.

"You know what the best thing about death is?" I glance at her.

She gapes at me. "Wow. I am surprised you put those words in the same sentence."

"Yeah. Wow," I echo, studying the horizon. "It's when it strikes once and quickly. The worst part is when someone is dying slowly, miserably, in agony. When, before death, you face the ugliest side of human nature."

I go quiet, remembering the night the Savages from the town attacked our village.

"It's not all paradise here, petal. Shit happens."

"Like what?"

I shrug. "Like hurricanes. Food shortages. The attacks of the Savages, who occasionally show up drunk or high. It's…not pretty."

Rape. Killings. Robberies.

I don't say those words.

"Fights?"

Callie is so naive that I omit the darkest words to spare her.

"That's the least of it," I say. "They look for girls."

Callie goes quiet, afraid to ask.

"Olivia." The name makes my stomach turn at the memories. "We had Olivia with us until a year ago."

"What happened to her?"

"She is dead."

I don't explain. Callie doesn't ask.

I exhale and slide down on the boat bench, my hands locked behind my head as I study the sky for a moment, trying to drown out the memories of that fucked-up night.

And when I look down at Callie, her eyes are roaming my body and dart away quickly when I catch her.

You like that, petal?

But there is no bitterness at the thought. Only regret.

She tells me more about the Change.

I study her when she talks, looking away. Her nose and cheeks, shoulders and chest are already burnt by the sun. I curse Maddy who didn't properly insist on sun protection, and now Callie's skin is not perfect. Neither is her hair, unbrushed and messy and frizzy unlike the flat-ironed perfection from before.

But I like her better this way. Here, she is closer to me. Now, we might be back on good terms.

The sun is setting behind the island. It colors the ocean with an orange glow and reflects on Callie's skin. This is the most peaceful I've felt in a while.

The bright colors reflect on the water and the wet sand strip on the beach, left by the low tide, turning it salmon-orange

"We missed dinner," I say.

Callie meets my gaze. It's soft. It's forgiving. It lingers on me longer this time. Longer still.

I don't look away. The air between us burns with something that makes my heart clench the way it did back then, four years ago, when she wasn't yet with Crone, when I sent her those stupid flowers, when she batted her eyelashes at me and blushed when I called her petal, and I felt like something magical in my life was unraveling.

Until Crone ruined it all.

Callie's pretty lips stretch in a little smile as she finally casts her eyes down.

"Yeah," she says, nodding. "Dinner."

That's human kind—existential dilemmas and basic instincts.

"Yeah," I mimic her, and we both smile.

Fuck me.

It took four years and a world war to see Callie Mays smile at me again.

19

KAI

THE NEXT DAY FEELS LIKE A NEW BEGINNING.

On the island, we get up early and go to bed early. There isn't much to do in the dark.

We are working on building a new bungalow. Some of us have to share rooms. Others, like me and Bo and Maddy, have one to themselves. The pier stretch was ruined by the storm some time ago, so slowly, we try to rebuild.

There are hardly ever any arguments about accommodations or food or anything else. In two years, we learned to work together. Most of the time, we are tired.

Most arguments are about booze and trips to town. Or the conversations about the Change and going back to the mainland. Which, for one, is impossible. Two, dangerous. Three, there is always this dilemma of what's better—being trapped on the island or have freedom in a lawless land ridden with radiation and violence.

My paradise feels like one when I see Callie at breakfast.

I am still self-aware around her, but it's different. She

smiles more and laughs at Ty's jokes. And her laughter makes me wanna build ten bungalows in a day.

After breakfast, Katura comes to help us with building.

"I am not gardening. Screw that shit. I want to do this," she says, wearing boots, shorts, and a tight tank. Her braids are gathered in the back by a bandana. This chick has balls, for sure. And the looks. She is hot. What is she doing on this God-forsaken island?

The sun is scorching. We are shirtless, sweat dripping down our bodies. Now and then, we take a dip in the ocean, then get back to work.

"What do you say we go dive for lobsters this afternoon?" I suggest.

"Hell yeah!" Guff doesn't fish but loves food.

The guys are all for it, and in the afternoon, we hop in the boat and take off. It's a longer trip, about an hour off the coast, then another hour diving with spears.

But we come back in the evening with fifteen monsters. Everyone is ecstatic. Only Ethan shakes his head.

"Fuck me, that's a lot of cleaning," our cook says.

But everyone helps. We fire up the grills. Music starts playing on the speakers. Hammocks are swaying. Local beer is poured.

"Baby, cook that fish the way you do it," Ty coos, rubbing against me playfully as I fillet the fish until I threaten him with a knife.

I cook. For the first time in months, I feel like cooking.

Because *she* will be eating it.

And, hell, she does, licking her fingers from that chili-honey grilled tilapia and the grilled lobster with lemon.

All eighteen of us—twenty one again now, to be correct—sit around the two dining tables groaning as we suck on the lobster tails and eat fish without utensils.

Sublime trickles through the speakers. Jeok tells a joke. Santino argues with Jordan, then throws an empty lobster shell at him.

Ty moans like a girl. "Fuck, this is so good." Butter drips down his chin. "Kai, seriously. I want to have your baby."

Even Dani, who is always silent, laughs loudly, and Ty rips a fat piece of lobster tail, dips it into the orange sauce, and offers it to her. "Try it, angel."

Angel? That's new.

She eats it off his fingers and laughs again, nodding. And Ty glows like a Christmas tree—the fool is in love.

"Good?" he asks Callie who sits in front of him.

"Yeah. It's amazing." She licks her fingers.

"Kai cooked it," Ty says proudly and winks at her. "He would have been a good boyfriend. If…"

He goes quiet.

"If it weren't for the Change?" Katura asks.

"Nah." Ty waves her away. "If he were better at oral, maybe."

Bo starts sneering. Maddy chuckles. And in seconds, the entire table bursts out laughing.

"Fuck off," I blurt, turning red. He is such a liar.

"What's up, sunshine?" Ty looks at me, feigning surprise. "Is that chili too hot and got your face all red?"

I shake my head, avoiding looking where Callie is, and wanna kill the bastard.

"Just spread that lobster tail shell wider and dive in with your tongue," Ty teases.

Everyone is laughing loudly. The other table turn their heads and grin in our direction.

Fucker.

I throw the shell down onto my plate. "Thanks, bro. Ruined that one, didn't you?"

"A little fishy, you say?" Ty carries on.

And then everyone roars with laughter.

I tackle him, we both fall off the bench, and we wrestle, goofing around as everyone cheers or boos.

This feels like family.

The sunset.

The breeze.

Reggae.

Smoke from the grill.

Laughter.

Happy faces.

I catch Ty in a headlock, which takes me only seconds.

"Hey," he says in a strained voice as I strangle him playfully, making him helpless. "Wrestling won't get you a girl, you know?" he says, and then I break down in laughter.

I love this human being. And tonight, I love life.

We get up, pushing each other, both grinning.

"Awe, hell," Ty exhales, looking down his bare torso.

We are both covered in sand and streaks of oil from greasy fingers.

"Maddy, darling," Ty coos, "will you wash our dishes? Droga and I gonna go take a dip."

And then he is running toward the water, his blond hair

flapping in the breeze. I am right behind him. Several others follow.

He turns, running backward, his forefingers pointing at me as he shouts, "I love you, baby!"

Fool.

Laughing, we dive into the orange-pink sunset water.

Life is amazing.

In moments like this, we feel lucky.

Such moments are rare, and when they happen, we hold on to them and each other.

20

MADDY

THE THREE NEW ARRIVALS FIT IN PERFECTLY WITH US. They work, clean, and help out with chores. It's been days, but we still haven't had the second meeting about their stay here.

All the while, everyone tries to stay close to them and ask questions.

About the Change.

About how things went down.

What it's like.

We are all curious. We've seen the news when the Change hit. We spent weeks in mourning and tears and discussions when we tried to track family members, only to find out that many of us didn't have any.

That came with the feeling of helplessness. Then the desire to fuck off to the mainland. Then the news that all the means of transportation had stopped.

A private jet came—the big daddy, Secretary Crone. He held a meeting like we were bootcamp kids, explaining what was happening in the world and that this spring break was going to be much longer than the pandemic one. With nowhere to return to.

He spent hours in Archer's villa, arguing. Eventually, Archer stormed out, all curses and rage. Then Daddy flew away, taking Anna Reich, who was a congressman's daughter and Archer's current girlfriend, with him.

When the first boat came days later, many had a chance to go back. Only about twenty people left. By then, the coastal areas of the mainland were destroyed, because the bombs caused tsunamis that sent nearby islands and coastal towns underwater. Protective equipment became mandatory. Martial law and curfews were the new normal. People were sent to inland areas. Looting and riots became the new way. And those who broke the law were sent to interment camps because prisons were full.

The fallout. Overloaded hospitals. Brutal violence.

The suicide rate was seven hundred percent higher.

The pandemic several years back seemed like an innocent joke.

There was no end to the atrocious news. So most of us stayed.

And then all hell broke loose with Archer and his crew and the new rules and the fighting and that fateful night when the Savages came to claim their island and Kyle and several others were killed. And then the fight between Kai and Archer happened. Kai wasn't even with the springbreakers, but the camp divided, and those who didn't want to lick Archer's boots left for the Eastside.

"You used to go to Deene, right?" I ask Callie one morning as she joins us for yoga at sunrise.

"Yeah."

She doesn't say much more, and I don't push.

Except, something is happening between her and Kai. They used to glare at each other like enemies. That night at the bonfire, drunk Katura said something about Callie's past that sent her over the edge.

The next day, Kai and her went on a boat ride, and things changed. Now there are occasional smiles and meaningful glances between them. Two days later, they sit on the beach in the evening and talk for the longest time.

"The boy is in love, eh?" Ty leans over on the dining room beam and watches the two on the beach as I sit with a cup of cold tea and talk to Bo.

"Is that what it is?" I pry. "They knew each other from before, yeah?"

"Something like that." Ty passes a joint to me as he squints at them in the distance.

I take a tiny drag. I don't smoke often, but occasionally, it helps me forget about the world outside.

And Jesus, if Ty, who is a natural gossiper, isn't secretive. They say he and Kai go way back. I was surprised when Ty left Archer's crew to come here to the Eastside. Now he is the gatekeeper of Kai and Callie's secrets.

It's all right.

Many of us have our own.

I look at Bo for confirmation, but he only shrugs his shoulders with a smile. He and Kai are close too. Kai somehow brings all the guys together.

I expect Ty to walk away but he doesn't like he is looking for company or a talk.

I know Ty on evenings like this. He would usually go hang out with Kristen and probably score a quickie. But he lingers around now, searching for something.

Someone, to be exact.

Dani.

Right.

Dani still won't talk much. Except for when she is with Ty, who is obsessed with her.

One evening, he comes to talk to me.

"What do I do to make her smile more?" he asks.

And I see it then.

Oh, Ty…

He paces around and pushes his blond hair back in frustration as he stares at me like I am a couples' counselor.

He fusses over the girl, takes her to walks, to the springs, brings her flowers. The rest of the guys sneer at him and make crude jokes. But Ty doesn't bat an eyelash.

I smile when I watch him.

He is falling for her, fast and deep. Just like everything else that Ty does—he dives head in.

It's cute and charming. Except Dani is like an empty shell.

"Did you talk to her? What happened to her since the Change?" I ask him.

"Yeah. Her family is gone."

"There is always a trauma behind it all," I say. "Hers might be different. Or her view of it is. Talk to her more," I suggest.

But it's hard to prioritize someone else's trauma. We all have our own.

There are days, evenings, and nights, when we go quiet and don't talk to anyone. Paradise can block out grief and emptiness. Until it feels like you are suspended in time. That you've been tricked. That it's a fancy lie, and the world is ok.

It torments you. It kills you with doubt.

Once in a while, I see Ty on the beach by himself. He is quiet. The sunshine Ty is alone, sitting on the sand, his elbows resting on his knees, head low.

In those moments when I watch him from afar, I know that those who smile and laugh the most and try to cheer up others often fight the darkest battles. And when I spot him one night on the beach, in the dark, and go to check on him, he is drunk and laughs when I shine my flashlight at him. But his face is wet, and I know he is crying.

But what can I do?

We all have traumas that rip through us with claws so sharp that they make our hearts bleed. Mine started before the Change. In a way, the Change made things better for me, or so I'd like to think.

Katura, on the other hand, asks more questions than anyone. She goes on hikes and disappears into the jungle or behind the rocks north and south of the beach. She joined the boys on a fishing trip one morning.

"She didn't care about the fish, that for sure," Kai said later. "She looked around, studied the beach like she was mapping out the island."

I don't like that.

That's why when I sort out the kitchen storage one afternoon and see Katura hike toward the path that leads to the springs, I set the boxes I've been stacking aside and quietly follow her.

I know every path within a mile radius of the beach, so it's not hard to know which direction she is going and how to track her. I take a parallel path along the main one, scanning the trees to see her t-shirt flicker among them. The jungle is full of noises during the day. But I've been here long enough to listen to the right ones, and I can hear her footsteps until they stop.

Hiding behind the trees, crouching to get closer, I watch Katura as she looks around, then sits on her haunches and pulls a pouch out of her backpack.

She survived a boat crash and saved her backpack. Atta girl! This ingenuity comes with proper training, and I admire her for that. But it's too out of place. She is only nineteen, she said. And she is hiding from everyone to look at whatever she smuggled with her.

Katura pulls something out of a plastic pouch, carefully sets the bag aside, and inserts something small into a rectangular device she is holding.

I swallow hard, watching her from behind the tree.

If she made it to the Westside on that boat, there would have been a proper search. Whatever it is that she brought with her would have been taken away. Unless she had another way of hiding it.

But why would she?

I think I know what she is holding in her hand. I stare in disbelief—no one on this side of the island has it. Unless you have connections to the outside. Unless you came here for a reason other than to join the paradise crew.

She presses the button.

In seconds, a beep sounds, and Katura pulls—

An antenna.

Shit.

I was right.

It's a satellite phone.

21

KATURA

THREE MONTHS EARLIER...

"We can't go to the island and extract. They have radars. The Secretary of Defense made sure his son's playground is armed to a tee. We have to play by the rules."

My uncle's voice is business-like. I feel excited. It's the first time he's talked to me like this. Hell, it's the first time they've asked me to do something on my own. Of that scale.

My dad is typing away on the computer at his desk in the corner. Our cabin in the mountains of Pennsylvania is several miles from a small town in the valley. A town that is more or less decent and carrying on after the Change.

This is also the first time I hear about Zion Island. And the story is out of the books.

"Plus, we don't want casualties." Uncle taps the pen against his thumb as he sits in the armchair, his feet crossed at the ankles on top of the desk. I am on the other side of it, and I feel like it's a job interview. "If the secretary finds out we invaded his son's precious haven, he might get angry.

Tsar is not exactly friends with him. Besides, we are not sure his daughter is there."

"Name?"

"Milena Tsariuk. Her father is Aleksei Tsariuk, goes by Tsar. You get the idea. His reach is pretty wide and strong worldwide."

"Why didn't he just talk to Secretary Crone?"

"He did." Uncle smirks. "The secretary sent a request to his son. Archer Crone said she is not on the island. He has extensive records of everyone. This is a tricky situation. She might not even be on the island. Or—"

"Under a different name," I finish.

He nods, leans over to grab a folder, and tosses it to me.

Besides a number of pages that I will read later, there is a picture of the girl.

Short light slick hair with bangs. Fine Easter European features. When you know the heritage, it almost jumps out at you. Mother Russia makes girls with pretty faces and guys who look like serial killers. I got the best of two worlds—my mom's pretty face and my dad's bronze skin and dark thick hair. Ukrainian and Puerto Rican—a rare mix. *Fire*, as my uncle often says with a smile.

This Milena Tsariuk is beautiful but has too much makeup on, which makes her look like a doll.

"She has an accent, though. How hard is it to track her?" I ask.

"She doesn't. She moved to the states as a teen."

I mull over it. This is exciting, and my heart already pounds in anticipation. But I have my doubts. "There are thousands of applicants wanting to go to the island. Well, considering the looks and skills, it narrows down to hundreds."

"You have a portfolio that no one can beat, Kat. You are an asset. I'll try to use some leverage. But honestly, if you can't get in, fuck, who can? And you'll fit right in."

"I'm only nineteen."

"They like young ones. You know the reason they do it every several months—they get bored with their own. They need help. Fresh blood. People die…"

I snort.

Uncle looks at me like I have a third eye. "Thirteen of them died since the Change. Seven during the fight that went down with the locals. That's unofficial info."

"No shit," I mouth. The number is so minuscule compared to the Change. But in paradise, it seems horrifying. "Someone actually came back?"

"Yeah. Twenty or so. The ones who still had family—pretty much the ones from the most influential families, surprise-surprise—were shipped off to the mainland."

"How did they know about their families?"

"Kat, come on. Public records. Database. Connections. There is a tower there and a data center, remember? The secretary's kid does a thorough check of everyone who is there and who arrives. Plus, there is more to that island than it being a hideaway."

"Tell me."

"The Chancellor"—he snorts at the word—"that's what they call Archer Crone. The spring-breakers, the Elites, are on the Westside. It's the resort part. About two miles by one mile deep. It's like Kardashian bootcamp there. Jersey Shore but with a lot more money. Not that you know either. You are too young. They had a falling out with a bunch of their own when the Change happened, and about twenty or so of them moved to the Eastside to the small self-sustaining resort. They are called the Outcasts."

"Dramatic."

"Right. The northern part of the island is the local town. Population about five thousand. Much less by now, probably, because of the diseases and fighting and lack of local law enforcement. It's a shithole. Drugs, booze, crime, prostitution. All the good stuff. Nothing you haven't seen in Bangkok but no one to regulate it. And they got blocked by the Chancellor. So they depend on him too. Nothing moves in or out of that island without his say-so. There are cameras everywhere. They use StingRay-type technology to create local cellphone network. The place is wired to a tee. The secretary sent contractors to work coastal security."

I whistle in surprise.

Uncle nods. "The central part is tropical forests and mountains. There is a cabin there. Belongs to an expat."

"Do I need to know about other parts besides the Westside?" I wonder.

Uncle stares at me for some time. Dad in the corner types away on the computer that is hooked up to the satellite dish outside the house and doesn't look up. He is proud of me, I know. And he is worried. Though I've seen enough shit in my life to handle the rich brats who play Lords of the Flies.

Uncle finally exhales. "This sounds like a game, Kat, but

you need to be prepared. Shit happens. They might not let you leave. You might get in all sorts of situations."

I snort. "I can handle it. They are immatures with guns."

Uncle's gaze hardens, and he leans over. "Listen here." There is no trace of patronizing or condescendence in him anymore. No joking either. "Archer Crone was a star quarterback. The secretary's son. The entire campus at Deene was under his thumb."

"Yawn."

"He was the best," Uncle continues. "But football was his hobby. Not his strongest side."

"What was?"

"IQ over 170."

"Oh," I mouth. Fuck me.

"His mother and brother died in a crash when he was twelve."

"Mental trauma?"

"You'll find out. But here is the thing, Kat. Zion's Westside is not exactly a resort. Crone and a couple of others developed blood-testing equipment that creates a personalized formula for the medication to prevent gene mutations after the fallout."

I swallow hard. That sounds like a sci-fi movie.

"Sounds intense," I say with a forced smirk, though I am not so sure it's a game anymore.

Uncle nods. "Heard of the Gen-Alpha Project that failed back in 2018?"

"Yeah."

"Wonder why so many wealthy smart people invested

money and didn't make a buzz when the project went belly up?"

I don't answer.

"The public part of it was just a venture. The actual info and studies were meant for times like this—the Change."

"You are telling me that the Secretary of Defense knew what was coming?"

"Irrelevant."

"You are telling me that twenty-four-year-old Crone and a bunch of his friends are the masterminds of the medical field?"

He nods, blinking slowly. "Yep. Why do you think that island is so armed? It's not just the secretary's money that has sponsored it for the last two years. And not just the investors' either. Crone is a genius. You shouldn't underestimate him."

I cock an eyebrow.

Uncle cocks one right back.

Damn.

Silence sinks between us for a moment.

"Kat, you are not Batman. But you are the best chance we got. The money we get if we bring the girl back will let us move to Australia. Or South America. It will open doors. Tsar will move us anywhere we want."

I know. I am tired of this country that is growing wilder by the day. I want to be elsewhere—the parts where it's more or less decent. Most importantly, I want to finally prove that I can use everything that Dad taught me.

"Two years on an isolated island makes one desperate and harsh," Uncle continues. "Trust me, they are not as soft as you might think. Archer Crone might sound like a privileged star quarterback. But he is brilliant. And vicious. So buckle up, Dorothy, and listen."

And I do. Because I am curious and excited as fuck.

I grew up with a sense of adventure. Learning how to hunt, load weapons, shoot, jog for miles through the mountains, fight, do first medical assistance, cook, grow shit, camp in the wild, and make fire without matches. That's only a part of it.

I was home-schooled.

When I was eleven, my mom died. My dad, who was a Navy SEAL, came back and we lived in Arizona for some time. Then we moved to Thailand.

Bangkok can teach you a lot.

Especially when you are thirteen, and your dad is a private contractor, and your sitter is more concerned with her new boyfriend, so you are running around with the local street gang, a lady-boy for a best friend, occasionally doing drug deliveries. Because you are brazen, only thirteen, and it's a wild world, and you want to explore every part of it. The youngest kid doing deliveries is six, so you should do much better. You learn the streets by heart, and the bosses give you pocket money and nod with a smile when you make a delivery, then laugh when you ask if you can do anything else.

Occasionally, you spend nights in random undercover apartments because the sitter canceled, but your dad has to go to work. So he takes you with him.

You sit in an armchair with a girl not much older than you, whose tits fall out of her netted leotard, her stiletto heels longer than your arms. She is the star of a "pussy shows" at Patpong, popular among tourists. Her makeup is smudged, but she smiles at you.

"You shouldn't be here," she says.

One of the undercover guys, loading his gun, comes over and ruffles your hair, then turns to her, and his smile vanishes.

"Neither should you, Pinky. And if we don't capture that *chao pho*, you are as good as dead."

Chao pho is a big crime boss, and the girls work for him, you learn.

There are four more girls next to you, barely wearing any clothes, men's suit jackets draped over their shoulders.

The undercover men with guns and your dad discuss the capture.

You hear the word *raid*. It sounds exotic.

You eat your green tea ice cream and study them all curiously. You don't want to be one of those pretty girls with bright makeup and funky shoes. You want to be one of the men who wear vests and baseball hats and look like bad-ass guys from movies.

That's the night you learn another word.

Sex trafficking.

It sounds dangerous.

A week later, you ask your father about the raid and the girl you made friends with and find out that she is dead.

Your father doesn't hide the brutal facts of life from you. He knows that the more realistic you are about life, the better the chances of your survival.

Two years later, you move back to the US, to a small

town in the mountains of Pennsylvania, boring as hell and too quiet. You do everything your father teaches you. You play games in a shelter built underground. You follow him into the Appalachians with only the clothes on your back and learn how to make a fire, a shelter, and survive for weeks. You learn the skills that seem only useful in movies.

Because you want to be Wonder Woman.

Most importantly, because your father says that one day, they might *save your ass*.

And one day, they do.

22

KAI

In the days following the episode in the cave, everything changes so rapidly that it feels like Christmas in May.

Callie and I talk again the next evening. We sit on the beach and watch the sunset. Everything is quiet and resting after a hot day. Nature starts getting ready for sleep. But my body is on full alert next to hers.

It kills me.

I try to stay away.

Day after day.

It only gets harder.

I go fishing, surf with the boys, and stay busy in the workshop. But since the cave, we don't have to pretend we hate each other. And we don't. Callie pulls me in like a fucking magnet. She is constantly around. Her slender body is everywhere, no matter where I look.

Soon, she becomes the one thing I think about when I wake up and when I go to bed.

Right after I jerk off thinking about her.

Fuck. Me.

The first time it happens is on the day of the cave incident. I am in bed, hot and naked and wide awake. I think it's stress relief. And because my fucking stress has blond hair and blue eyes, naturally, it is Callie who opens her legs for me, her pussy taking my cock as I pound and pound into her.

My mind goes wild with the fantasies. I want to rip her apart. I want her to cry, scream, pant, and moan in pain and pleasure. More than anything, I want to hear my name on her lips when she comes all over my cock. I want to fuck her like I hate her. And then make love to her like we've been dating for months.

While I think about it, I jerk my cock in my hand with so much intensity that I come in less than a minute.

But then I wake up at dawn with a boner again.

Dammit!

Guess whose face is right there in my mind when I stroke myself to oblivion?

And then she is outside one morning, at dawn, walking on the beach in her lime bikini with fucking strawberries that I want to rip off her with my teeth.

Ty, Owen, and I are about to take off fishing.

"Can I come with you?" she asks.

No.

I need to think about the catch and not her half-naked body next to me.

But fucking Ty grins. "Yeah. Hop in! Maybe Kai will show you how to handle his rod."

I want to kill him. Callie laughs and slaps him on the arm. And my face turns bright fucking red.

Ty notices. "It's suddenly too hot in here, no?"

The motherfucker winks. And I want to wrap his blond hair around my fist and dunk his head into the water.

He is glowing, too—something must be happening with him and Dani.

I try to focus on fishing, but there are glimpses—Callie's slender legs with scratches and sand stuck to her feet. Her already tanned skin that is in beautiful contrast with her bikini. This wouldn't be high damage to my already fucked up mind if I didn't catch the tiny glimpses of white skin on her breasts that are covered by the lime triangles.

Fuck.

I've seen her breasts before. That night of the Block Party when I made up my mind to undress her so she didn't sleep in her own puke. Silk dress. Bra. I remember my hands hesitating when I lifted her senseless body on my bed and unclasped her bra, then turned away and pulled it off. But the goddamn thing got caught on her arm, and when I turned just for a second to free it, her beauties were staring at me. I covered her right away with the blanket. But Callie Mays' breasts were something I couldn't unsee for the longest time. They were like unsolicited porn images that startled me in the middle of other thoughts, however grim they were after that night.

And here she is again.

Every day.

Breakfast.

Lunch.

Dinner.

Her voice is almost tangible against my skin. Her stares at my tattoos that I catch once in a while make me tense up.

And then she sits with the girls on the beach at sunset and watches us surf.

"You have a new addition to your fanbase. Besides Kristen, of course," Ty jokes as he paddles, lying on his board, up to me and grins. "Does she know about the accident?"

I turn away, scanning the rocks in the distance. "Doesn't matter."

"No?"

"It doesn't fucking matter, Ty," I snap. Like I need any more pity. Especially from her.

"You know, some of us lost everything after the Change."

Shut up. I shake my head. I hate this emotional shit.

"And still…" Ty doesn't let go. "You play cool. Like we are at Deene and we have a lifetime of opportunities to fuck up."

"Cut it out."

"But we lost them all. And when something good comes our way, it's a miracle."

"Yeah. A miracle," I echo bitterly.

"Why don't you pull your sorry head out of your ass for once and tell your girl how you felt years ago?"

"She is not my girl." But my heart—the motherfucking traitor—starts fluttering in my chest.

"She can be. You don't think it's obvious how you two look at each other?"

"Dude." I turn to look at him and smash the water with my palm, sending splashes into his face. "Fuck off, yeah?"

He shakes his head. "Damn, bro, you need a cross?"

"What?" I frown.

"It's a good prop for a martyr." He smiles. "Maybe you can go on a hunger strike to show how misery is your best friend and—"

I kick his board hard and send him into water, but he laughs when he reemerges.

"Cheer up, fool!" he shouts and crawls back onto the board, swinging his head to shake the wet hair off his face.

We sit on the boards, rocking on the waves that are not high enough after the storm for proper surfing and watch the beach.

"How is your angel?" I ask.

My question is not sarcastic, and Ty is too open in his affection. He likes the girl a lot. It's obvious and cute. I've never seen Ty obsess about a girl like that. Not in Deene. Not with anyone, though he is all smiles and bows and winks with everyone, including Kristen, who fucks everyone.

Guys make fun of him and Dani. "Team not getting any" is always bitter about those who get lucky. Ty is not just in for some luck—he is head over heels.

I am "team not getting any" for sure. For over a year now.

We used to go to town and visit Candy and her girls and buy liquor. But the town is miles away. After what happened to Olivia, we only go there for trading. That place took a dip for the worse.

Even the local expat, Bishop, is said to have retired to his cabin in the middle of the jungle, because the town is a shit-hole. Bishop is a legend. No one bothers him. And what he does up there is a mystery. Maybe he went nuts, who knows.

Anyone can go nuts after the Change.

Even in paradise.

23

KAI

ONE DAY, OVER A WEEK SINCE THE BOAT CRASH, MADDY TAKES me aside after dinner.

"So, that girl, Katura, yeah?" she says, narrowing her eyes at me. "You know how you thought it was super weird that she kept studying the coast when you took her fishing?"

"Yeah?"

"She has a satellite phone."

I stall. "What?"

"I saw it. She didn't come to the island for fun or fresh air."

"No shit. I'll tell Bo."

And Bo studies me for some time in silence when I spill the info. We sit in the workshop and smoke a joint.

"So she came to spy on Archer, or the entire island, whatever the deal is." Bo is calm and calculating something in his mind. "Here is the thing though. I know age is not an indicator. She might be a trained assassin for all I know."

He passes the joint to me. "But if she thinks she can sneak past Archer, she is in for a big fucking surprise."

I nod.

As much as I hate Crone, the fucker is genius. He might have been into chicks and drugs and booze and football, all mula and fun on the surface. But at home, he had a library the size of fucking Congress. He could speed read and had a photographic memory. He spoke fluent Spanish and was brilliant in chemistry. He invented two party apps that went viral and did some day trading. He wasn't your typical rich kid—he's been making money since he was thirteen.

I admired him. He was like no one else. Behind the spoiled kid who liked to tell the world to bow and paraded hot chicks around, he blew me away with his random conversations.

I'm still not sure how our friendship started. Crone always had a big crew. An inner circle. And another cohort of fans. But within a year, we became best friends. He was like a brother who, when everyone headed like a herd of sheep to some hot happening, would pull into my shabby driveway and say, "Come on, bro, fuck them all. Let's go for a ride."

There was this invisible thread that tied us together. Things we shared were at times too shameful. Stories that no one else knew about that we told each other, drunk or high, when we roamed the city and the most random places.

We got drunk in Tijuana one spring and got into a fight with cartel mules. We raced sports bikes. We went to Ultra Fest and partied with some big-name DJ, then flew with him to Tulum for a wild week, then ditched him, rented a car, and drove up across Mexico.

Then Callie came along. Crone saw the way she and I looked at each other.

That's when something snapped in him.

I think, for the first time, he felt really jealous. Deep affection was his issue, after what happened to his mom and brother. And he decided that if he couldn't have the happily ever after, no one would.

It all went downhill. If we'd sorted it all out the day after the Block Party, life could have been different.

But the next day was the beginning of the end.

I know Crone better than he knows himself. He thinks he has his shit together. But that accident with his mom and little bro left him forever scarred. It made him vicious when something made him feel vulnerable.

Katura doesn't know that, but she should. She will find out. I hope it doesn't break her free spirit. I pray Crone doesn't fuck up her ego.

I ask Callie about her.

"She never said anything," Callie says as we walk toward the greenhouse one morning after breakfast. "But she didn't lose anyone during the Change. And she is too independent to want to be locked away here. So it makes you wonder…"

"Yeah. She has a family?"

"Well." Callie smiles as if remembering something.

Fuck, how I love Callie's smile. She is wearing flip-flops and a surfer's tank that comes down just barely below her bikini bottom. Her hair is tied in a loose bun on top of her head, and I want to throw her over my shoulder, carry her into my bungalow, and fuck her senseless.

S-s-stop.

"Here is what she told me," Callie says, stopping by the entrance to the greenhouse, then looks inside to make sure no one can hear and crosses her arms over her chest. "Her dad and uncle are former Navy SEALs," she says in a low voice. I chuckle in surprise. She nods with a half-smile. "Yeah. They did some contract jobs in Asia. They built a bomb shelter in the mountains of Pennsylvania a year before the stuff went down."

"No shit…"

"She's lived in Arizona, California, in Thailand for several years. She knows martial arts, first aid, shooting all sorts of weapons, speaks a little bit of Russian, fluent Spanish, and some Thai."

"Holy shit," I murmur.

"I mean. I thought she was adventurous. I didn't think twice about it when we were on the way here."

"Right."

We stand in silence for a moment, and I need to leave before I make it too fucking awkward.

"See you later, yeah?" I blurt.

I walk away, knowing that Callie watches me. And I already can't wait till lunch when I see her again.

Fuck, petal, this is getting harder by the day.

Both being around her and my cock that twitches at the unsolicited fantasies of her that disrupt the course of my day now and then.

Bo is already in the workshop when I walk in.

We have three regular guns that we scored in town some time ago for protection. We made twelve handguns from random parts. We have knives, blades, bows, and arrows with metal tips, though not many are good at them, and we haven't had a single practice since the new arrivals.

Well, fuck, since Callie showed up in my life, I haven't had a single coherent thought in my head. Just images. Memories. Feelings. They crowd my mind and heart like a jungle full of parrots in the morning.

I exhale loudly as I take off my t-shirt, ready to start on the new gun.

But before we start, I tell Bo what I learned about Katura.

"If she is an important asset, Archer will come for her," Bo says. "But I have a feeling, he will come for Callie before anything."

Yeah, I told him the story the other day. I had to. Another meeting was about to happen.

Bo looked at me intensely when I finished the story about the Block Party, ran his palms over his dreads, and said three words.

"We are fucked."

And then there was the meeting where Bo talked to all three girls. Separately. All three said they wanted to stay for now. And when the rest of us voted for or against letting them stay, all eighteen of us voted for.

Dani smiled at Ty and looked away as if embarrassed, and the fool grinned like a Cheshire Cat.

Callie smiled to herself. No matter how much I stared

her down, she wouldn't look at me, though at some point she blushed.

Katura didn't react much.

But now Bo and I stare at each other, knowing that as soon as the fucking Chancellor finds out about the missing cargo still alive, he'll come for it. And we better be ready to stand up to him. Though the mediocre stash of weapons we have is nothing against his heavy arsenal.

Still.

I think of Callie and him, and my heart thuds with unease. There is only so much you can do against AK-47s and sniper rifles. And there is nowhere to hide on this island.

Most importantly, when Archer Crone wants something, he gets it.

And there is a reason he brought Callie here.

24

CALLIE

"We are going to the waterfall!" Maddy announces when she walks into the bungalow where Katura, Dani, and I rest after lunch.

Katura jumps up right away, excited. "How far is it?"

"About a two-hour hike," Maddy says.

"Who else is going?" I ask.

Katura snorts and looks in my direction. "You mean, besides Kai? Do you even care?"

"Shut it," I snap, smiling.

"Kai, Owen, Ty"—Maddy nods at Dani who blushes right away—"Kristen, Maddy, Mia, Santino, Jeok, Ya-ya. Maybe a couple more. Others will stay here. We never leave the camp without at least several people on guard."

I'm in.

And in about twenty minutes, a bunch of us are walking up the hill and the path that leads through the jungle.

Katura might be right. There is a sense of adventure when we hike up. We chat and fool around. Ty goofs around as we walk. Jeok finds a long bamboo stick and sharpens it into a spear. Kristen laughs too obnoxiously with Ya-Ya and has her arm wrapped around Kai, which makes me wanna slap it away.

The knowledge of him being just ten feet behind makes me giddy and makes the day so much better. But I remember how he shook on the boat. How his body tenses when I am around. We might have cleared the misunderstandings, but he must still despise me.

The jungle finally opens up onto a rock platform.

I gasp in awe.

"Holy hell," Katura whispers.

We are on one side of a river that is about forty feet wide and surrounded by stony banks. Up ahead are the falls. They are glorious, falling down about forty feet, the water cascading in mesmerizing waves, the mist like magical fog rising around it.

"Follow me, bitches," Ty shouts and dives from one of the rocks into the water.

"Is it deep?" I ask.

Maddy shakes her head. "Not here, no. Up to your waist. But closer to the falls, the bottom is caved in about ten feet deep. These guys know all the spots."

Everyone disperses down the bank and into the water. There are shouts and squeals and goofy screams and splashes that are mixed into the humming of the falling water. Birds fleet above.

It's paradise.

I don't care what they say—this place is magical. And for the next two hours, we all sink into a state of carelessness.

I stick to Maddy.

Dani sits on one of the flat rocks just a short distance away, feet dangling in the water as she stares up at the waterfall.

Kristen and Ya-Ya goof around with the boys. I can't help watching Kristen. She is tall, slender, cute, and too nonchalant about what she says or does. I know the type—everyone's friend, everyone's girlfriend.

I sit halfway in the water that is cool and rushing past me as I lean back on the hot stone. Maddy is bobbing in the water in front of me.

Maddy tells me about her when I ask.

I study Kristen talking to Kai, who laughs loudly at something she says.

It startles me. I love hearing him laugh.

I never judged girls like Kristen. We all have habits and things we enjoy. But I think of Kristen and Kai together, and I am so freaking jealous that I want to drag her away from him by her hair.

"So, Kristen slept with Kai then, too?" I ask as I watch them.

"I wouldn't worry about it." Maddy swirls in the water and spits out a little trickle of it. "She likes men. Men like sex. It's what they do. It's a win-win for everyone."

"So he did sleep with her."

Maddy turns to look at me. I can see her smiling gaze but can't hold back my frustration.

"Well, I shouldn't be saying this, because the details are none of anyone's business." Maddy smiles coyly as she pushes off the river bottom and takes a swim toward me, reaching me in several powerful strokes. "Kai doesn't fuck anyone. At least here, in the village. He prefers blowjobs. And no kissing. He is simple."

The words make me uncomfortable and excited all at once. I'd seen the girls at Deene that he hung out with. Pretty. Popular. In and out. I saw him with Julie at the Block Party and the way she sucked his face.

And now the raunchy details…

I feel a wave of arousal wash over me. Kissing. Blowjobs. When I think of Kai right after those words, they make me feel exactly the way I do when I try to sleep at night with two other girls in the room and think of him, wanting to touch myself.

"Did you date any of them?" I ask.

Maddy squints at me.

I shrug. "Sorry. Is it none of my business?"

"It's all right. I didn't."

She sinks into the water and reemerges, wiping her face with her palms.

I don't ask anything else.

Instead, I watch Ty, who crawls like a monkey up the rocks in the distance and to the top of the falls. He stands on top of the cliff, and my heart ceases to beat.

"Tell him to stop," I murmur in a slight panic.

Maddy only laughs. "Chill. He's done it a hundred times. It's deep there. Watch."

And Ty, the freaking fearless ray of sunshine that he is, pushes off the cliff and jumps.

He is like a bird. He folds his arms above him, his hands

together in a spear, and dives into the water with a sharp splash worthy of an Olympic medal.

Everyone cheers.

I grin. I freaking love him.

Freaking Ty!

Dani is about twenty feet away, motionless, staring in that direction.

Ty's head pops up above the water about thirty feet away from us, and he swims brass style in our direction and toward Dani, who is perched on one of the rocks like a bird.

He pushes himself up on his hands on the stone platform she is on, water dripping off him. "You wanna try, angel?"

She shakes her head with a smile.

He pushes up and twists, taking a seat next to her, and shakes his head like a dog, showering her with water.

She laughs, shielding herself.

"He is trying," Maddy says, watching them with a smile. "He is really into her."

"And she is really messed up," I add.

Maddy nods. "Yeah, looks like it. But he might get through to her."

I look around and see Kai floating in the water, his face up toward the sky.

"Kai is the best," Maddy says. "He can do flips and all kinds of crazy shit. He is fearless. He is being shy tonight."

She smiles at me.

I want to see Kai dive. But his presence is enough.

What the hell is my problem?

It's like four years ago.

I can't control my emotions.

The awful thought of what he'd done kept me at bay for years. And now that I know he actually saved me from the worst at his expense, the feelings are back.

I study him as he ducks into the water, then comes out onto the shallower surface, up to his waist.

When he is not looking, I study him quite a bit, learning his tattoos. There is a tiger on his back. Some mythical creatures in dark vibrant colors on his legs. Scales. Floral ornaments. Bold shapes. Card suits.

He is like God.

Inked.

Glorious.

Strong.

I want to be next to him.

I want to wrap myself around him.

I drink him in as he wipes water off his face, then rakes his hands through his hair. And I want to do it for him.

He turns abruptly, his eyes on me. The seconds that our eyes stay locked burn me to the core, and I look away so he doesn't see me blush.

I am so screwed.

25

KAI

IT COMES FROM OUT OF NOWHERE. AS ALWAYS.

Suddenly, the sky gets darker, and I'm thinking, fuck, we stayed too late. The dark clouds start rolling from behind the jungle on the Eastside.

"Oh, shit!"

"Guys!"

"We have to move!"

Everyone starts scrambling, making their way to the bank and the path that leads to the village.

We are over two hours away. And if the downpour starts, it will get dark before we reach home.

But no one seems too concerned, giggling and pushing and shoving as they dress.

"Guys! Watch your step! Stay close!" Maddy shouts.

She is a fucking camp counselor and our mother. She is younger than most, but everyone always listens.

The heavy drops land on my head and skin like pebbles.

"Ooooh, shit!" The boys howl.

We all know that we are a little too late.

And then it comes down fast and hard like a wall, and the girls squeal.

We are used to tropical showers. We embrace them. And now we have new people in our camp. It's exhilarating. There is no waiting this out—just running through it.

The downpour starts, and we *are* running. I don't want to make it too obvious, but I watch Callie from the corner of my eye.

She is giggling, following Maddy, me following her.

I grin.

Yeah, this feels like adventure.

I've been to this waterfall a hundred times, but with her, it feels different.

The rain drums against the big palm leaves. It showers onto us. We are wet. And everyone is laughing. Like it's the biggest fucking miracle that's happened.

The guys make war cries.

Ty is playing Tarzan or whatever he is doing, running around and beating himself in the chest with his fists. Then he grabs Dani by her hand and hurries up the path, making her laugh.

We slip and slide and wipe our faces again and again and squint because the rain already soaked us wet.

There is something magical about a moment of happiness that takes over you suddenly, like a storm. An unexplainable euphoria. It wipes away the past and the future and even the present. It lets you laugh and live in the moment.

Ty is howling like a fool. Katura is behind him, making

war cries. Maddy, Mia, Santino, Jeok, Ya-ya, Kristen, and Owen are all cheering.

Callie is behind them, on purpose or not, and I close the procession.

The branches and leaves slice my face as we dart along the path to the village.

The air around us is thick with rain. The sky is dark, and the path through the jungle is even darker, the trees closing above our heads, leaving just a tiny slice of the dark sky.

The world somewhere else is falling apart.

But fuck!

Euphoria sweeps over us. And we are desperate young souls trapped on this island, running toward something we are not sure of.

"Watch the stump!" someone shouts ahead.

Someone roars with laughter in response.

We only have this moment.

This minute.

This fucked-up sense of happiness takes us away from the memories and grief.

This island traps time. It traps us away from anything that can hurt us. And though there are plenty of things that can damage us here—fuck, we try to harness them, because once in a while we feel powerful.

This is our world.

We cry.

We live.

Ty screams in delight somewhere too far ahead now.

Katura oh-la-las.

The cheers are suddenly so powerful, echoing all over,

that we take over the rainy jungle with them, cackling and chirping like a pack of rowdy parrots.

Someone slips and falls. We laugh hysterically. Because if we don't, we break down and sink in misery.

Here, we are kings.

We are the Outcasts.

We are the lords of the fates.

In these moments, we feel like we are invincible. Because the rest of the world falls to shit, but we are still alive and healthy and happy and young. And we drink and fuck and love and tell stories.

Callie is just a bit ahead of me. She is caught up in the moment, but then trips, and falls to the ground, slipping onto her back with a loud squeal.

I almost trip over her but catch myself.

"You all right?"

I forget the awkwardness between us at this moment when I take her hands and yank her up.

The touch, wet and warm in the tropical rain, is just as powerful as it ever was. This girl is a witch, I swear.

"Yeah. Crap." She gets up and wiggles her shoulders, grinning.

I take her by the arm and spin her around, then peel her wet shirt up.

There is a scratch on her back. Nothing major.

"You cut yourself," I say. "It'll be fine."

And she turns to face me.

Rain is pouring, plastering her hair to her face.

She smiles. And so do I. For no reason whatsoever. Or perhaps the awkwardness of this situation.

I still hold her arm, and she doesn't pull it away but takes a step closer instead.

It's just a step.

One.

Little.

Motherfucking.

Step.

But her blue eyes are on me.

She is smiling, rain running down her face.

I take a tiny step closer too.

And she closes the final distance and licks the rain off her lips.

Everything else suddenly shifts away. There is only this—pouring rain, her body in that soaked shirt and shorts, her face too close to mine, her eyes searching mine for something.

The adrenalin of momentary happiness takes over.

I cup her face and kiss her.

I fucking kiss her.

And she answers.

I don't know if it's her taste or the taste of the rain.

But it's exquisite.

Fresh.

Overpowering.

Charged with happiness.

I place my hand on the back of her head and pull her closer as my other hand lets go of her arm and wraps around her waist.

I deepen my kiss, sliding my tongue between her lips.

It's the rain, I tell myself.

It's the island, I am sure.

It's the momentary spike of serotonin.

It's the happiest moment on this island.

I don't want to let it go.

I don't have to.

I don't care if she pushes me away, but she doesn't.

She wraps her gentle hands around my neck, and I don't even care that she is touching my scars. In this moment, she can touch anything she wants.

The energy of the kiss changes so abruptly that one second we are gentle and cautious, the next one, I am pressing Callie so close to me that I almost lift her off the ground.

The kiss is ravaging, greedy and deep. We dive at each other like our life depends on it, like we need to breathe through each other's mouths. It's tongues and lips and teeth and dripping rain and a little moan that escapes her. I catch it with my mouth and deepen my tongue as if the rest of those little sounds she makes hide somewhere deep inside and I need to get all of them.

Petal…

Fuck…

Why couldn't we have it back then?

Why couldn't we be together?

Why couldn't we get what we both wanted? Because that's how it always felt—that we were meant for each other.

I kiss her like it's the last time. And her lips are so fucking good that I feel like I'm melting. They are soft. So is her tongue, sinking into my mouth with so much need that I know for sure—she wants this as much as I do.

The rain is getting harder.

It's soaking us.

It trickles down my face and onto my lips that are taking hers like there is no tomorrow. Maybe there isn't. We lose our balance and step around as we kiss like we are in some crippled dance. I take it together with her heat and her tongue. I take it all. And I won't stop until she does.

"Yo! It is going to get dark soon!" Owen yells from somewhere up ahead but too close.

Callie pulls away abruptly as if caught. Her eyes are blazing at me, but she starts smiling and wipes the water off her face with both hands.

And then she laughs like a lunatic. And that's how I feel —like I am losing my mind with her.

I missed that laughter.

It's a rainbow in the middle of this storm.

She turns and starts walking up the path, and I follow.

Fuck you, Owen. What the fuck?

The moment is gone.

And though I know it might be just a spontaneous burst of serotonin or dopamine—whatever the fuck it is—I hope I get it back.

26

CALLIE

I AM SO HAPPY, I FEEL LIKE I AM ON DRUGS.

I just kissed Kai.

I grin, walking through the rain. I don't even care that I just fell like a loser and hurt myself.

Everyone is ahead. I don't see them. But I don't care. Because Kai is right behind me. I slip and slide and I try to slow down so I can have another moment with him. Or at least be close to him.

It's getting dark. The clouds are black. The jungle suddenly seems hostile.

I stop and turn around.

Kai is walking up, inked, so fucking glorious that I feel like I am a tribal woman with a tribal man at her side.

"Do you know where we are going?" I ask. I can't see anything upfront. It's like a wall.

"Yeah," he says when he reaches me. "Follow me." He smiles and nudges me with his arm.

God, that arm.

I want it around me again.

I am soaking wet. Rain runs down my body. This is unbelievable and magical, and I don't feel like going back to the shelter. I want to stay here and kiss Kai again.

It's really hazy when we finally get to the familiar wider path I recognize. By now it's a downpour. It's hard to see. The night is coming down fast.

I turn to Kai. "Where are we going?" I have to almost shout against the rain and squint at him because the water pouring down my face blinds my eyes.

"My place!" he shouts back.

Excitement spikes through me at the words.

Yes, your place!

And I follow him.

We finally reach the point where the path opens up to the village beach.

I can't see anything, shielding my eyes from the rain because it's pouring like a shower onto me. We trot toward his bungalow, and somehow, I am the first one to reach it.

When I rip the door to his place open and walk in, it's like a vacuum.

His body slams into mine, pushing me inside, and the door shuts behind us.

"Jesus. How often do these happen?" I ask, squeezing the water out of my hair and sinking into the silence of the room.

Kai pulls his shirt over his head and tosses it onto a chair.

I stare at him. This view never gets old. Guys walk shirtless around most of the time. Yet, seeing Kai is different.

He is mesmerizing. Doesn't he know that?

I am used to a different image of him. But this—*this inked beauty*—is enchanting in all the bad and good ways.

I peel my eyes away and turn around.

The rain clatters on the roof and the trees outside, but the inside is stuffy and quiet. I kick off my shoes and study the interior, which is basic. A low queen bed, a dresser, a desk, a couple of wicker chairs, and a low wicker table. Kai's clothes are scattered around, but nothing else makes this place personalized. He spends most of his time in the workshop.

Music starts trickling in from somewhere, and I turn to smile at Kai.

"Nice," I say, suddenly feeling too self-aware.

He takes a towel from the hook on the wall and tosses it to me, then takes another one and starts drying himself.

I do the same but can't take my eyes off him.

What now?

I want this moment alone to stretch. And I don't know what I want next. Except I don't want to be anywhere else but here with him.

"We should look into that wound on your back," he says.

"Sure," I blurt.

And I am thanking God for the downpour. I hope the storm comes down onto this island so I can be buried here with Kai in my arms.

It's an atrocious thought.

But suddenly, I feel like the last years of fighting my hate and desire came down to me being on this island with him.

27

KAI

"Your wound might get infected. So take off your shirt," I say softly, not looking at Callie.

I walk to the first-aid box in the drawer by the bed. We all have those. Plenty of shit happens, and we know better than to leave wounds unattended. There is no doctor here besides Maddy.

The memory of the kiss still burns my mind, though the scenario changed. "#41" by Dave Matthews Band trickles from the speakers, breaking the awkward silence.

When I come back with the box, Callie still stands next to the desk, staring at me like I am an alien.

"What?" I pull the Neosporin and a Band-Aid out. "I don't have proper mirrors, petal," I say, taking a step closer and cocking my head. "So unless you have an extra-long arm and a third eye on your back, take off your shirt." I pause, holding her gaze. "Or do you want me to do it for you?"

I am being cocky.

I don't know if that's the kiss or something else that makes the air between us so sexually charged. It's probably just me. We are alone. In my bungalow. It's a downpour outside. And I hope that no one—fucking Ty or someone—comes to check on us. I want to be alone with her. For this brief moment. In this small space.

Callie casts her eyes down and pulls the shirt over her head.

It's right there—her exposed skin, the jagged tan lines, her neon bikini top with strawberries.

I don't hide my open stare. She is too close to me, and it's dizzying.

She turns around with her back toward me.

Right, we are doing first-aid care.

I take her towel from the desk and wipe her back, which is wet from the shirt. Cleaning her is arousing as fuck, and I can't hold back a smile.

Her skin is already tanned, her shoulders slightly burned, the white skin peeking from the edges of her lime bikini top. I want to lick those white lines off her skin to make it perfect.

S-s-stop.

I don't know if it's adrenalin, but I feel confident, unlike any other time around her. She is in my domain. Four years ago, I would've been too nice, talking some nonsense to distract myself. I've always been a good guy. Girls always came along. Archer got the feisty ones. I got the nice ones. I didn't care.

Until her.

She is silent. I gaze at the scratch just beneath her bikini strings. It doesn't need dressing. Maybe a swipe of an alcohol pad, that's all. But hey, what wouldn't a guy do to touch the girl he likes?

"Is it bad?" Her voice is low and soft, making my skin hum.

"You'll live," I say with a chuckle and toss the towel away.

My body rises to the awareness of her standing next to me. Alone. Unprotected. Willingly. I want to push her just a little to see where it goes.

So in one swift motion, I undo those ties on her bikini top and pull them down.

Her hands fly to hold her top at her breasts.

"Kai," she snaps and wants to turn, but I place my hands on her waist to keep her in place.

I bring my lips to her ear. "They were on the way. Relax," I say softly.

I love when she says my name.

I grin as I squeeze the ointment on my finger and touch her wound.

She flinches. The more I rub it in, the more her breath quickens.

So does mine.

Damn. Who would've thought nursing is so arousing?

The skin on her back is perfect to the touch. Her damp blond hair is pulled back and hangs like a messy rope along her spine. I push it to the side, just to touch more of her, my fingertips brushing her skin.

I squeeze more of the stuff on my fingers and rub it onto her scratch again.

She turns her head sideways as if trying to see what I am doing but says nothing.

I am gentle. Careful. I don't want to spook her. And the more I touch her skin, the more I feel that energy rising inside me.

It's not lust. Or that, too. But there is something else. The feeling of caring for her. I want to wrap my arms around her and hold her. I want to slide off her clothes and kiss her naked body. I want to pick her up, carry her to my bed, and wrap her in my sheets so that she smells like me. Besides other things, of course, that I want to do to her in my bed that make my cock stir in my board shorts. I want to dry her and make her wet in the right way.

The more I rub that stuff on her, the more I get aroused. And soon, my cock is rock-hard and pitches a tent in my board shorts.

I need to stop this, but I don't want to.

Her skin breaks into goosebumps, and I chuckle.

"What's funny?" she asks quietly.

"Goosebumps. It's not cold here. Are you turned on, petal?"

She doesn't answer.

And fuck, I wish she did, because I would have stopped. I would have pulled away. But her silence is a signal. And I do hope I read it fucking right.

I take the Band-Aid and rip the protective cover, then take the excess medicine off her skin, wiping it on my shorts, because there is a swamp of it, the mess that I've made—the fucking Dr. Droga—and put the Band-Aid on.

It's done.

But I don't say the words. As soon as I do, she will flee to the other side of the room or try to leave. And if she does, I will go mad here by myself thinking of her.

I am shameless, I know. Desperate, for sure.

I put my hands on her waist, lean over, and kiss the skin around her scratch.

Her entire body shivers as my lips touch her skin.

My heart pounds in my chest as I expect her to push me away.

But I do it again.

And again.

And once I inhale the scent of her and kiss that skin, I beg the universe for her not to stop me.

I let the tip of my tongue slide between my lips and follow those kisses up her back to her shoulder. Carefully. Slowly. Like I am stalking the prey. But she is not my prey. She is a trap. And she caught me a long time ago. I want her to want me. Because I've wanted her for so long it seems like a never-ending story. Right now, I am begging in my mind for her to submit. Just this once.

Let go of the past and just be with me.

It's like a mantra on repeat in my head.

My kisses reach her neck. My nose brushes against her damp blond strands, and she tilts her head, exposing her neck to me.

Yeah, she wants it.

Excitement spikes through me like an arrow.

The air around us is still, salty, and sprinkled with light music and the sound of crashing waves from outside.

I bring my lips to her ear. There is so much I want to say

and I don't because I don't want to scare her. My feelings will do that. She will run. Like she did four years ago.

But her head turns. Her face tilts up. An inch. Another inch.

Her eyes are closed, unlike mine. Her lips, full and delicious, slightly parted, inch closer to mine. And when they meet mine, I am on a highway to hell and paradise.

Forget the highway.

It's a race track that rewinds four years to when kissing Callie Mays seemed like an impossible dream.

When being next to her was magical, and nothing else mattered.

28

KAI

I have to restrain myself from attacking Callie like an animal as I take her lips. I suck on her lower lip, then sear her mouth with a kiss that is no match for my want for her.

My lips push hers open, and I slide my tongue in.

Some invisible walls start crashing between us, in slow motion.

Her tongue sinks into my mouth, meets mine, and that's it—the world around vanishes.

Callie is mine.

At least for this moment as our mouths fuse in this kiss.

I won't let her get away this time. She thought I was a monster. She blamed me for something I didn't do. If it's my fault, I will fix it.

The rain rams against the roof. But the sound goes away as I get lost in the kiss.

My hands slide up her torso. Slowly. Carefully. Inching up. Until they reach her arms still holding her bikini top.

But they give way under the pressure of my hands sliding up. And in a moment, I cup her breasts.

Fuck…

I buck my hips against her. My hard cock in my shorts is pressing against her back and wants so desperately to break free and make acquaintance with her.

I squeeze her breasts gently, and she moans.

Callie Mays moans in my arms.

I fucking dissipate at the sound, deepening my kiss.

I am like a dinghy caught in a powerful tide. Capsizing. Being swallowed by the warm water. Drowning.

I sink my tongue deeper into her sweet mouth, and she moans again. There is no doubt she wants me.

Fuck yes!

I try to be gentle, though I want to throw her onto my bed and fuck her.

We kiss for the longest time while I knead her breasts and stroke her nipples with my thumbs. Her hands slide up to cover mine, and it's as if we are pleasuring her together.

I finally pull my mouth away from hers, just an inch apart.

"Petal," I whisper. "Have you ever been touched?"

If what Katura said is true, Callie hasn't been with anyone.

Her breath is warm and jagged, and I love it. She smells like the waterfall and rain and coconut oil. It's hot in the hut. I want to rip the rest of her clothes off and mine, too. Right now, I want her hands on me, and I hate being touched.

"Touched how?" she asks.

"I guess it's a no," I say, my heart fluttering at the answer.

No guy has touched her.

Good.

Because I would have burned with jealousy.

"I want to touch you," I whisper. Just a touch. I don't want to go farther where she doesn't want to be. "Do you trust me?"

And that's a heavy word, considering some pretty fucked-up things she thought about me.

"Yes," she whispers.

That's all I need.

Slowly, I turn her around to face me. Our foreheads are almost touching, and it feels intimate.

"Let's take this off."

Slowly, I start unbuttoning her shorts, and she doesn't stop me.

I don't look away. Neither does she.

The air between us burns with want that was always disguised by something else—awkward smiles or silly conversations that never carried any meaning.

That's what people who have feelings do—they hide meaning behind nonsense. And I am done with nonsense for tonight.

Her shorts are wet from the rain. I slowly pull them down her hips. She pushes them further, letting them drop onto the floor, and steps out of them. I hook my fingers under her loose bikini top and pull it over her head and toss it aside.

I pull her closer to me and kiss her again, then lower my

head and kiss her one breast, then another, then catch one pink nipple in my mouth and tug at it softly with my lips.

Her hands weave into my hair, and I close my eyes, reveling in the feel of her touch.

She is warm and damp. I want to dry her with a towel, then drag her to bed, make her wet in all the right places, and fuck her brains out.

But that's a no.

So I stop, bring my face up to hers, and search her eyes for a signal—something to tell me she is not ready for this.

Her gaze is shy but open and is a definite yes. Her hands are still in my hair. And I drop my gaze down to her lime bikini bottom.

"Strawberries, huh," I murmur.

"It's from the communal stash," she murmurs as if in apology and bites the corner of her bottom lip.

My gaze slides lower to her thighs pressed tightly together.

And then, nothing else matters.

"Open your legs, petal," I say softly, the words making my already hard cock swell with need.

She widens her stance.

The fucking strawberries—they have to go. They are closer to her skin than I am.

I bring my hand to her bikini, hook my forefinger under the fabric, and slide it to the side, exposing her pussy.

She is bare.

Fuck.

Who was she getting ready for like this before coming here?

But that thought is lost too as I brush my finger along her delicious slit. Moisture coats my forefinger—she is wet, and it's so fucking arousing my entire body is one big hard-on.

"Look at this pretty thing," I murmur as I stare down.

I can stare at her pussy for eternity.

It's perfect. Bare. Slick as I run my finger along the slit and the little petal that peeks out.

Petal...

I stifle a grunt. I want this beauty in my mouth but I don't want to push it with her.

I want to open her pussy lips and tease her, then shove my cock inside her and fuck her brains out.

And that's out of the question. But I want to play.

My shame was lost somewhere ten minutes back. I stare openly at her naked body, her panties pushed aside. She is so fucking delicious that I feel like I am about to come in my shorts.

Her gaze on me is shy but burning with need, her hands cupping my neck like she is afraid to let me go.

I bring my hand to her pussy and run my finger along her intimate flesh, barely touching her. I can hear her tiny gasps, but I don't look up. I am fucking hypnotized. It's like a peep show. The lime fabric of her panties is like a curtain pulled aside that opens the view of her sex. I spread her pussy lips and run my fingers up her slit.

Callie is soaking wet. Holy hell is she an ocean. She gasps louder this time, and I raise my gaze to meet hers—I want to see her enjoy it.

She is flushed. Her rosy lips are parted. Her chest rises

and falls in heavy breathing. And I can't help it. I dive in to meet her lips with mine, and my fingers sink deeper into her flesh.

She cries out.

"You like this, baby girl?" I murmur against her lips.

Fuck. I might like this more than she does.

Not hearing the answer, I stop.

"Tell me you like it, and I will go on."

It's only a matter of seconds that she gasps "yes" into my mouth.

29

CALLIE

OH MY GOD. OH MY GOD. OH MY GOD.

My mind reels with shock and desire and excitement as Kai touches me down there, and I want to whimper but try to hold myself together. Barely. Because his touch sends a shiver through my body. I've fantasized about it in my screwed-up dreams back in the day. I've wanted to kiss him for as long as I remember.

Right now, I don't want him to stop.

He might be looking for a lay.

But I don't care.

I want this.

This room.

This time alone with him.

It's for the best when we don't talk. We don't say harsh things. We don't bring up the past. This moment of us kissing is like a bridge between when I met him and couldn't forget his dark burning gaze ever since and now when his hand is cupping my pussy and saying those filthy words that make my mind spin.

"Callie, tell me it's okay," he whispers.

"Yes," I whisper back, catching his mouth in a kiss again, pushing myself into his hand, and right now, I don't care how pathetic and desperate I look.

I want Kai Droga.

Always have.

When he pulls my bikini bottom down my hips, I wiggle to help get rid of them.

And now I am naked.

He hooks his hand behind my thigh and lifts my leg, wrapping it around him, opening me up. Then kisses me deeply, and his fingers are down there again, between my legs.

I wrap my hands around his neck and melt in his arms.

It's his smell, his broad form next to me, the hardness of his muscled body, and the softness of his lips on mine. His tongue casts some sort of spell on me. The softer it swirls into my mouth, the more prolonged its swipes are, the more want seeps out of me. Need coils inside me.

His hand is on my breast, stroking so gently I want to whimper. His other hand is between my legs. It feels nothing like mine. Mine is a tool that can bring the heat down. His is the magic that sends fire through my body, turning into a blaze.

He is dark and strong. I want him to wrap himself around me, take me to bed, and do anything he wants. Now. Forever.

The heat inside me starts building. I slide my hand

down to where his is, cover it with mine, and our fingers start working together, intertwining, sliding around my wetness, working in sync.

It feels amazing.

It spikes my arousal.

The fact that we are touching me together ignites the heat between my legs.

And it explodes.

I am free-falling.

I come and come. I shamelessly roll my hips to get the most of his fingers, sinking my tongue into his mouth like I can get another orgasm.

I've never come this fast. I whimper, and he takes my lips harder, his tongue lunging deeper into my mouth.

When the climax subsides, both our hands are still between my legs, our fingers gliding softly together in circles.

I want to hold on to this moment because as soon as I pull away, it will be broken.

I want all of him. I want to go down on my knees and do what other girls do to guys. I want to spread my legs and let him do what I thought was done to me only to find out I was a virgin.

Take me.

I don't want to offer. I want him to ask me. I want to know that he wants me. That this isn't just an island entertainment or redemption for the crappy history between us.

I am breathing heavily when Kai pulls away from me and lets go of my leg wrapped around him. I stumble, trying to stand on two feet, though my body is limp and boneless. He holds me by my waist, steadying me.

Our eyes meet, and his are burning as if in fever.

He drops his gaze down, studying my nakedness, and now I am too aware of my body, bare in front of him.

He adjusts his manhood in his shorts, and I drop my gaze down to see a bulge there.

Oh.

He is hard. Like really hard.

"See what you do to me, petal?" he murmurs. "Now I have to go take care of myself."

Go where?

I don't want him to go. I want to *see* him. Just like he sees me.

"I want to watch," I blurt out without thinking, and my heart slams in my chest.

His eyes snap up to meet mine, and there is a question in them.

"I want to watch you do it," I repeat quieter, my heart pounding like a war drum. "Here. Now."

A tiny smile curls his lips.

His eyes are the abyss I slowly drown in. I can gaze at them for hours. Somehow, his tattoos feel powerful and dangerous. And I want them to rub against me.

I tick my chin up, not breaking the eye contact.

Kai hooks his thumbs under the waistband of his board shorts and pauses, his gaze never leaving mine.

I look down, then up at him again, remove my hands from him, and take a step back, leaning against the desk behind me with my hands.

There is no mistake in the way I look at him that I want to see him. It takes all my courage not to cover myself. I've never been naked in front of a guy. Or a girl, for that matter.

This is an offering. And a dare.

Slowly, Kai tugs his board shorts down, just below his hips, letting his erection free. I bring my gaze down—

Holy hell…

I stare at it, and now I understand what he meant when he said that if he did anything to me back then, I would've felt it the next day.

He is big. Very big. Smooth. Perfect. I'm not sure he would fit inside me without hurting me. If he were inside of me that night, he would have ripped me apart.

I swallow hard but don't take my eyes away from his hardness even when his inked hand wraps around it and starts stroking it softly.

I've never been with a guy. Never been that close to a naked guy. I've seen plenty of raunchy videos, sure. But this —he—feels special.

His white erection is framed by dark curls on his groin and tattooed abdomen and is even more pronounced.

"I want you to sit on that desk, petal," he says softly.

His voice is low and husky, charged with that animal magnetism that is overpowering.

I raise my eyes at him, and he gives me a backward nod.

I do what he asks, the desk surface cold against my butt.

"Open your legs," he orders softly, all the while stroking himself. "Wider," he insists until my thighs are wide apart, feet dangling in the air. His gaze drops to my pussy. "Now show me how you play with yourself."

Need coils inside me at his words. I am so wet that I feel the liquid seep out of me.

How would I—

"You touch yourself, don't you?" Kai takes a step closer, his hand stroking his cock only a foot away from my opening. "Show me. Come on, petal."

I swallow hard. I am embarrassed and aroused at the same time. This is like some porn movie, but it's so erotic that if he wanted to take me this very moment, I would've let him. I slide my hand down between my legs and start softly touching myself.

I burn with shame. This is too open. This is not lovemaking. This is raw. Carnal.

But Kai is hypnotized. I can see by the increasing rhythm of his strokes that he likes what he sees.

His other hand glides up my thigh, stopping at the junction, and his thumb slides up my slit, touching my fingers.

"Fuck," he whispers, steps closer, bringing his erection an inch away from my fingers. Then the inch is gone, and his tip is touching my fingers.

We are both staring down, our foreheads almost touching, as we watch, transfixed.

It's hands, fingers, his ink, and my wetness, his hand jerking violently at his erection and my fingers rubbing my pussy, both of us nudging our hips at each other.

This is madness. Was it the kiss or the rain that flipped an invisible switch, and we are both like two cats in heat?

The ink on his hand is dark against my white skin, his sex against mine. The sight is so primal that I feel the arousal spike through me again. I want him inside me, where it burns.

His hand starts jerking faster, the tip of his cock tapping my fingers that catch its smoothness now and then.

And he groans.

"Fuck," he exhales, and a shot of hot liquid spills down my fingers. He tilts his cock up just a little and squirts more liquid onto my belly.

He exhales heavily again, pressing his forehead to mine, and closes his eyes, going still for a moment.

When he finally opens his eyes, they are on mine.

He pulls away slowly, tucks himself in, and smiles.

But the smile doesn't quite reach his eyes when he says, "And you still have your cherry, petal."

30

KAI

I shouldn't have said that.

Fuck.

I am a moron.

What's wrong with me?

I walk over to the wash basin, take a towel, and bring it over to Callie, then wipe her belly and between her legs, then take her hand and wipe her fingers, one by one.

The hot moment between us is gone. As if we were thrown into some sexual trance and forgot who we were.

I should say something nice. But then, I am not the nice type, right? She thought so for the longest time.

Callie gazes at me too timidly now.

I feel uneasy. I was never good with words. With her, I always fuck things up.

The disappointment in her eyes tugs at my heart in the wrong way. The words were harsh and unnecessary. As if I took what I wanted and pulled back.

Dammit.

I toss the towel into the basin and, without looking at her, go to the nightstand and pick up a cigarette.

I glance at her as I light it and exhale the smoke, watching her fumble with her bikini, her shoulders hunched.

She is embarrassed.

Fuck, dude.

I feel like a jerk.

Her bikini is wet just like the rest of her clothes, and before she puts it on, I take one of my shirts from the shelf and bring it over to her.

"Wear this. The rest of your stuff will dry by morning."

I stand by the desk, smoking and watching her.

This girl was made to be adored. I wasn't meant to be the one. But I don't fucking care. I want to pull her into my arms and kiss her more. Again. Till morning.

And here is the fucking problem. What does *she* want?

She never says anything.

I feel like I did four years ago when I stopped her in the hallways and talked awkwardly, melting like a fool under her smiles. Until, one day, she showed up with Archer, his arm wrapped around her waist. And I almost punched him but didn't say a word, the world suddenly crashing around me.

I am in over my head again. I promised myself I wouldn't touch her. And here I am again, being a fucking fool and dreaming of something—someone—who is not supposed to be mine.

Callie stands in my gray t-shirt that comes down to her thighs and looks around awkwardly.

"I should go," she says.

I can hear the rain hammering outside. She could walk to her bungalow, sure. She'd be soaked by the time she got there.

But that's not the problem.

I want her here. I want her with me. This night. Right now. I don't know how to fight the awkwardness between us, and don't know how to tell her that I am going mad around her. I'm fucking weak, yeah. A deep cigarette drag burns it all inside me. I am so desperate and so afraid that she'll see it that all I can do is pretend to be an indifferent dick.

"You are staying here tonight," I say with intended harshness in my voice.

She looks at me in submission. "I don't want you to—"

"Petal." I lock eyes with her, burrowing into her as I take another deep scorching drag that for a moment burns away my hesitation. "You are staying here."

She nods.

I walk toward my bed and throw the sheet open, nodding toward it, then dim the lamp, walk past her toward the wicker chair and sit down, stretching my legs and closing my eyes.

The cigarette is hanging off my lips. I feel the smoke curl into my nostrils. I hear every little movement, Callie's soft steps as she pads toward the bed and gets in. The rain rattles against the leaves outside. Its whisper is soothing. But my heart is beating wildly.

I know what would happen if we talked. She would talk about that night again. And I don't want to. I want silence. I want to think of her pretty naked body splayed open for me. Her hungry eyes as she studied my nakedness. I want this night to be about me and her and not the memories of the past. I want to stay in this moment of knowing she is in my bed, though I shouldn't be getting in there with her.

I don't know how much time has passed when a whimper comes from the bed.

Is she crying?

I look in that direction and see her on her side, hands tucked under the pillow, her shoulders twitching.

Another whimper.

What the hell?

"Callie," I say softly, but she doesn't respond and goes quiet.

A minute passes, and I hear it again—a whimper, louder this time, then a murmur.

I stand up and walk over to the bed.

"Callie," I whisper.

But this time she doesn't go quiet. Her eyes are closed, but her feet and shoulders jerk just slightly. And she whimpers again.

Nightmares. She is having nightmares.

The realization is a relief that she is not upset. But it's followed by my heart clenching in the strangest way.

Nightmares come from pain.

I am an expert in it.

The worst pain is not second-degree burns.

The memories suddenly rush over me as I stand by the bed and watch Callie.

Getting tattoos is torture.

"Nothing intricate. No straight lines, bro. The smooth skin patches can be done with designs, yes, but the ridges and grooves will work better with solid color and bold shapes."

The voice of the tattooist is monotonous. But my heart is pounding. The guy was highly recommended, used by outlaws and ex-prisoners.

"I've done a dude who had ninety percent of his skin scarred after an explosion," the tattooist explains. "So you will be a piece of cake. If you can afford it. More importantly, if you can handle the pain."

Oh, I can handle fucking pain. It's nothing compared to the horrified stares of several chicks who ended up in my bed after the accident and saw glimpses of my scars. When you are a monster, you can't show up anywhere like this. No beach. Forget being shirtless. Turtlenecks and scarves in the winter. Long sleeves in the heat of the summer. Neck to knees—my backside and left side look like someone chewed me up and spat me out. Thank God for my face and dick that were left untouched.

So do I care if my new skin comes with pain?

Well, the tattooist is right. Because when the needle touches my scars, it's like a razor slicing through my flesh with excruciating slowness.

But the worst pain is the memories. One in particular. Looking at myself in the mirror at the hospital after they took the bandages off for the first time.

It still haunts me sometimes. Though the nightmares were replaced with the grief of losing my family when the Change happened.

Perhaps Callie was right. Lucky means not seeing your loved ones die in front of you, slowly and painfully.

When another whimper comes from Callie, and her entire body trembles, I understand it now. Her memories are monsters.

I want to chase them away.

I am not sure I know how, but the girl took my heart in her hands a long time ago and still holds it, squeezes it gently but tightly every minute I spend with her.

I hate it.

And I can't stop myself.

She is the reminder of the worst but also the best in my life. She makes me feel things that unravel my dark heart and, for a brief moment, make me forget hate and grief. I want to feel something besides hopelessness.

With Callie, I feel strangely alive. I want to cherish every moment of her next to me because I know—there will be a time she will leave.

So I turn off the light, get in the bed next to Callie, press close to her, and wrap my arm around her.

She stills when I do so, but her breathing is even.

"Goodnight," I whisper, knowing she is asleep.

I close my eyes and sink into the feeling of her in my arms when a barely audible whisper comes from her:

"Goodnight."

31

CALLIE

When I open my eyes, the room is too bright.

I overslept.

I sit up and look around.

Kai is gone. I am pretty sure he slept in the bed with me. And I am pretty sure I didn't dream about him spooning with me.

I smile and bite my lip.

The sheet is pushed to the side. His gray shirt I am wearing is hitched up to my waist, leaving me completely bare down below.

Oh, God.

I blush and pull it down.

Was I sleeping like this when Kai woke up?

Embarrassment washes over me, and with it, the realization that I was almost naked in bed with him.

And yesterday…

Shit, shit, shit.

The memories flicker in my mind with the intensity of

the parrots' trills and whistles outside. I am not sure I can look Kai in the eyes today.

I hear shouting outside, scramble out of bed, and find my bikini and the rest of my clothes neatly stacked on the nightstand.

It's even more embarrassing, knowing that Kai folded my clothes.

When I open the door to the outside, it's too bright. And suddenly, the memory of the walk of shame at the frat house is back.

There is no one around, but I feel exposed all the same.

Until more angry shouting comes from the direction of the kitchen.

Not good.

Almost the entire village is gathered in the dining room, sitting, standing around with arms crossed, raking their hair, or staring absently around.

Ty is in Jeok's face, both shirtless and barefoot.

"It's us against them," Jeok snaps. "We gonna be fucked!"

"Don't be a fucking pussy!" Ty pushes him in the chest. It's the angriest I've ever seen him. "No one forced you to come to this side. No one forces you to leave either."

"They don't belong here!" Kristen comes up to stand next to Jeok, glaring at Ty.

And then everyone starts shouting.

"They will destroy the village!"

"The girls have to go!"

"They should have a choice!"

"He'll come for them, and it will be war!"

"We already lost three people!"

"Shut your mouth!"

"You wanna tell them how it really is here? Tell them about Olivia!"

That name again.

"Let's vote!"

I come up behind Katura, who stands watching this all with sardonic amusement, arms crossed at her chest.

"What's happening?" I whisper.

She turns around. "There was a note pinned to the kitchen table this morning. It said, *I want back what's mine.* Signed, *The Chancellor.*"

Her eyes widen in mock surprise.

Shit.

I swallow hard and look around for Kai. He is discussing something with Bo as everyone around continues talking loudly and all at once.

Maddy, who is next to Katura, turns to me. "That's not all," she says, a grim look on her face. "They killed all the chickens."

"Oh," I mouth.

"Yeah. Oh," Katura echoes mockingly. "We have to go."

"Where?" I ask, and my heart starts pounding.

"To the other side!" she snaps. "Before this village is burned down."

My heart sinks. "No," I protest.

"Oh, yeah?" Katura smirks. "I assume you spent a night with your boy toy, and now you wanna stay."

"Whatever."

"So did Dani, I guess."

I turn to meet her gaze.

"Yeah." Katura rolls her eyes.

I shake my head and, despite the thoughts of a different kind that preoccupied me only minutes ago, I push through the crowd to make my way to Kai and Bo.

"Do we need to leave?" I ask straight off the bat, my heart pounding at the words.

Bo shakes his head and looks away.

Please, say no.

But he doesn't say anything.

"Listen," Kai says to Bo, "there should be a way. We can send a message." He rakes his inked fingers through his hair but doesn't look at me, so I have a moment to study him.

Shirtless. Barefoot. Shorts hanging low on his hips. Gorgeous. And concerned.

I hope that's what I see.

I should be concerned about other things and not Kai's body.

"What message?" Bo asks, staring him down.

"I don't know, Bo. We can ask what he wants instead."

He.

Archer Crone.

"Oh, yeah? And how do we do that?"

"Write a note." Kai sounds so confident that I almost believe we can sort this out. "I'll hike to the Divide and pass it on. Right now."

My eyes drill into Kai. I am so grateful and so desperate not to go that I want to wrap my arms around him right now and kiss his face.

He still doesn't look at me.

"If the girls don't want to go, that is." His last words are quieter.

"Exactly," Bo says, then turns to the rest of the crowd, which is too loud and angry and arguing, and raises both hands in the air for attention. "Listen up!"

There is another meeting.

Dani, Katura, and I are in the center, like we are on trial. Neither Dani nor I want to leave. But Katura just shrugs.

"If you want to send a message, I can deliver." She stands there with her arms crossed at her chest, a proud smirk on her face. "I can deliver it straight to the Chancellor's hands. Yeah?"

She stares at Bo and knows that everyone stares at her right now. That's Katura's power. She thinks she is some freaking missionary or conquistador or both. She doesn't know Archer or what he is capable of.

The voting starts. And it's eleven to seven against us staying.

Both Kai and Ty are angry and shake their heads. But I understand those who awkwardly look away and avoid meeting our eyes. It's not their war. They want peace. They want to keep this side of the island safe because this is the only place they have.

"Fine!" Kai rakes his fingers through his dark hair. "We write a message and Ty and I will hike up to the Divide and pass it to the patrol. Then we wait for the answer and go from there."

"It's a three-hour hike," Maddy says.

"So fucking what?" Kai gives her a backward nod.

He is pissed off. His jaw is set. He looks just like he did in the first days when we tried to avoid each other. Except now we don't. And right now, he is on my side, wanting to keep me here.

Right?

My heart thuds heavily in my chest.

"I'm coming with you," Katura says, her expression forever-amused like she just struck a good bargain.

"Whatever," Kai blurts out. "We are leaving in ten."

In less than ten minutes, they are ready, walking out of their bungalows and toward each other.

Kai and Ty look different. Hiking boots. Jeans. T-shirts. Baseball hats low over their heads. Backpacks.

"Why the backpacks?" I ask Maddy, watching them from a distance as Bo walks them over to the main path, discussing something, and Katura follows behind.

I beg Kai to look back at me. As if it's the last time I will see him.

"Things happen in the jungle," Maddy explains indifferently. "It's about six hours there and back. Plus, we are not exactly friends with the patrol. Unless there is someone we know. We can only hope for the best."

She nudges me with her elbow. "Look what you made them do." She smiles, but my heart only starts beating faster as the guys disappear into the jungle.

I run to my bungalow and look at the waterproof watch I have stashed with my old clothes.

It's nine in the morning. This means that if everything goes well, they should be back by early afternoon.

I braid my hair into two pigtails to keep it off my shoulders, put the watch in my shorts' pocket, and go find Maddy. We have to clean up the chicken coop. We have to peel and process coconuts. And I throw myself into work, constantly checking the watch, counting seconds and minutes in my mind.

I've never waited for anything like I wait for Kai to come back.

32

KATURA

Well, well, the little village is getting a soap opera action.

An hour into the hike through the path in the jungle, sweat soaks my tank top and beads on my face. But this change is exciting. Finally, some action.

"There are cameras," I say when I spy the fourth hunting cam on one of the trees right on the path.

I am walking behind the guys.

Ty doesn't look back at me. "They will see us coming. Probably for the better. We took the cameras around the village down when we moved there. This is technically the middle territory."

I snort. "Well, there is a camera just at the beginning of the path that goes north. I saw it the other day."

Now, both Kai and Ty turn to look at me.

"Yeah," I say proudly. "You should do another check."

"What are you doing roaming the paths by yourself?" Kai asks instead.

Is that concern in his voice?

So sweet.

Or, perhaps, suspicion. I smirk. "Maybe I like nature."

That's part of the answer.

"That's probably how the Chancellor knows you survived the crash," Ty says with a note of accusation.

Whatever.

Kai pulls a water bottle from the side of his backpack, takes a gulp, then passes it back to me without looking.

"I have my own, thanks," I reply.

They have no idea.

They think they are tough as shit, living on the beach for two years. Well, try surviving on the streets of Bangkok when you are fourteen. Or get thrown into the Appalachian Mountains in just your clothes for a week.

Yeah, dipshits.

I appreciate the concern. They turn to check on me as they walk. But they barely talk. Probably not wanting to share whatever it is guys discuss when girls are not around. Because the two of them are doing this hike for pussy. That's a no-brainer.

And I am going with the flow.

This island trip is getting interesting. I don't have a timeline. The original plan went out the door as soon as the boat crashed. I sent Uncle a message on the satellite phone saying just that. I am good with wherever this goes. In fact, if I went to the Westside by myself, I would've scored some points from Archer. But then, he might be a psycho, or a perv, or God knows what. And I've dealt with those cocky privileged little shits before.

So, bring it on, I say to myself as we walk.

I've figured out plenty of things about the Outcasts. The word is right. They seem to have their shit together more or less.

Emily and Owen are an item. So are Alaina and Austin.

Mia used to date Qi Shan from the Westside.

Kristen is the go-to girl. She's probably moved here because she likes boys and doesn't like competition. She has a thing for Kai, though until recently was cozy with Ty and Jeok. And Zach, I think.

Ya-ya is a mystery. The girl is quiet but cocky as fuck. As per little snippets of stories here and there, she had some beef with some kid called Axavier on the other side. Her name is Yara, and she was supposed to graduate as a Juris Doctor after spring break. President of Black Students' Law Association. Intern at a private security firm. All that fancy-pants stuff. Now, her conversations barely go beyond discussions of fallout and dinner menu.

Jordan, Zach, and Jeok had a fight with Qi Shan and Marlow from Archer's inner circle. I need to learn more about Archer's crew in the West. Several people died during that fight. The Savages from town were involved. Some shit went down.

Guff is the big heavy-set dude who sleeps in a hammock half the nights.

Maddy has some medical background. She is the Godmother of the place. Bo is the grandpa. I laugh at the thought.

Kai and Ty are thick as thieves. They've stayed in touch after some beef with the Chancellor back at Deene. Kai is an

Outcast in the true sense of the word. He flew to the island by himself for whatever reason and got stuck here when the Change happened.

A year ago, there was an incident with the Savages from the town. Two people died. Olivia is some dark fucked-up story. Another kid killed himself. Everyone is hush-hush about it, sour faces and all. They don't know what death truly is. On a mass scale. Or how fucked up some humans get when they have a gun and there is no law. Or what humans do when they live on the law's blind side, like many in Thailand.

It's getting brighter around—we've been hiking uphill toward the top of the island this whole time. My muscles are tense. Feels good. I control my breathing. The boys will get tired before I do.

It's been about three hours, and when we reach a wide intersection at what looks like the highest point of the island, we stall.

"Where does the other road go?" I ask, looking at the path that crosses the main one and disappears in either direction.

"North. South," Ty explains, looking around.

No shit, Sherlock.

"What are we waiting for?" I ask, annoyed, looking around, my eyes rising slowly to scan the trees.

And then I see it.

Cameras.

Not the hunting ones. Proper motion-activated, color footage.

Well, well.

"Shhhh... Don't make any sudden moves." Ty brings his forefinger to his lips, silencing me.

I am all ears.

There is a crack of branches somewhere in the jungles.

A pack of birds flap their wings wildly as they flee out of the green canopy.

And there are clicks.

One.

Two.

And I fucking know these sounds.

Rifles.

Oh, shit.

"Put your hands up!" a voice shouts from the distant bushes. "Now!"

Seriously?

My heart thuds in my chest. It's anticipation. Adrenalin. I didn't expect that.

I do as I am told, my head turning to look for the person the voice came from.

The boys raise their hands too. They are taller and broader than me, but they obey.

Oh, shit.

The bushes rustle, then shake, in all directions, and four guys step out with rifles in their hands on all sides of us.

I whistle, turning around, studying them.

Cargo pants tucked into military boots. Tank tops. Sunglasses. Young, maybe five-six years older than me. Buff and by the sight of them, arrogant as fuck.

Who are they? Peter Pan's boys?

The youngest-looking one tilts the sunglasses to his nose

and studies me with a wolf whistle. He is the only one wearing black jean shorts that go below his knees. A loose tank over a muscled body. His dark hair is tied in a bun at the back of his head. Leather bracelets around his wrists. Beaded necklace around his neck. Tatted arm. A Cali surfer-boy turned Legion fighter.

Jesus.

He is hot.

This island is a fairyland for horny girls.

His rifle slowly points downward as he approaches, too lazily for someone with a dangerous job.

Yeah, babe, lower your gun, and you'll lose that and your balls.

If any of them touch me, I swear…

Slowly, he rolls a toothpick in the corner of his lips, and his eyes shift to Ty. The surfer boy straightens, and his face turns vicious.

"Down on the ground!" he barks so suddenly spit sprays out of his mouth, and I almost jump. "Fifty pushups! Now! Move your ass!"

My heart bangs against my ribcage.

His glare is murderous.

His mouth is curled into a snarl.

But in seconds, his lips start spreading in a smile, and Ty slams into him in a bear hug.

"Mother! Fucker! You!"

They sway in a big hug like fucking flowers in the wind, then push off each other and study each other up and down.

"What up, douche?" Ty asks, grinning.

"You can chill," Kai says behind me.

Only then do I lower my hands and notice that the other three guys stand to the side, guns lowered, studying me more than the boys.

The one talking to Ty turns to me again and pushes his sunglasses onto his forehead. "And who is this lovely creature?"

He cocks his head and steps toward me and around me like I am a doll.

I turn as he walks around me, not letting him get behind me, staring onto his smiling eyes. He has a several-day stubble, sharp features, a chiseled body, and a tattoo that snakes around his bicep. Are all rich guys so muscled and perfect? Or just on this island?

"You done staring, sweetheart?" I ask, giving him a backward nod.

He grins at me, baring his perfect white teeth. "Are *you*? Let me guess"—he turns to Ty—"new arrival? Lost and found?"—then nods to Kai—"What up, bro?"

Ty grins at me. "This is Nick Marlow." He nods at the guy.

So, this is Marlow, one of Archer's close buddies.

The guy's smile is the same—cheerful and curious as he brings his sparkly eyes to me. Yeah, definitely hot as hell. "Let me guess." He cocks his head. "Ka-tu-ra Or-tiz." He punctuates every syllable.

Oh, I see. They know. Like we are celebrities.

Ty's smile vanishes. "So you've heard."

"Oh, we've been waiting." Marlow blinks slowly and

puts the rifle across his shoulders, his hands hanging on either side of it. "Where are the other two?"

Ty glances at Kai, who stands with his hands in his pockets with an indifferent but tense expression, then looks at Marlow.

"Well, here is the thing." Ty pulls off the backpack and takes out a piece of paper that Bo wrote for Archer. "Got a message for Crone."

Marlow carelessly flicks the paper open with his fingers, scans the message, and exhales. "Fuck, Ty. It's not gonna cut it."

Ty looks away. "I know. But that's it for now."

Marlow shakes his head, then turns to me, and that cocky smile is back. "How about we pluck this *se-ño-ri-ta* to come with us?" His playful eyes study me up and down, and only now, with his sunglasses perched on his forehead, do I notice that his eyes are almost transparent blue. Gorgeous. Like the mist of the waterfall.

But his confidence rubs me the wrong way.

"*Se-ño-ri-ta*," I mimic him, "is not interested."

Marlow might not be bad, but the other three stand at a distance with their rifles at their sides, and they are like Commandos with frat attitude. I've seen that type after the Change. Not a chance I am going anywhere with them by myself if I want to make it to the Westside with my panties on.

Marlow smiles at Ty. "You look rough."

"Well," Ty answers with his sunshine smile. "I don't have an army of minions to serve me. And now you guys killed our major source of food, so…"

"Yeah. Last night's patrol. Crone's orders." Marlow looks down as if in apology and kicks the ground with the metal tip of his military boot.

His clothes and boots are new. Not a speck of dust.

He whistles to his goons and walks briefly toward them. "Sorry, guys," he says as he rummages in a backpack that one of the guys hands him and comes back with granola bars, apples, and energy drinks.

You kidding me?

We take a seat on the side of the grassy intersection, and I devour the bar and the energy drink like a kid who just got the first ice cream in her life.

"There is more where this comes from," Marlow says and winks at me.

"Marlow," I say, chewing, my mouth full. "Is that Russian?"

He shrugs. "Russian, Polish. Whatever you want it to be."

I give him a backward nod, taking a gulp of the energy drink like I've never had one before. "*Govorish po-russki?*" I ask him if he speaks Russian.

His eyebrow cocks in surprise. "*Dlia tebia, solnyshko, shto ugodno.*" Anything for you, sunshine.

We both smile. I like this one.

In a minute, he and Ty get up and step aside, only fifty feet or so. It's hard to hear what they say but they shoot shit for some time while Kai and I chill in the shade and the other goons stare at us.

"Secretive, huh?" I look at Kai and nod toward Ty and Marlow.

He shakes his head. "Don't want the others to hear," he says under his breath. "Crone is probably watching right now."

I scan the trees, find one of the cameras, and wave my hand with the biggest smile and, "Fuck you," under my breath.

When we finally get up, say goodbye, and start walking, I hear Marlow's voice behind us.

"Hey, kitten! Last chance to stay!"

I know he is grinning. So I don't turn but raise my middle finger in the air and hear his laughter.

It's three hours back to camp.

And now the boys are talking.

They discuss the people they know, whatever Marlow told Ty. I stay quiet, no questions, because I want to find out as much as I can.

The Westside got attacked by the town thugs three weeks ago. Surveillance was disrupted. Several guards were hurt. The attacks are getting more frequent and thought-out, though Archer has patrol in town too.

He is angrier than ever, often flying off the handle and doing drugs.

The boat wreck washed up ashore.

There is another survivor from our crew, some IT kid.

Someone died several months back after an epilepsy attack.

Another girl died, pulled away by a strong tide.

I take it all in, and one thing is clear—the Kardashian bootcamp is not as well-off as I thought.

33

CALLIE

He's back!

My heart thuds to the sound of the words in my head.

"They are back!"

The news spreads across the village, but only Dani, Maddy, Bo, several guys, and I hurry to the Common Lounge.

"And?" Maddy asks impatiently.

Ty tosses his backpack aside in what looks like disappointment. "They know how many survivors there are. Another one is on their side. Marlow was on patrol," he explains.

"I miss that fucker," Owen says with a smile.

Ty keeps talking while Kai lights a cigarette and smokes, sitting on the floor next to Owen.

My eyes dart from Ty to Katura, who lights a joint and sits, slumped, on the low couch, her legs crossed at the ankles like she just came back from a stroll.

I look at Kai again, trying to read his face. My heart

beats so fast that I want to jump in the ocean that I am not a fan of so I can chill the hell out.

"So we wait," Bo concludes, hearing the entire story, even though many won't like the news.

Kai gets up and walks out, and I go after him.

"Kai," I call, trotting after him. He stops and looks at me, his gaze burning through my heart.

His shirt is soaked with sweat. The smoke of his cigarette tints the air around us. He looks like sin in jeans and boots, with the backpack over his shoulder. I want this sin wrapped around me.

"I don't want to go to the Westside," I say.

That's it, I said it. I want to see Abby, but more than that, I want to be here, with Kai and the rest.

"Thank you for trying to sort it out," I say, not looking away.

His expression changes. A tiny smile starts at the corners of his lips. His hooked forefinger reaches under my chin and taps it just lightly. "Sure thing, petal."

His gaze is soft, and we stare at each other for a moment that is turning too awkward when he turns to walk away.

I catch him by the hand and let go right away.

He doesn't like to be touched.

I know, I know.

"About last night," I say, and summon all my courage to keep my eyes on him as his search mine, willing me to go on. "I really liked last night," I say, though my heart doesn't like the anxiety that is rising in me and rebels against my chest. "I…" God, what else am I supposed to say? "I really liked it, yeah." I finally lower my gaze down to my feet, because I feel color rising on my face. "See you, yeah?"

Without looking, I turn around and walk toward my bungalow.

I really need to blow off steam.

I need a shower.

And I need to stop being so nervous around Kai.

34

KAI

I am so stirred up when I reach my bungalow that I think of jerking off.

Fuck, petal.

I was lost for words. Dumb. Quiet. Instead of telling her how I felt.

Let's fuck, petal! Because tomorrow might never come. Because Crone might shoot us all. So, let's take everything we can from each other. And go swimming. And kiss in the waterfall. And laugh. And sit by the bonfire because you like it though I hate it so much.

Of course, I didn't say it.

I tear the sweaty shirt off me and toss it onto the chair, then kick off the boots and change into shorts.

I need a shower.

I need to jerk off.

I need food.

And a joint.

And most importantly, her.

I can't unsee Callie's body. Not when she was wasted after the Block Party and I tried to undress her, catching a glimpse of her bare breasts. Not this morning when I woke up to her in my arms, the shirt I gave her hitched up to her waist, her naked butt up in the air.

God fucking help me! I don't know how I didn't jerk off standing by the bedside, staring at her bare butt for what seemed like an eternity, wondering if I can come just by studying her perfect behind. Because my cock was rock hard. It screamed for release.

And I am hard again at the thought of it.

I grab a towel and walk out, then make my way across the sandy patch between the bungalows to the back that is shaded by the palm trees and nestle the outside shower stall.

And I slow down.

I see Callie go into the shower, and the fact stops me in my tracks. I've been torturing myself for too many nights, jerking off at midnight to the thoughts of her, and now my body starts responding again.

I can't stop thinking about that shower stall now.

She is in there.

Naked.

I want to feel her body pressed to mine again. If only for a moment.

I can see her head up to her shoulders. She turns on the water and raises her face, letting the water stream down her shoulders and down where I can't see her.

My brain tells me to put the breaks on, but my cock has

a mind of its own. I should stop myself, I know, but I don't. Because by now, she is the gravity of this island.

I come up to the shower door, look around, open the bamboo door, and step inside, then slowly strip off my shorts.

The sweet thing doesn't even notice me at first. Water cascades down her naked body with her back to me. Tanned. Burnt at the shoulders. White in all the right places.

Callie runs her hands along her blond hair. She didn't undo her braids, and the sight of them makes me hard. I want to tug at them like a naughty fucking puppy.

She might freak out and push me away. I'll deal with that too.

But I am naked and too close to her. My cock hardens at the sight of her under that cascading water.

I stretch my hand and touch her just lightly on the back.

She jerks, turning sideways, and right away her hands cover whatever she thinks she can cover. She gapes at me for a moment, then her face relaxes, and her eyes acquire that same intensity I saw the other night when we were alone.

"What are you doing?" she asks quietly.

There is no hostility in her voice.

I take a step closer.

Naked. My cock rock-hard. She doesn't look down. Her expression is more inquiry than shock.

"I am taking a shower, petal." I stretch my hands to catch the shower water and smile, taking another step closer to her. "I really felt like taking a shower."

And then her hands fall down to her sides, and she turns to fully face me.

I don't look down. It's a challenge. But I don't want to challenge her. She is in way over her head. She won't handle this the way I want to.

But holy fuck am I wrong.

Callie glances down, then lifts her gaze at me, and it's burning with something new. There is a confidence in her that I haven't seen before. There is want. And there is a dare.

"Is that all you want, Kai? To take a shower?"

She says my name in that seductive voice, and I want to fuck her right here and take her cherry in this shower stall.

"What do *you* want, petal?"

We've been playing this game for far too long. Dating back four years. Though back then we were too young to voice what we wanted.

"I want to stay on this side of the island," she says. I know. "I want to stay here with you."

This is the first honest admission from her that makes my heart race.

"I know what you like, Kai," she says. "I want to do it to you."

I cock an eyebrow, not quite sure what she means.

She is trouble. Or at least I hope so.

And then she goes down on her knees.

Fuck, is this real?

My erection is right in front of her face. She is too straightforward. Is she drunk? High? She is not, I know it. But something *has* changed since this morning. And it's not the last night when we went to bed feeling awkward around each other after what we'd done.

It's the imminent danger. The fact that whatever tore us apart years ago is back.

I feel it too.

I know it.

It's desperation.

I see it in Callie's gaze.

She is trying to be brave. And seductive. And she wants to please me for whatever reason, and I hope it's the right one. She wants to take it all before it's taken away from her.

I could almost feel Crone's eyes on me when he watched through his cameras at the Divide. I know he did. This is Callie's "fuck you" at him. And there is a scary thought in the back of my head that I might once again lose the only thing that matters.

I don't want to ruin it. I should work it out step by step, because I want this so fucking much, I can feel my cock seep pre-cum already.

I gaze down at Callie on her knees.

Easy, buddy, I tell myself.

Step one.

"Have you done it before?" I ask softly.

She shakes her head, staring up at me.

I can tell. Her hands are at her sides but not touching me. Her gaze is hesitant.

The water is too strong. I reach for the knob, tone down the shower to a trickle, and turn my eyes to Callie again.

She is so sexy on her knees, but I know she feels vulnerable.

My heart leaps in anticipation. Then stops. Then thuds again against my chest.

Don't ruin it, Kai.

She's probably seen porn stuff. Or not. Who knows? She's always seemed shy. And a virgin. Hell…

Step two.

"Give me your hand, petal," I say softly, stretching my hand to her and wiggling my fingers

She puts her hand in mine. I fold her fingers except for her forefinger and the middle one, lean over, and take them into my mouth. I slide them all the way in, then suck on them as I pull them out, then slide them in again, then slide them back out as I suck gently.

"Like that," I say, letting go of her hand.

I can't believe that I just showed a girl how to blow me. And it's sexy as hell.

Callie nods just slightly.

Step three.

Slowly, I take my erection in my hand and stroke it gently. With my other hand, I cup her chin, stroking her jawline with my thumb.

Callie brings her eyes down to my cock, and my cock goes from hard to steel hard.

She brings her hand to my erection and brushes her fingers along the length of it, pushing mine away.

I tense, stifling a groan.

She flicks her gaze at me as if in confirmation, then her lips part, and she takes the tip of my cock in her beautiful mouth.

35

CALLIE

Kai's erection is pale compared to his other skin and stark-white in contrast with his tattoos. It's smooth to the touch, large and heavy.

I study the sensation of it being in my mouth. I can't take all of him in, and I don't try. He doesn't urge me, letting me go at my speed.

I've never done it before. He knows. He won't mock me if I don't do it right. I want to please him. I want to feel close, if only in this way. It's the wrong reason, but hell, in this world of wrong morals, this is the last of my concerns.

He groans as I release his cock from my mouth, sucking just like he showed me, then take it in my mouth as far as I can. I wrap one hand around the base of his cock. The other touches his thigh.

He takes it in his and brings it to his balls, gently closing my fingers to cup them.

"Like this, petal," he says quietly.

I keep taking him in, out, then in again. He gently takes

my head between his palms and bucks his hips just lightly into my mouth.

"Suck at the head a little," Kai orders softly.

And I do, my tongue exploring the smooth skin of its tip. My lips roll over the rim of his head, and he groans.

I like having this power over him. I've never been with a guy. Never touched one. Not without clothes on.

Knowing that Kai enjoys it is liberating and arousing.

I am nervous. But being naked with him turns me on, and I feel my sex contract with want.

I suck harder. A moan escapes him. I do it again.

Slowly, I learn by the sounds he makes what pleases him, what makes him thrust his hips at me just a bit harder. It's a reflex—wanting more. I feel it. And use it.

His fingers stroke my wet hair gently. It's surprising how soft his touch is, considering his build and snarky attitude.

"Suck it more, baby girl," he whispers.

His voice is strained.

And that *baby girl* makes heat pool between my legs.

He is letting go.

I do what he says, then tug at his balls and massage them.

He groans again.

That's right.

I try to take as much of him as I can in my mouth, and he holds my head tighter and bucks his hips at me.

"Fuck," he hisses.

I start sucking harder, taking him into my mouth and releasing his cock almost up to the tip, then taking it in again. I tighten my lips and increase the pace. And I put my hands on his hips to steady myself.

He is so lost that he doesn't realize that I've touched him where I am not allowed to. I keep working on his hardness, but my mind goes to the texture of the skin on his hips. Parts of it are jagged and rough. Others are unnaturally smooth like plastic.

Shock and surprise spiral through my body. And I want to make him happy, really happy right now.

"Fuck, baby girl." He groans. "Please, don't stop."

Kai Droga is begging me not to stop.

And I won't. Because this is the most intimate I've been with a man. The most open. The only man I've known. Kai.

My lips start getting numb. It's a new feeling. But I keep going.

His hands get tighter. His little thrusts into my mouth deepen. But I go with it. I want this. And I want to know what he is like. *What* he likes. What makes him tick. What makes him let go and relax.

I keep sucking him off. My fingers keep roaming his hips and glide back toward his ass. I look up, and my eyes meet his.

There is nothing of the usual Kai left in that gaze. There is intensity, want, and need. It burns as if in fever. The plea for me not to stop startles me. I keep his gaze. I want him to forget everything that was before and only live in this moment. Because in this moment, he is glorious, powerful, and mesmerizing, towering above me like a dark angel.

Our eyes stay locked as I take him in. It must tip him

over the edge, because I feel his thrust that is too forceful, and suddenly warm liquid gushes into my mouth.

It startles me. It floods my mouth with so much intensity that I forget to breathe.

Kai lets out a long raspy groan, and I swallow and swallow, making sure that it doesn't spill out of my mouth. When it stops coming, Kai stills, and I let go of his hardness.

His hands shift to my shoulders and pull me up to my feet.

I stand naked in front of him, not knowing what to do. The shower is still trickling. It's colder now. Only now do I register the cool breeze from the ocean on my skin. It's refreshing against my face that is burning with the realization of what we just did.

But I keep Kai's gaze. It's not hostile or cocky like it usually is, and not withdrawn like it was the last time were together, but warm and somewhat confused.

His hand reaches my face, and he strokes my cheek with the back of his fingers.

My skin hums at his touch. It's too tender for what we just did. I try to smile. My heart flutters. He leans over and kisses me, deeply, slowly, though I know I still taste like him.

We kiss for the longest time. His arms wrap around me, bringing me flush against his strong body, so tightly that I stand on my tiptoes.

I want mine wrapped around him, but I know better. So I wrap them around his neck, feeling dizzy and happy as our tongues swirl together.

I love kissing him. His lips take mine just the right way. His tongue is hot and soft, seductive rather than forceful.

But when he pulls away, the cocky Kai is back.

"You did well, baby girl," he says with a tiny smile.

The words tug at my heart with pride in the strangest way.

I still remember the texture of his scarred skin under my fingers.

And I think, *I see you now, Kai.*

But I don't say it.

He will only hate me for that.

36

KAI

Alright.

There is a blowjob. And there is *the* blowjob from the girl that you are head over heels for. She could be worse than a blowup doll, and you would still come in seconds. There is something magical about the touch of the girl you desperately want.

I stare at Callie and don't want to let her go. I want to make this special. But how the fuck do you make a shower encounter special?

She did so well. So eager. So gentle.

"You were perfect, baby girl," I murmur.

The longer I kiss her, the harder I get again.

But I'm not letting her go. Tomorrow, this island might sink, and the world might go up in smoke. I want all of it to disappear. Because suddenly, this shitty outside shower stall is the sexiest place I've ever been.

I want her. I want to know that when she leaves these

twenty square feet, she will think about this moment over and over again.

I break away from her sweet mouth, right away wanting to come back to it. But I have other plans.

I push her back gently until the back of her knees hit the wooden shower bench.

"Sit down," I order softly.

She obeys.

I love how willing she is, naked and beautiful, her tanned skin glistening with water drops. Her blue eyes stare up at me with want. Her breasts beg to be in my mouth. And it's only a matter of minutes until her pussy begs for the same.

"Open your legs," I say, towering over her as my cock stands to attention being so close to her.

Callie Mays and I are naked together. Again. The second time can't be just pure luck, can it?

She obeys, spreading her legs just a bit.

"More," I command.

And she spreads them even wider, her pink pussy on full display for me.

I grab my erection in my hand and stroke it softly as I study her for a moment. And then, slowly, I go down onto my knees in front of her.

She doesn't take her eyes away from mine. Those beautiful blue abysses are gazing at me, and if it wasn't for something else I wanted, I would have stood on my knees before her and gazed at her for eternity.

I don't stop stroking my cock as my hand reaches toward her pussy and strokes it gently.

She flinches. Her rosy lips part in a tiny gasp.

"Do you like when I touch you, petal?" I ask.

"Yes," she exhales softly.

I part her pussy lips and slide my fingers back and forth across her slit.

She shifts her hips a little.

"Lean back on your hands," I order.

She does. Now she'll be able to roll her hips—in a moment I will make her whimper. I lower my head and give her pussy one long swipe with my tongue.

She exhales loudly.

"That's right," I murmur, still holding her pussy lips open with my fingers. "Like that, yeah?" I give her slit another long swipe.

"Faster," she exhales.

I can't help smiling—my petal tells me what she wants, and I like it.

"Yes, ma'am."

And then I hear a familiar voice that is too close to the shower.

"Yo! Anyone there?"

I freeze. My heart jolts in surprise. Callie jerks in panic.

Fucking Ty. He is like a bumblebee that startles you in the worst moments possible.

I pause and raise my head to meet Callie's panicking eyes. "Do. Not. Move," I whisper a warning.

I get to my feet, and as soon as my head rises above the partition, I meet Ty's lop-sided smile only several feet away, a towel hanging off his shoulder.

"Man, you taking a shower lying down or what?" He snorts.

I feel Callie shifting, so I lean just slightly and cup her pussy, holding her in place.

She stills.

Ty can't see her. And that's just great. Because I start sliding my fingers up and down her slit, not taking my eyes off Ty.

"Just playing around," I say with a smile and wink at him.

Paranoid, Callie grabs my wrist to stop me, but I slap her hand away, and my fingers find her slick pussy again.

"Don't waste the water, yeah?" Ty is about to turn around, then stops.

He frowns at me in suspicion.

I grin at him, stroking Callie's pussy.

He must've noticed the movements. His nose suddenly wrinkles. "Wait." His face turns into a disgusted grimace. "Maaaaan, are you jerking off? Dude!"

I cock an eyebrow, and he shakes his head, turning away. "Why are you fucking talking to me then? Jeez. Do it at your place." He starts walking away, then turns his head. "Or go find your blondie and give your right hand a vacation," he blurts as he stomps off.

I look down at Callie to meet her gaze. "Sound advice," I say with a grin, not a bit baffled at the admission of it.

Except my right hand is where it wants to be. My fingers are still on her pussy, and her eyes are blazing at me with want.

Several blond hair strands wet with sweat and water are

plastered to her face. Her braided pigtails are adorable, hanging down onto her breasts. Her legs are wide open for me. She is still leaning back, her back arched, her breasts out like they are asking for my attention.

"Where were we?" I murmur, drop to my knees, and my mouth is on her soaking pussy again.

I run my tongue slowly along her slit, then spread her pussy lips with my fingers and start flicking my tongue against her clit.

She moans beautifully. God, is there anything this girl does that doesn't fascinate me? Her skin glows orange and pink in the last traces of sunset. Her breasts and pussy have those white triangles from her bikini.

She is glorious.

Like a goddess.

A fairy.

I suck on her clit gently, and she moans.

"You like that?" I ask, then take her clit between my lips and tug at it gently.

How did I not like doing this to anyone before?

I cup her ass with both hands and raise my eyes at her as I tug at her clit again. Her unfocused gaze drops down to meet mine, then slides down to her pussy, watching me lick and tug at her clit, then meets my eyes again. I can see the arousal in her eyes that widen and hungrily eat up the sight. She is a voyeur. I like it. I love pleasing her, watching her fall apart slowly. It's more erotic than anything else.

She leans with her back onto the bamboo shower wall, opening her legs wider for me.

I want to finger her but I can't. I want to fuck her, but it's off-limits. But the one spot further down is not. So I keep licking her as my one finger runs along her slit, gathering the moisture, and slides further down between her butt cheeks to find her back entrance and starts massaging it gently.

"Kai," she whispers, lifting her hips to avoid it.

"Easy, baby girl. Let me do this. You'll like it."

And holy hell she does!

As soon as my finger starts massaging her back entrance, she starts breathing heavily. Her back arches, and she rolls her hips at me.

"Good?" I ask as I watch her.

She starts moaning.

"Shhh," I warn her. And when I resume lapping at her little pussy, she starts shuddering, trembling under my tongue so beautifully that I feel like I will come too.

I don't.

But she does.

Her hands grab the edge of the bench.

Her toes dig into the floor.

Her hips rise, pushing her pussy into my mouth. I lap at her wetness, wanting to take a bath in it. My tongue is doing a mad dance on her pink flesh.

And then she whimpers, trying not to be loud.

And comes.

And comes.

She tilts her face up, her mouth open in a silent moan like she sees God. Her body goes rigid. And I keep licking and sucking on her clit and circling it until I feel her body soften up.

"Kai," she whispers softly.

I stop and hold my breath, knowing that this very moment, I am still on her mind.

I watch her as I plant little kisses on her pussy, calming her. Her chest rises and falls heavily, her breasts perky and moving in sync. I want to play with them, and that's next on my agenda because I want to keep her in this shower as long as I can.

I want her to open her eyes and meet mine. And when she does, I give her pussy a gentle kiss, smiling as I shift upward.

No, it's not the color of sunset—it's a scarlet blush that colors her cheeks. Or a post-climax flush. Whatever it is—it's me. I used to get hard, thinking about her blushing.

And I am sure as hell hard now, kissing my way up her body to her cheeks.

Her beautiful eyes are some wild green color as the blue mixes with the pink-orange of the sky. I cup her face and kiss her so she can taste herself on my lips.

I am as hard as a rock again.

But I hear voices getting closer.

Dammit.

This is the wrong time. Soon, everyone will line up for the shower. I don't want her to feel embarrassed when she leaves it with me.

And before someone kills us for wasting all the water, I tear my lips from her reluctantly.

"We'd better hurry up," I say.

She smiles awkwardly as she nods. But I can see it in her eyes—she wants this again as badly as I do.

I can feel my scars tingle under the water. They are a reminder. I should stay away. But I can't. Because once I let go of the hurtful past, I want Callie more than anything.

37

CALLIE

I CAN BARELY CONTAIN MY EXCITEMENT.

The first blowjob is not an achievement, right? Then why does it feel like I took one more step to something called intimacy?

I want more of Kai. More of what is happening, because something is. I want to tell myself that it's desperation. That he just needs a good lay.

But that's not how it is for me. Being with him stitches together everything I felt for him before that was broken, ruined, but now becoming whole again.

I am silly.

Gah!

What am I thinking?

But when he is around, I don't want to be anywhere else. I don't see anyone, lose focus, and the world shrinks down to my heart fluttering like a little hummingbird, and the butterflies in my stomach, a hundred of them, and my treacherous body that swirls with want like I am a cat in heat.

At dinner, I try to avoid looking at him. But when I am filling my bowl with the salad from the buffet, inked arms appear on each side of me.

"Excuse me," he says softly, takes my plate from my hands, fills it up, and gives it back to me.

His big form presses onto me from behind, and I grin.

"You guys gonna get it on right here, or can I get some salad?" Ty's voice is laced with a soft chuckle.

Kai's hands disappear, and without looking, I go to my seat, trying to hold back a grin and blushing like a fool.

His glances at me at dinner are too short but way too charged with the knowledge of the shower episode. I fumble more than an awkward girl in front of a room full of men.

I want to ask Kai if he wants to hang out but don't want to sound too needy. And then Ty and Guff and the whole gang of guys are gathering at the workshop, and it is too late to talk to Kai alone.

That night, I lie next to Katura on our mattress and I can't help thinking about what happened. I want to tell her, but she won't care. She's done it many times, I'm sure.

So I contain my thoughts as much as I can, because when I let them run free, my panties get soaked, and I feel shame, lying next to Katura with my pussy wet for Kai Droga.

I lie in darkness, eyes wide open, for the longest time. The breeze from the open window caresses my skin. I listen to the purring of the ocean outside. And that's how I fall asleep, looking forward to tomorrow when I will see Kai again.

I wake up the next morning to an empty bed. Katura is gone, which is weird because I am usually the first one to wake up.

The air outside is humid. The birds are wild. There is no one around as I walk through the morning village, rubbing my eyes.

Katura sits on the beach, watching the waves.

"What's up?" I ask as I join her.

Then I see it—boots, cargo pants, backpack.

"It's time," she says.

"For what?" My heart gives out a heavy thud, and I am wide awake.

"I need to get going."

The words are ambiguous. When Katura gets up and heads to the main path into the jungle, anxiety sweeps over me.

"Katura! Where?"

I know where she is going. She's had a fixation on the Westside for some time, but I want to stretch time. When she gets to the Westside, there will be Archer and questions, and he will come for me and Dani because that's how we got here in the first place.

I trot after Katura, who walks in that usual military stomp that is faster than my trot. Her fingers are hooked under the straps of her backpack. She is determined.

"Kat!"

I don't want her to leave. Not just yet. I am already out of breath, and she looks like she is taking a casual stroll. The distance between us is growing.

"Kat! Wait up!"

I stop and lean with my hands on my knees, panting.

She turns around abruptly and puts her hands on her waist.

"Listen, babe." She stares at me with what looks like pity and irritation. "You are adorable. And a good-hearted human. But I need to get to the Westside."

I push off my knees and walk up to her. "Will you tell me why?"

"Why?" She smirks. "We came here for this, remember? And your cousin is on the Westside. Though a certain someone seems to have bewitched you here."

"They say it's not what you expect."

Katura exhales loudly in irritation and cocks her head. "You don't know until you are there. Pull your head out of your ass, babe. You've only been here for less than two weeks, and already you are happy cleaning fish and gardening and running in the rain with your boy toy."

I blush at the mention. "And what do you think they make you do there to work your way around that place?"

"You don't try, you don't know."

Gah! She is stubborn. And right. But she doesn't know about me and Kai and Archer. Now that I think about it, meeting Archer petrifies me.

"So let's stick around," I plead, "find out more from the others, and figure out a plan."

I know there is no plan.

"I have a plan." She smirks.

Well, shit. Of course, she does.

She narrows her dark eyes at me. "It's about the boy, isn't it? Kai. You know him from before. And not just from going to the same school."

I exhale loudly. "I know him, yeah."

"You like him."

"Yeah."

"Yeah." She chuckles. "Wanna tell me what this is about?"

Katura takes slow steps closer, studying me with that prying stare that seems to pierce me and extract my thoughts.

I look down at my feet and dig the dirt with the sole of my sandal. "I used to go to Deene."

"Right. That's where a lot of the Westside comes from."

"Right. So did Kai."

"Right. But something went sour."

I look up at her. "Why would you say that?"

She rolls her eyes, then throws her head back and exhales in frustration. "This is excruciating." She looks at me again and cocks her head. "You glared at each other like the worst enemies when we got here. You avoided each other for days. And suddenly, you are cuddling away in his bungalow."

"Whatever." I hate that Kai and I are so obvious. "It's just… The guy who runs the Westside…"

How much do I tell her?

"Yeeeeah?" Katura mocks me now. "Come on, girl." She rolls her head, seemingly annoyed. "Spill it already. You know him, don't you?"

I finally give up. "I used to date him."

38

KATURA

Well, fuck.

I take in a deep breath. I want to laugh, but can't because the blondie is visibly uncomfortable. And there is waaaaaay more to this story. I can feel it in my gut. Sunshine Ty didn't spill the beans no matter how I coaxed him, so it must be important.

Then something dawns on me.

That makes sense. There is no way Callie was chosen to come here for her looks or skills. Psychology major—sure, useful. Not! There are better candidates. Uncle showed me the applications of those who were chosen to come to Zion. I studied them. Callie had—maybe, and that's a stretch—a thirty percent chance. One in a thousand.

But here is the trick.

The Chancellor is her ex.

I stare at Callie as she stares at me with some sort of apology in her eyes.

Now I know Mr. Chancellor's type. Pretty. Blonde.

Gentle. Though as per stories, he is in about anything that moves. But now I know about his ex. And I can surely work with this. The fucker will give out the info I need under the light pressure of my foot on his Adam's apple. Star quarterback or not.

"So why are you not there?" I ask, trying to fish out more info.

It's strange. I would have run to my ex in a heartbeat if he were in charge of the island my survival depended on. I would have sucked his cock and fucked him. As many times as he wanted. And had fun doing it, too.

But not this girl.

"We had a falling out," Callie says, avoiding my eyes.

I laugh. Jesus, getting her to tell the story is like pulling teeth. "C'mon. Don't take me for a moron. Falling out, my ass."

"Well…"

She goes quiet, and I can't handle it.

"Just fucking say it already! You lost it all and you still choke on boy memories. Seriously!"

"I slept with Archer's best friend," she blurts out.

"Oooooh-ha." I cross my arms over my chest, smiling. "That's precious. That's the boy you don't remember the night with? Damn, girl."

"Well, it's complicated." She goes quiet, and my patience is gone.

"You know—" I start backing away up the path because I am done with this bullshit. I learned that bullshit and half-stories get you in trouble and create exactly the shit this girl ended up in. "I'm off. Done." I raise my hands in the air and wipe them against each other as I keep backing away. "Keep your fucking secrets, Callie. Be—"

"It's Kai," she blurts out.

I stop.

At first, I don't understand where Kai comes into place.

She purses her lips. "The boy I spent a night with when I dated Archer. It's Kai."

I can't stop a smile from spreading on my lips as I gape at her. Her arms wrap around her torso, hugging it. She won't look at me as if I am some fucking moral judge.

"It's Kai," she says barely audibly and stares at her feet as she digs the ground with the tip of her foot like she can dig herself out of this story.

I approach slowly. This is five-star soap opera right here. "All right. You can't tell me a story and omit parts of it." I won't deal with bullshit. "You are not eighteen," I say, knowing that my voice is harsh. "You are a fucking grownup, Callie. And if you want me to stick around for a while, I wanna hear all of it. It's important, considering, well, that your two ex-boys are in enemy camps. So spill."

And she starts talking.

I listen.

When she stalls, I ask questions.

When she hesitates, I press on. Because that's how interrogations work. That's how you get the full story. I need every detail.

Hers is a story of young elite students getting fucked by mind games and feelings and rivalry and this stupid "oh, he/she can't possibly like me, so I'm just gonna hang out with her/his best friend." That's how you ruin your best years.

And holy shit is it stupid. Like they don't have common sense.

But she talks.

And talks.

And I let her.

"So he didn't spike and rape you after all," I confirm after she is done.

She shakes her head.

"Are you sure?"

Her eyes snap at me, and she gapes.

This doll doesn't even know what a dick is or where to find it.

"Chill. I'm just making sure," I calm her. "You like him, huh? Kai?"

"Yeah." She exhales heavily, but I can tell it's easier for her to talk now.

"In love?" This question is for me. Others' love stories are exciting.

She bows her head and doesn't answer.

Precious.

"Yeah," I echo.

I know the answer. This girl has all sorts of things twisted up in her mind. I've never felt special to anyone. Nor have I liked anyone too much. But I can imagine. I watched *Cruel Intentions* and *Mean Girls*. I've never gone to public school, probably for the best. My first guy was a street runner in Bangkok. My second—a bar owner in a small town, twice my age. They taught me to use guys for my own satisfaction. I learned that the world can end any day. So, I use it. And I use men.

But, hey, a good love story is never boring.

I stare at Callie for a short while. She is beautiful in all the right ways. And with a heart like hers, I can see how mean boys can get vicious.

But the fucking Chancellor, huh?

And Kai.

My, oh, my.

"Did you sleep with him yet?" I ask, wanting juicy details now.

"Who?"

This girl.

I will strangle her one day.

"Who? What are you an owl? Seriously, babe."

She shakes her head.

"What's stopping you?"

She is quiet. Petal, really. I get the name now. I heard it on Kai's lips. Precious.

"Let's go." I nod toward the village and start walking. She follows me obediently. "You know," I say as we walk down the path, and I repeat the words I've been taught over and over again. "When you don't go for what you want, one day, you realize you missed the biggest chance of your life. The Change taught us all."

I look over my shoulder to meet her eyes. She is staring at me like I am a therapist who just made the biggest revelation of her life.

"You got a second chance, babe. Don't fuck it up," I add.

I turn away with a smile but feel a pinch of envy. I wish I'd meet a man I really liked.

She has one.

She is the lucky one.

And now I should consider my moves with Callie by my side.

First, I need to make several trips to the Westside and observe from afar. I can ditch the cameras. You can learn a lot by watching people who don't know they are being watched. This is why I agreed to stay on this side. These are the good guys. The other side... Well, Archer Crone doesn't exactly have a stellar reputation, besides his IQ and athletic skills.

Second, I should watch out for Callie to make sure she is safe. She can be my trump card on the Westside once I get there.

Archer Crone already knows that his cargo is here. But I don't have beef with him. This girl, on the other hand...

Two boys.

Two sides.

It can turn nasty.

I need to play it right.

Callie is a powerful connection between the opposing sides.

I know Kai already.

But now, I am really, really curious about the Chancellor.

39

CALLIE

Dani picks the weeds in the garden like every single one of them is a precious gem.

I watch her for some time.

She is so delicate that I feel like she belongs to a fine china cabinet. She likes wearing dresses, even when we do work around the village. She looks like she needs protection, and Ty is definitely taking the lead in that department.

He is all over her any chance he gets. He makes her smile. He takes her for walks, on boat rides, and for a swim. She didn't spend last night in the bungalow. Whatever magic Ty is using—it's working. She seems more cheerful, but something holds her back.

Trauma is a monster. It clings to some people stronger than others. Some people don't have the strength to fight monsters. Some are ghost-busters. Others are victims.

I finally put the rake away, get up, and slide my feet into my flip-flops. "Dani, let's go for a walk."

She looks at me without much emotion. "Sure."

The other girls glance up but don't say anything.

I take her toward the path that goes to the waterfall. It's wide and sunlit. The trees whisper. It's secluded. And it's nice to be in the shade, away from the scorching sun.

Dani looks around like she is on a boring date.

"Do you want to talk about what happened back home?" I ask.

Her brown hair is in a ponytail. Her sunflower dress is too loose and hangs on her skinny shoulders over her bikini. Her knees are dirty, and she picks her nails as if it's the most important thing at the moment.

"We all had something happen to us," she replies. "We just deal with it differently."

"And you can't deal with it. Is that what it is?"

Talking to her is like pulling teeth. I feel like she won't break. Not with me. Not right now. Not by daylight.

"Do you know how it feels when you watch your family members being tortured and killed and think it's your fault?" she finally says.

I halt, turn, and look at her.

Trauma has shades.

So does violence.

So do atrocities.

"What happened after the Change is not our fault, Dani."

"Did you ever think that being spared and surviving is not a blessing?"

That's not what they tell you in counseling.

"That it's actually the biggest punishment," she adds quietly, her eyes cast down to the ground. "We think that fate was unfair to them. But they are the lucky ones, you know?"

She looks at me then. God, she needs counseling, reassurance, and a shrink.

We resume walking up the path.

"You can't think like that, Dani. Life is…" Ugh. How do I explain it? Not that I know. "A psychologist whose family was burned alive during the second world war said that the meaning of life is in overcoming the challenges and finding new beginnings."

She smirks. Even her smirk is gentle.

"You know," I say as we walk slowly, "Ty really cares about you."

She smiles and bites her lip.

There.

Thank you.

It's a sign, a good one. Five points for Ty. She likes you, buddy.

I smile as I gaze up the path. "The purpose of healing is realizing that your loved ones who aren't with you would be glad to see you happy. That whatever defines our fate and life—some other power, karma, whatever it is—meant for things to be this way. When you find someone who cares and who you care for, you need to make them happy. Because that's your redemption. Your ticket out of trauma."

"Do you care about Kai?" She looks at me with curiosity.

There we go. Of course, she had to ask. I smile, I can't help it.

"Kai and I go way back. Something I thought he did

four years ago ruined our lives, took us to hell, and I blamed him for it for a long time. And then I found out that what I thought was a betrayal was actually an act of kindness. That he went through a lot of tough stuff because he tried to keep me safe. And… I really liked him back then."

"And now?"

My chest tightens at the thought. I look at Dani and I smile. "And now it's different. Way different."

We walk in silence. Emotions start inside me again. My feet kick palm leaves and branches out of the way like I can kick those emotions away so they don't overwhelm me.

"Now I realize," I say, "that in this dark world, Kai is one of the very few people I care about. Maybe, the only one. And I so desperately want to make him happy. You know, if you can't ease your own pain, you do it for others. Somehow, it makes your own pain subside. It's the weirdest thing."

I look at Dani, and she gazes at me with a strange look like I just told her a secret.

She nods. "Yeah," she says quietly. "It makes sense."

I stop, then step up to her and, without saying anything else, hug her.

"That's how healing works," I whisper in her ear.

Her skinny hands meekly wrap around me, and she sniffles.

I hear a crack in the jungle.

And birds fleeting out of the bushes, a pack of them.

Suddenly, it's too quiet.

Something is wrong.

OUTCAST

A voice, alien and raspy, comes in from the bushes. "Look at them two beauties."

I push off Dani and whip around.

"Well, hello there."

His grin is brown like he is missing teeth. A dirty t-shirt, shorts, and sneakers. He looks like a predator, slowly walking out of the bushes, his tongue licking his lips as he grins. He fixes his baseball hat with one hand. The other—

Holds a knife.

"Easy, birdies, easy." He crouches like he is about to jump.

"Our lucky day." Another voice comes from feet away, and another thug, almost identical but heavier, scowls at us as he pushes a tree branch away with a hand holding a knife, too.

My heart starts pounding in my chest. Dani stares at them in some stalled surprise.

"We should go," I whisper.

The thoughts flicker in my head—we are ten minutes away from the beach, we don't have any weapons, and there is that overwhelming fear at the thought of Olivia.

What happened to Olivia…

I start panicking, backing away down the path and tugging Dani with me.

"Run," I whisper, whip around, and dart down the path.

Only to slam into someone else's arms that grip me with painful strength, whip me around, and a hand presses to my mouth.

"Well, hello, pretty."

I try to scream, but the hand is too tight around my mouth.

"Shhh, sweetie. Be quiet, and you might enjoy it."

Nasty breath fills my nostrils, and my heart jolts in panic.

I scream, but it only comes out as a muffled moan. The hands around me tighten.

And there is Dani, who stares at me as one of the guys comes up from behind her and pokes her ribs, making her jump and whip around in shock.

They cackle—that nasty laughter of predators who know exactly what their prey will or will not do.

Dani won't do a thing. She is the weakest of us, and she is paralyzed as the guy strokes her cheek. She jerks away, but he catches her, widening his eyes, and blows out a "Boo." And she trembles.

I try to fight, but there is no way I can do anything against a guy.

So I do the only thing possible. I suppress the gagging from the stench of stale booze and piss and bite into the hand over my mouth.

"Fuuuuuck!" the guy shouts.

For the flimsiest second that he lets me go, I pull away from him, start running, and scream.

"Heeeelp!"

I scream as loud as I can because that's the only thing that can save us.

And I run like I never ran in my life.

But then something slams over me and tackles me to the

ground, the impact so sudden and painful that it takes the breath out of me.

A slap on the face comes next.

It's blinding.

Loud.

Painful.

My face catches on fire. Tears burn my eyes.

A hand wraps around my throat too tightly, cutting off the air.

"You fucking scream again," the guy hisses, "and I will gut you like a piglet, you fucking whore."

Hands yank me up, grab the back of my hair in a fist, and that stench in my face is back as he says, "You make a sound, and I will break every fucking bone in your body."

40

KAI

Maddy's shout across the beach comes like an echo.

"Guys!" She is running toward us. "Someone screamed in the jungle!"

She is panting. Bo and I pause and start walking toward her.

"Someone screamed in the jungle," she repeats. "I am not sure it's anything. But—"

"Where are the girls?" I bark. "All of them!"

Bo and I start trotting.

We've been here before. Shouts are not fun when they come from the jungle.

"Is everyone accounted for?" Bo asks as he gains speed.

I see a pack of girls coming out of the garden, all of them looking around.

But I am looking for one.

Callie.

Maddy trots behind us. "Callie and Dani went for a walk."

My heart slams in my chest.

"Walk where?" I ask, not realizing I am shouting as I trot.

Maddy looks at me with her scared eyes. "Up the path to the waterfall."

And I am running like I never ran before.

"The workshop!" I shout to Bo though I don't look at him. "I'm taking the guns! Get the guys!"

Adrenalin spikes so high that I fly like the wind.

Workshop. Crates. Three legit guns. They are loaded. I don't bother with the rest. Time is precious.

As I whip out of the workshop, I shove one of the guns at Bo, and another at Guff, who is next to him.

"The Savages!" Bo roars.

I hear shouts, girls calling the names, and guys running from all directions.

But my eyes are on the waterfall path as I dart barefoot toward the opening to the jungle.

I run like a motherfucker. My heart races. Blood pounds in my head.

Hold on.

I don't know who I am talking to, but I pray this is all a misunderstanding.

"Callie!" I roar as I run. Because if she is there for some fun, I don't care how stupid I look.

"Dani!" I hear a shout behind me, and it's Ty.

They couldn't have made it far.

Wind swishes in my ears.

My footsteps thud through my body as I whip up the path, faster and faster.

I will fucking fly if I have to.

And then I see flickers up ahead.

There are people.

Too many.

Figures I don't recognize.

And then I do as I slow down and someone whips around.

She is in his arms.

Callie.

Her eyes are full of panic. A nasty arm is wrapped around her waist, another hand pressed to her throat. With a knife.

I slow. My gun is up as I approach. It's one step at a time as I cock the gun and point it at the guy.

He stops, anger in his eyes, his lips curled in a scowl. "You do anything stupid, amigo, and I will slice her pretty neck," he hisses.

Callie is a shield.

I hear multiple thudding footsteps behind me that slow and stop.

My body is trembling in rage, but my hands are steady like iron bars as I look at the Savage.

My gaze shifts to Callie, who is staring at me wide-eyed.

Don't move, baby girl.

I look at the thug again.

He is scared. But he has a knife. The fucker thinks he can get away.

Easy.

"Let them go!" the voice behind me shouts.

It's Ty.

"Calm down," I tell him, not taking my eyes off the group ahead—four guys, Callie, and Dani.

Dani looks like she is about to cry. But the guy who holds her doesn't have a weapon. He doesn't need it with her. She will snap at the slightest pressure.

Bo passes me, both his hands on the gun that points at the guys. He is slow, careful, knees bent as he crouches toward the guys.

I follow.

"Everyone keep calm," Bo says, his voice is calm and measured. "We can resolve this peacefully. Let the girls go, and you can go where you came from."

There are crunches behind us. Many. I know there are guys behind us. I pray Ty doesn't do anything stupid because of Dani. We are on it. And as long as the Savages don't fuck up—

"Put your guns down," the one holding Callie growls, and she whimpers as he presses the knife closer to her throat.

Fury spikes through me. I want to blow his brains out, shoot him to mush, rip his throat out with my teeth.

I see red.

I want to shoot the motherfucker in the face.

But he has her.

And she is the only thing I care about right now.

"Drop. The fucking. Guns," the nasty baseball hat growls.

"Bo?" I say quietly.

He lowers his gun slowly. "Let them go," he says in his calm low voice. Fuck, he can be a negotiator alright. "It's a long way from home. And we'll track you. All. The way. Down."

My eyes are on the guy and the knife.

And then there is a movement.

It's a flicker.

Callie's leg rises and bends at the knee, and her foot rams back into the guy's crotch.

He roars. She pushes him away.

In a split second, I aim at the guy who stands by her other side and shoot.

The sound is loud, sharp

"Kai!" she shrieks.

I aim at the other one and shoot.

Then I dart toward her to cover her from whatever might come and pull her in my arms, shielding her, yanking her away from the fucker that held her, and pull her onto the ground.

And all hell breaks loose.

41

CALLIE

THE SOUND OF THE SHOTS IS DEAFENING.

Something wraps around me and yanks me to the ground.

I am panting.

It's Kai.

There is another shot, and a scream, and dozens of feet stomp the ground.

There is a commotion, a roar, swearing, and a scream, Dani's.

"It's alright, baby girl. It's alright," Kai's familiar voice seeps into my ear, though it's hard to hear with everything that is going on.

Kai lifts me off the ground, and I whip around, frantically looking for Dani.

She is standing to the side, shielded by Bo and Zach.

One thug is on the ground, crouching.

Two are running, being chased by our guys.

The one who held Dani holds a knife in front of him, but

he is scared, backing away from our guys who step toward him.

And Ty—

He darts to the thug, swings a bat in his hand, and sends him down to the ground, then tosses the bat away, straddles the guy, and punches him.

Once.

Twice.

"Mo-ther-fuc-ker!" he roars, every syllable a punch, the guy's face turning red as he tries to push Ty with his arms that are weak and useless.

Another punch.

Again.

Another roar as Ty mindlessly pounds the guy's face, who is motionless on the ground and doesn't respond anymore.

"Ty!" Owen shouts.

Bo, Owen, and two more guys run up to Ty and drag him off the guy as he keeps swinging, cursing and roaring.

"Leave it!" Bo barks. "Stop!" He shakes Ty.

Ty looks around like a madman, then sees Dani.

She stands with her arms wrapped around her and gapes at him, tears running down her face.

"Angel," he whispers.

It's as if a switch in him was flipped at the sight of her.

His hands are bloody. His long blond hair is whipped across his face. Shirtless, blood spattered across his chest, he flings himself at her and cups her face.

"Are you okay, angel?"

He presses his forehead to hers and strokes her hair.

"It's okay, angel. It's okay. I'm here. Yeah? I'm here."

I don't realize it, but tears start rolling down my cheeks as I turn to look at Kai.

He is silent. His gaze on me is unblinking.

"Are you okay?" he asks quietly.

I am trembling as I nod and look around at the other guys.

They stare at the body on the ground. It's lifeless. Bo approaches it, drops down on one knee, and feels the pulse.

"He is still breathing," he says.

"Fuck," someone exhales.

My heart is still pounding. Kai rakes his hand through his hair, staring at the body too. "What do we do?" he asks.

I am shaking and wrap my arms around myself trying to stop it. Only one phrase lingers in my mind.

What happened to Olivia?

There is no sign of the other Savages. Just this one. Did they just leave him?

"We are bringing him with us," Bo says.

"Seriously?" Zach shakes his head.

"Come on." Bo nods and bends to lift the guy's upper body.

Kai goes over and helps him.

A minute later, we are on our way down the path.

In silence.

The only voice is Ty's whisper as he has his arm around Dani and murmurs—angel, and something else—on repeat.

I am in shock all the way to the village where the girls stand in a pack in the dining area.

"What is this?" Maddy gapes at the unconscious guy, whose arms are wrapped around Bo and Kai's shoulders.

"Scum," Bo says. "But he is still alive. We should see to it. Please, Maddy."

She runs to the cabinet that holds the first-aid kit like she is saving one of her own.

That's a lesson about humanity. It comes into play in every war. No matter what happens, some have compassion. Whether it's to an enemy or any human being whose life is at stake—some will do anything to save another life.

And then you have peaceful times when seemingly normal human beings will harm anything at every opportunity they get.

In Ohio, where I came down with my aunt after the Change, looking for relatives, a small town was looted by the nearby residents. There was a white family, snobby, rich, with connections. They could talk their way into any deal any other time. Just not out of the ruthless ways of the monsters who one night raided their place, beat the father to a pulp, and kicked them out. As they stood, all four of them, with no place to go, on the side of the road, a Hispanic family that lived in the projects on the outskirts picked them up and gave them shelter. Law enforcement is helpless when masses rise and loot. After the Change, in small towns, anything went.

Moments like this teach you about humankind. There is a human in every one of us. And there is a beast. It's a scale. Some have it tuned by a moral compass. Some let it go. When shit happens, when law enforcement is not in sight, when the power scale tips, the dark side inside humans can cause an eclipse in the middle of a bright day.

We all sit at the dining tables. Quiet. In shock. The entire village is here. No one is talking.

Half an hour later, Maddy comes out of the Common Lounge where they put the guy.

"Broken nose, cheekbone, brow. Bullet wound to his shoulder. He is not awake. I am not sure he will live," she says as she wipes her hands again and again with a cloth like she can't get rid of the blood that is not there anymore.

The ocean is peaceful. It's dinner time. The smell of food lingers in the air.

And that's humanity for you again. The banal needs—eating, surviving—mixed with the moral dilemma.

"Should've left him in the jungle," someone says.

"Yeah."

"Agreed."

But Bo's lips are pressed tightly together as he stares at the joint between his fingers, then, without looking, passes it to Kai, who sits quietly next to him.

Kai doesn't look at me. His body jerks barely visibly from time to time as if in recollection. But I can't forget his gaze when he pointed the gun at the man. The steely determination—it haunts me in the most beautiful way. So do the gunshots that deafened and could have taken a life. But at that moment, I knew he did it for me, and my heart swells for him.

Katura straddles the bench at the table and stretches her hand to take the joint out of Kai's hand.

She looks at Dani as she takes a puff. "How are you?"

Dani nods. She seems fine. Ty is not. He is silent, not smiling, not looking at anyone, even her.

My heart still throbs. My knees are weak.

I look at Kai, and his hands are shaking as he tries to light the cigarette, then curses under his breath, gets up, and walks away.

Dinner is served. But everyone is quiet.

Bo is grim.

"They might come back for revenge," Owen says.

"Fuck," Zach murmurs. "And now we have that piece of shit to deal with." He nods toward the Common Lounge.

Bo shoves food in his mouth without visibly caring what it is. "Zach, Jeok, Guff, Owen, and me," he says quietly, his eyes on the plate. "We are all up on guard tonight. Five people a night. That's how we gonna do it from now on."

Everyone nods.

I feel like the world is crumbling around me. This was supposed to be paradise. It only takes some time to learn that every paradise has a bottomless pit that opens its hellish mouth to swallow whatever falls into it.

After dinner, a bunch of guys light the bonfire. Darkness falls. Tonight, it's menacing. It feels like back home when the Change brought out the worst in humankind. Especially at night.

Everyone gathers around the bonfire. There is no music. No laughter. Only soft whispers and quiet chatting.

The memory of Olivia is in the air. I still don't know what it is, but now, I have an idea. It's terrifying. Nauseous. It makes me wanna throw up when I think about what could have happened if we weren't saved.

For some time, everyone just sits and stares at the bonfire. There is a feeling of an imminent end. As if it's the last day. There is a feeling of a tragedy avoided.

But then there might be another one coming, more terrifying. There is a lot more scum in town.

When will they come again?

42

CALLIE

I can't get rid of the images of the Savages in my mind.

There are other thoughts, too. *What if it was my last day?*

This philosophy never does anyone any favors. If anything, more often, it leads to recklessness. But in moments like this, it makes all the difference.

Kai is not around, and it bothers me.

I don't want to wait for what is to come.

No tomorrow.

No promises.

Screw dreaming and planning.

The Change taught us that God laughs at our plans.

Katura is right—when you miss a chance, and you have a second one, take it.

I see a shadow in the distance on the beach. I don't know it's *him*. But I feel it. He is like a fishing reel, reeling me in. A hook that doesn't hurt but tugs and tugs no matter what I do, pulling me away from my thoughts and routine and toward him.

I rise from my beach chair at the bonfire and walk into the darkness toward the figure.

It's Kai.

He sits alone by the shore, only ten or so feet away from the water, where the waves can't reach his feet, and the sight breaks my heart. I want to be with him. In his happy moments. In his grief. When he feels like he needs to talk to someone.

I walk on the sand, my feet sinking, the breeze whipping a loose strand of hair across my face. I come and sit down next to him on the sand.

"What's up, stranger?" I nudge him softly with my shoulder.

We stare into the blackness of the ocean lapping at the shore just several feet from us.

He turns to look at me.

We are alone. I want to say so many things, and I don't. Because words never did us any good.

But then, silence did the worst.

"Are you all right?" I ask.

I can feel his gaze on me, and when I turn, he doesn't say a word. He gets up, and my heart falls, thinking that he will walk away.

Instead, he sits down behind me, his raised knees on each side of me, and wraps his arms around me, pressing me so tightly against his chest that in seconds, my heart is ready to explode. From all the feelings that suddenly rise in me. From this tender gesture.

His cheek presses against mine.

I close my eyes and inhale deeply.

He is silent. But words and feelings crowd my head and heart. I press my hands to his arms, and we sit like this for some time.

Kai, say something.

Tell me things.

I turn my head and find his lips. He kisses me softly. No tongue. It's so gentle and warm and loving that I can almost feel what he is feeling. Our breaths mix, our lips touch, let go, then touch again, just brushing against each other, emotions suspended between us.

It's the most innocent kiss and the most important yet.

Why now?

Why not back then?

But I don't say it because this moment wipes away the past.

Kai is like a rose with thorns. You have to work around the thorns to get to the smooth parts. I want to. So desperately, it hurts.

We are wrapped in the darkness of the island night and the soft purring of the ocean at our feet.

His forehead touches my head. "I was really scared earlier," he says quietly.

I tense. He's never admitted anything like this before. And here is the soft part of him as his thorns fall off, one by one. Moments such as this are precious. They make my chest tighten and tears burn my eyes.

"Me too," I say. "Everyone was. Because of what happened some time ago, right?"

His hand slides up to stroke my hair. He is so gentle right now that it rips my heart. I am used to him being snappy. Cocky. Slightly hostile in his silence. Careful, maybe. Just not tender like this. I want to touch him so desperately, but I am afraid he will just pull away.

"That's not why I was scared, Callie. When you screamed…" He stills. "Fuck," he exhales. "I felt like back then, the day after the Block Party, when I knew I royally screwed up and something bad was about to happen."

My heart is a hundred drums that beat all at once, then pause, sinking me into the silence that closes around me.

"I can't stay away from you, Callie," Kai says softly, his lips hovering next to mine, his hand tugging gently at my braid. "I try. Because I feel that once I get close to you, something bad will happen, and I will lose you again."

Again.

The word tugs at my heart in the best and worst ways. But the meaning of it dissipates, because I melt at his touch.

"Nothing will happen," I murmur and capture his lips with mine in another soft kiss. I so desperately want to believe it, because I've lost too much in this life already.

"You drive me crazy, Callie. And give me hope that I don't think any of us can have in this shitty world."

"It's not shitty. Not when you have someone—"

You love, I want to add.

I feel my chest burn with emotions that make it hard to breathe.

Kai kisses the corner of my lips, then my cheek. I want to run my hand over his body and make those scars that he is so ashamed of disappear like magicians do in fantasy movies. But I can't even touch him. He doesn't like that.

Katura's advice is still in my head. So I do what I feel

like, even though my heart slams in my chest at what I am about to say.

"I want to be with you, Kai. Tonight."

I'm such a coward. I am using this one trump card. The one that every guy in the world falls for.

But I don't care.

I want Kai.

Always have.

Even more so now. I want to heal his wounds and the sadness—the one that takes over him when he thinks no one is watching and he smokes and drinks like it can burn that sadness away. And I want to see more of his coy smiles that are so out of place on a guy tatted up to a brim. I want to hear his laughter when he surfs and jokes around with Ty.

I want all of him.

His face is so close that even in the darkness I can see his eyes searching mine for confirmation. Or at least that's what I think.

"Can I stay with you tonight?" I ask.

Please, say yes.

He gets up, stretches his hand to take mine, and pulls me up.

"Petal, you are asking for trouble," he says as he caves my body with his.

I laugh nervously. Trouble is what I want. If it has his face and body and heart. If it's name is Kai Droga, the boy I've wanted for as long as I remember.

We walk toward his cabin, my hand in his, and I don't care who sees it.

His place is familiar now. I've been here once. I dreamt about it.

The door closes behind us, and the rest of the world disappears. Kai turns on the dim lamp, then walks to the speaker and turns it on. Soft music starts trickling through the room. I don't need music. Only him.

He comes over and wraps his arms around my waist.

"I almost lost you today," he says.

He didn't. I'm here.

I put my hands on his shoulders, touching the fabric of his shirt, the muscles under it taut and hard. I inhale the scent of him, salt and cigarette smoke.

This moment feels special. I stand on my tiptoes and kiss him.

His hand slides to the back of my neck. So familiar. So endearing. I melt. I dissipate at the kiss when his tongue sinks into my mouth.

"Kai," I say when I pull away from him.

"Yeah, baby girl."

I smile.

I know his degrees of intimacy by now.

I am Callie when he is serious or too vulnerable.

Petal when he is casual or bitter or funny or playful.

But when he feels close to me, it's baby girl.

Funny how you learn a person by his words.

"Kai," I whisper his name. I know he likes it. I learned that too. "I want you. I want to go all the way."

But when I try to kiss him, he pulls away and stares at me.

"You know what I mean," I say. I know he does.

"Are you sure?"

God, how could I think this guy could do anything against my will? An angel dressed in the suit of a devil.

"Yes. So sure you have no idea."

I chuckle as I rise on tiptoes again to kiss him.

43

KAI

What the hell, bro?

I kiss Callie, and I am already hard. But when she says the last words, I try to relax but I can't.

I am nervous.

What the fucking fuck?

I've wanted her for years. My fantasies about her are borderline psychotic.

But when she says she wants to do it with me, my mind stalls.

She wants me to be her first. And it's a big step. Because I know deep in my heart that I will be the first and the last. But if anything ever happens to her, I will never forgive myself.

And the thought—*that thought*—is heavy as fuck.

I pull away and look into her eyes.

There is trust. Want. A softness that I only see in them when I kiss her.

She is so cute, and I know that she is way more nervous than me.

Man the fuck up, Kai, I tell myself.

I've had more girls than I can count. But this one with blond hair braided in pigtails that drive me nuts and the blue eyes that make me want to go down on my knees before her and unravel all the emotions that stay pinned inside—she is the one who turns my world upside down.

"Do you have any idea how crazy you make me, baby girl?" I say.

Of course, she doesn't. I want her to say something, to laugh, to smile, so as to break the intensity of this moment. But my heart is in full-on tornado mode.

"You haunt me day and night," I say, rubbing my nose against hers. I can't keep this shit inside me anymore. Not after what happened today. "In my bed, in my workshop. When you sit on the beach in the evenings and watch me surf." I rub my cheek against hers, closing my eyes and trying to calm my feelings that are ready to spill over. "Not a minute passes by during the day that I don't think of you. It's insane," I finish with a whisper, planting a soft kiss on her cheek.

I pull away.

"Callie Mays, you've been haunting me for four years now."

I chuckle, but she doesn't smile back.

"You too," she says, barely audibly.

And I know I am fucked for life.

The only thing that can break this spell is pure, raw body contact.

When I grab the hem of my shirt and pull it over my head, the coolness against my skin shifts the feelings away. If only for a moment. I pick up the hem of her tank top and slowly pull it up and over her hands and head that she raises obediently, and drop it onto the floor.

Her shorts are next. Her hands are hesitant as she tries to help, our eyes locked the entire time. The shorts drop to the floor, and she steps out of them.

She has two bikinis. But it's this one that's always on when she is with me.

"I am starting to get jealous of these strawberries," I say, smiling. "They are too close to where I wanna be."

She chuckles and bites her lip. And when I undo the strings and pull her top off, she casts her eyes down.

Her breasts are perfect. Her nipples are inverted but start hardening when I bring my hands to them and brush them with the back of my fingers.

Fuck…

Nipples are even more arousing when they look like cat eyes until you touch them, and suddenly they start coming out of hiding. So fucking hot! Petal is full of surprises.

She is blushing as she looks down.

I tap my hooked finger under her chin.

"Look up, baby girl."

When she does, I have a full hard-on. These eyes made me come in seconds so many times during my solo rides.

I kiss her softly, trying to be as gentle as I can, though I want to tear her apart. I pull away again and take one of her pigtails, slide the tie off, and start undoing her braid.

She tries to help, but I gently push her hands away.

"Let me do this, baby girl. I'll undo you piece by piece."

And while she blushes and nervously licks her lips, I undo one braid, then the other, then run my inked fingers through her hair, loosening it.

Who would have known that my tattoos would undo Callie Mays?

She is so fucking hot that I am done playing games. I need to be closer to her.

I hook my thumbs over the waistband of my shorts and slowly tug them down, letting my hard-on free as the shorts slide down to the floor.

I deal with her bikini bottom next, tugging them down and sending those strawberries to the floor.

I bring one arm under her knees, the other around her back, pick her up in my arms, and carry her to bed.

It's the first time she is sober when I carry her. Both of us are naked. The thought lingers in the back of my head and dissipates when I lay her down on my sheets, cover her naked body with mine, and kiss her.

"Are you nervous?" I ask softly between the kisses.

"I think I want you more than I am nervous," she murmurs.

I take her hand and bring it down to my erection, letting her touch it and get used to it. It's been in her mouth but not in her hand, and my cock feels rock-hard, about to burst, when she starts stroking it softly.

I slide my hand between her legs, sinking into her wetness. She is soaked. That fact alone makes me want to sink my tongue into her pussy instead of her mouth.

The more I play with her pussy, the harder she rolls her

hips, gasping and whimpering into my mouth. She is drenching my fingers. But I don't want her to come. I want her to yearn for my cock instead.

"Kai," she whispers finally, "I want you."

That's it. My baby girl is needy.

I pull away and slide my hand under the pillow where I have a condom that I put there just the other day. I pray she doesn't ask. But she takes my hand to stop me.

"I have an implant," she says.

I frown. "What does that mean?"

"A birth control one," she explains.

I am not sure I know what it means, but the thought of being bare inside her is more than I can handle. My cock screams for her as I settle between her thighs.

"Knees up, baby girl," I say, then crown her soaked entrance and push in gently.

She looks away, her hands awkwardly on my shoulders.

I still.

"Baby girl, look at me."

She does.

That's right.

"Keep your eyes on me," I order softly. This moment is more intimate than anything I've ever had with anyone.

Her hands grip my shoulders harder.

"Don't be nervous. I'll be gentle," I comfort her, though I have no idea how to be. Except I thrust in, and there is a slight resistance.

A sharp gasp escapes her.

"Just hold on to me," I murmur.

One more gentle thrust, hitting an invisible barrier, and she bites her lip.

And then I slide almost all the way out and thrust harder, sinking into her.

She whimpers, her eyes widening with a pained look as she arches her back off the bed.

I hold my breath and still, searching her face for the signs of pain. When her body softens up, I start thrusting slowly.

"That's it, baby girl," I murmur as I continue slowly sheathing into her. "You are mine."

She feels tight and hot. I pray I don't finish too soon and want to close my eyes in pleasure. But I gaze at her as I keep thrusting, my forehead low, almost touching hers, my dark hair falling onto her face.

I rub my nose against hers. To soothe her. To calm myself. Because my heart is racing like *I* am the virgin here. And I keep thrusting slowly, sinking my cock into her wet hotness.

I *am* her first one. Fuck fate and circumstances and stupid misunderstandings and the four fucked-up years that kept me from her.

Nothing ever felt so good.

Nothing felt so special before.

I can tell it doesn't hurt her that much anymore, because her luminous blue eyes are full of wonder and are locked with mine as she studies the sensation of my cock inside her.

I don't know if it's anything special.

But it's me.

44

CALLIE

SHARP PAIN. THE FEELING OF BEING FILLED BY SOMETHING that's never been inside me. And then there is pleasure, soft and soothing as Kai sinks into me again and again.

He rolls his hips, thrusting deeper, and that's when I feel it—ripples of liquid heat starting inside me.

I come up to kiss him, and he answers so passionately that I know he is holding back so as not to hurt me.

I enjoy just being in his arms, knowing we are now forever connected with this first experience. The first for me, anyway.

He kisses my neck, then moves his mouth to my breast while his hand squeezes the other. I liked when he touched my breasts before. But now he kisses one softly, licks my nipple, then takes it between his lips and pulls it gently as he keeps thrusting into me.

I don't know why it's so erotic. He kisses the skin around my nipple, the tip of his tongue licking it softly. The sight of it starts a fire deep inside me that's coiling through my body. As if my breasts are connected to my core, and the pleasure starts softly rippling between my legs.

I moan, unable to look away. I roll my hips to get him deeper inside of me.

His eyes flicker up at me.

"You like your breasts being kissed, huh?" He smiles. Without taking his eyes off me, he licks my nipple, then takes as much of my breast as he can in his mouth, shoving his cock inside me deeper.

"Kai!" I moan, closing my eyes in pleasure. "Faster, please," I plead.

He starts thrusting faster, his mouth on one breast, then shifting to the other one.

The sensation inside me is different from any before like there is a wire going through my entire body, connecting all the spots that he touches—his hips against mine, his thighs between mine, his lips on my breasts. It all ripples through my body toward the spot between my legs where he feels full and large. It starts flaring into a fire.

"Don't stop. Please, don't stop," I whisper, chasing those fiery ripples.

"I won't, baby girl. Come for me."

His words are like a jolt of electricity that shoots sparks through me.

My thighs fall open. I buck at him, wanting to catch that one spark that is almost there. He pulls at my nipple with his lips.

And that's it.

Flames burst through me, engulfing me.

I cry out, and I am suspended in an ecstasy that I've never felt before.

Kai is pumping into me faster, feeding that fire that is blazing inside me, and then he thrusts one more time, and halts.

The world goes still for a moment.

There is that magical sensation of him being inside me.

And the strange tide.

Rippling.

Calming.

Slowly fading.

He presses his lips to my neck. His breathing is heavy. When he finally slides out of me and pulls himself up on his elbows, there is a soft smile on his face.

"I've wanted you for so long, baby girl, that I almost died right now."

We chuckle.

He pushes off me and rolls onto his back and pulls the sheet to cover us both. We turn our heads toward each other and lie in silence for some time.

I want to touch him, wrap my arms around him, and press closer.

I roll onto my side, prop my head with my hand, and study his tattoos. I've done it so many times but never studied his front.

God, he is so freaking gorgeous and his eyes are so mischievous that I feel like I would like to have him inside me again.

"Can we do it again some time?" I ask, smiling coyly.

I am fishing for more. For another date. Another

moment with him. To know this wasn't just a one-time thing.

He cushions his head with his forearm. The other snakes under me, wraps around my waist, and pulls me closer, where I have no choice but to put my hand on his chest.

I smile, meeting his gaze.

"I was hoping we would." His lips stretch in a smile, and he leans over and kisses me, gently sucking on my lower lip, his tongue stroking it but not going any further.

He pulls away and keeps studying me.

His gaze is too prying. We've never spent time together after any other things we did. And this is even more intimate.

I lower my eyes to his chest again.

"Do some of these tattoos mean something to you?" I ask.

"Some," he says.

He never talks much. Like there are secrets that he doesn't want to let anyone else in on.

His body is an artwork. Shapes. Colors. Ornaments. Creatures. There is a large butterfly wing over his left pectoral. But it doesn't look girlie, rather like a wing of the Phoenix on fire.

I frown, noticing another shape, a pink flower and petals scattered around it as if blown by the wind.

It's a peony.

Kai…

"This…" I swallow hard, feeling like it's a coincidence or maybe not. "This is my favorite flower," I say, glancing at him.

His smile is fading. His mischievous gaze turns serious.

"Yeah…" He stretches lazily.

We keep staring at each other, the air between us burning with silent questions but no answers.

"It's right on your heart," I say quieter, stretching my hand and touching it with my forefinger.

"Yeah…" he says. Nothing else.

I can feel the ridges of his skin. I want to feel all of him. So I fan my fingers and start sliding my palm down his torso.

He catches my wrist gently and pulls my hand away from his skin.

"You touch me where you are not supposed to, baby girl, and I'll fuck you again right now."

But his hold is gentle, almost too loose.

His smile is back.

My eyes flicker down, and there is a tent under the sheet where his erection is.

Holy crap, he is hard again!

I want him. Yes, I want to bring out more of him—that softness that hides behind the thorns.

So I pull my hand out of his grip, then smile, locking my gaze with his, and set my hand down on his chest again. I glide it down, pressing it harder to his skin, feeling every ridge, every inch of roughness under it, smiling playfully as I do so.

He grabs my wrist, and in a flash, I am on my back, hands pinned above my head, Kai on top of me. He brings his lips to mine, barely touching.

"I warned you, baby girl."

He keeps my hands pinned by one of his, and the other slides down and pulls the sheet from between us. His naked body is against mine again, heavy, weighing me down, his legs between mine, pushing mine apart with his knees.

Why does it feel so sexy?

Heat gathers between my thighs again. I can feel my pussy contract, want seeping out of me.

"Say yes, baby girl," he says, palming my breast.

"Will you let me touch you?" I tease.

He shakes his head, nuzzling my chin.

"Why?" I ask.

"Because I said so."

When he shifts, I feel his erection pressing to my entrance. But he doesn't move. His dark hair falls onto my face. His lips hover just above mine. His eyes pin me down.

"Yes," I say.

He pushes slightly into me, and there is that pain again.

I wince.

He stops. "Are you sore?"

"A little."

"Do you want me to stop?"

His concern is so sweet and arousing that I feel my pussy throb with need. I push into him.

"Don't you dare stop now," I whisper, and a chuckle escapes him.

He pushes into me inch by inch. I hold my breath through the slight pain. But when he fills me and starts thrusting slowly, the familiar soothing feeling flares inside me.

I like my hands pinned above my head. It stretches me so I can arch my back and press my breasts against his hard chest.

His hand on my body slides lower, between us, and he starts touching me down there, swirling his fingers around my clit.

And holy hell…

I whimper, rolling my hips. His hand and cock inside me work double magic.

"You like when I touch you down there, baby girl?'

"Yes," I exhale, closing my eyes and focusing on the sensation.

"Like that, yeah?" he whispers.

I revel in the feeling of his large form pressing down on me, his sweet heaviness, his hand on my pussy, his cock thrusting deeper inside me. He is impatient this time. More forceful. I like it. The deeper he goes, the faster his fingers work.

And it's there again.

I am free-falling into pleasure.

"You feel so fucking good," he exhales, then crashes his mouth into mine.

But I don't care for the words. I just want to feel. Him inside me. His hands on me. His lips. All of him.

The tension inside me builds, his fingers stroking just the right way.

And I come.

I moan into his mouth, tear mine away from him, and cry out.

Again.

And again.

Ecstasy ripples inside me.

Kai lets go of my hands, and I weave my fingers into his hair, pressing him closer to me.

He goes wild, pushing harder where it hurts a little. He grunts and murmurs something, pumping into me. I let my hands slide to his shoulders, gripping the skin under my fingertips.

It takes an eternity to break a spell. It takes a moment to get close to the one you want. Life is strange. Our story is even stranger. I feel like everything in my life led to this moment—Kai Droga in my arms.

He pushes into me one more time and falls limp on top of me.

For some time, it's just soft caresses and gentle kisses, his hand stroking my hair as he rubs his nose against my cheek. It makes me smile. I've never imagined Kai tender like this.

We don't talk anymore, sleepy and exhausted from everything that happened during the day.

Kai shifts onto his back, wraps his arm around me, and pulls me toward him. And when my hand slides to his chest, he covers it with his, and shifts it to his heart, where the petal tattoo is.

I don't even think of the scars under my fingertips, only about his hand over mine, and his heart beating under my touch. As loudly as mine.

45

KAI

I AM NOT SURE I SLEPT AT ALL.

When I open my eyes, we are in the same position we fell asleep.

Callie's body presses tightly against me. Her hand is on my heart. Where the petals are.

She is warm, somewhat familiar, though it's only the second time we slept in the same bed.

This feeling is so overwhelming that it leaves me breathless. It reminds me of how things used to be. The feeling of home. Happy dinners with dad and Lilly. Driving my sports bike in the fast lane. Lazy afternoons on the couch watching TV. Pizza and beer. Morning alarms. Late-night TV shows. Thanksgiving with family.

My name being called by someone I love.

Kai…

I want her to say it one more time. Right now, she is the only one in the world who can bring that feeling back. The only one who cares. That fact is heartbreaking and heartwarming at once.

My heart pumps like the powerful tide of the ocean that whispers outside.

It's already dawn, though I didn't notice it until the room grew lighter. We'll have to part soon...

Callie stirs.

She lifts her face and looks at me through the sleepy slits of her eyes.

I let go of her hand on my chest and cushion my head with my arm, studying her. My other arm is still wrapped around her. I fix the sheet over her and tuck her closer to me.

"You don't have to get up yet," I say softly and smile.

"Do you? If you do, I will, too," she says, her fingers stroking my chest.

"Last night was perfect," I say.

It's me telling her things now because I want to keep her close, and she needs to hear how I feel.

She nods.

"I can't stay away from you, Callie. You know that, don't you?"

She smiles. Her blue eyes send soft vibrations to my heart, which gets heavy again.

"I can't promise I won't try to seduce you any chance I can," I say.

She laughs then, burying her face in my chest. Her hair tickles my inked skin.

I grin.

This is heaven.

She tilts her face just slightly, so she can peek at me.

"Can we do it again later?" Her eyes are playful.

And fuck, I'm hard again.

It.

Cute.

"Yes." I smile. "Every day. Three times a day. Is that good enough?"

Her delicious lips stretch in a grin, and I'm thinking that I will probably push it and fuck her pretty mouth if I stay longer in bed.

I lean over and kiss her, slowly sucking on her lower lip.

I can't get enough of her.

"Petal, you are trouble," I murmur.

"I thought we figured out that's you, not me."

She giggles. For a moment, the words jerk me into the past. She doesn't know how right she is.

But then, she licks her lips, gazing at me seductively. She knows exactly what she is doing.

Tease.

She kisses me back playfully. And, fuck, she can touch me as much as she wants if I can have more of her.

The waves outside crash softly against the shore. The seagulls ka-kaw in the distance. The jungle around the cabin is the usual morning cacophony of crazy birds and insects.

It's barely past dawn—my favorite time when nature is waking up but the people are still asleep. So are their shitty attitudes and fucked-up plans.

Callie rests her chin on my chest, her fingers stroking the *good* part of it.

My fingers brush up and down her spine, feeling the texture of her skin. I focus on my senses. Inhale her scent. Feel her warm body press tightly against mine.

In another life, we could've been a couple. *This* could've been a romantic getaway. I could have been a national champion with a bright future, taking her out to dinners, laughing at jokes, having beers with friends on Friday nights, and working a stellar job by day.

For a moment, Callie's blue eyes make the world around me disappear. They take me back to the time when she danced like no one was looking, batted her eyelashes at me, and laughed effortlessly. When we were the kings of the world. Young. Indestructible. Fearless. Our future was bright and clear. Because we knew that, no matter how much we fucked up, we could always start fresh. We were invincible, or so it seemed.

That very night of the Block Party proved me wrong.

And in two years, life showed the entire world that it can take one crazy finger to destroy everything you knew and loved.

Maybe, that's why I don't want to let her go. Besides the feelings and all that emotional shit that simmers inside me lately, Callie reminds me that life can be bearable again. With hope and purpose. Like I just got a second chance.

She seems to sense my uneasy thoughts and cocks her head just slightly, her long blond hair shifting across my bare chest. She reaches my face with her hand and traces the outline of my eyebrows, then my nose.

"Where do you go this early in the mornings?" she asks dreamily.

She knows.

"Out and about," I answer lazily.

I know she's been getting up as early as me almost every day. I'd like to think it's on purpose.

She runs her fingers across my lips next, and I feel like kissing her every fingertip. I melt like chocolate under the sun at her touch. This girl is doing something wicked to me.

There is hesitation in her eyes. She wants to touch me more, in other places, and is afraid. So I lean over and kiss the corner of her lips, then her jaw, cheek, and temple. It makes my heart flutter like I am a fucking schoolboy. But I feel like doing it, and fuck it if I look cheesy. Because tomorrow, the world might go to hell. If it does, I want to spend my last minutes with this girl right here.

Callie is taken aback by my too-tender kisses. She giggles, hiding her face in my chest, but then lunges upward, cups my face, and kisses me like we are lovers who haven't seen each other in forever.

Her naked body rubs against my side. Her knee slides between my legs, nudging upward. And fuck, my cock is as hard as concrete in seconds.

I can't do this to her.

Can I?

I should ask. I want one more time with her to hold me off for a while. So I wrap my arms around her and press her closer as her demanding little tongue whirls in my mouth.

She is a fantastic kisser. Her lips are just the right amount of soft and hard. Her tongue has a magical spell over my cock that gets hard every time she kisses me.

And there it is again.

Our limbs tangle, and I am free-falling.

I want to hug this fucked-up world. Because now it makes sense. With her in my arms.

I hold her tighter and pull her on top of me.

She laughs, steadying herself with her hands on my chest.

God damn! That laughter makes my heart turn into a bird that is trapped inside my chest and flaps its wings madly.

She kisses me again. Her messy hair falls onto my face and neck. I inhale her smell, trying to get enough of it, and let my hands slide down her body and cup her sweet little ass.

I'll eat the fuck out of it one of these days.

It's a threat and a promise.

Because Callie is mine.

She should've been mine a long time ago.

The thoughts dissipate. The naughty little thing rolls her hips against my hard cock, and I groan, grip her ass tighter, and buck my hips at her.

Her hands touch my scars where she knows she is not supposed to. She is a sneaky little fox. But right now, I let her, because my cock rubs against her belly and it wants to claim her again.

My body rises to the awareness of her flush against me. I can't hold back. I shift, kicking her legs open until they are on either side of mine. I push her little ass up and position it so that her entrance is against the tip of my cock.

"One more time, baby girl," I murmur into her mouth and push into her.

She moans and rolls her hips, sinking onto me.

The parrots go wild outside the window.

"Early bird special," I whisper as I thrust my hips up, deeper into her. Her short chuckle turns into little whimpers as I thrust deeper yet.

"You all right?" I ask to make sure.

"Yeah," she whispers, steadying herself with her knees against the bed, and moves her little butt down, sinking herself onto my cock. Our thighs meet and find the perfect rhythm.

"That's right, baby girl. Just like that," I say as we fuck slowly.

I want to learn her every curve, every sweet spot. I want to fuck her hard and gently, fast and slow, with bites and scratches and softly licking the wounds afterward. I want to be her first in every way possible. And the last guy she ever touches.

Mine.

Finally.

Maybe I am losing it, but for the first time since the end of the world, there is a reason to go on.

The world suddenly feels amazing. Even if it's filled with ashes and anger.

The world with *her* in it.

We are sticky with sweat and lovemaking, grinding into each other, tongues lapping at each other like we can't get enough.

I might be in over my head.

Callie might just need a good lay.

But this moment with her in my arms lets me dream.

46

CALLIE

I return to my bungalow, and Katura studies me up and down like I look different.

"How was your night, babe?" she asks with forced indifference as she gets dressed.

"I followed your advice," I reply, changing into a different bikini and shorts. I want to save this lime green strawberry bikini—every time I look at it, I remember Kai's hands on me.

I feel the ghost of him between my legs. The slight ache. The sweet soreness. I want to sit on his lap at breakfast. And I want everyone to see him wrap his arms around me.

I am insane. Needy? I don't know. Aching for him? Definitely. It's as if I had a taste of life-saving energy and now want all of it.

Sex is sex. Yet, there was so much more to it last night and this morning. My heart tightens at the thought.

I smile, fixing my hair, but other feelings start simmering inside me.

I am so fucking in love that the realization makes my eyes burn with tears.

I notice Katura's half-smile. Her glances at me. There is no mockery in them. No condescendence as if she knows everything. There is curiosity and almost anticipation—like she wants me to tell her how it was.

Suddenly, I realize something—Katura has screwed plenty of guys and has done many crazy things. But she's never been close to anyone. That's where her indifference and nonchalance come from, and that fearlessness like she has nothing or no one to lose. She goes with the flow. Nothing ever anchored her to anyone. I have a feeling that when someone does, it will be a battle and the most glorious defeat. Or a win, however you look at it. I can't even imagine the guy who will tame someone like Katura.

I feel like the night changed everything.

But it didn't.

At breakfast, everyone is slow and grumpy. It's small talk. Eyes, squinting at the horizon. Picking nails.

Kai brushes against me in line for food but doesn't sit next to me. Is he supposed to? It's not high school. Right.

And after breakfast, he walks off with Ty and Bo.

I feel stupid.

Ya-ya, Kristen, Maddy, and I walk to the closest stream in the forest, wash our clothes, and fill up the water jugs for the kitchen.

They move the thug from town to a spare half-done hut to get him away from everyone's sight in the lounge. Maddy checks on him now and then. "He might not make it," she says, but no one seems interested in the news.

Lunch is the same. Kai smiles down at his plate the entire time.

"Can we talk?" I ask after lunch.

"Anything you want, petal," he says with that same smile that I can't quite figure out.

We walk along the shore. It is early afternoon. Hot, sticky, but cloudy. The breeze is stronger today. I wonder if a storm is coming.

The water splashes against my feet.

Kai is walking deeper in the water next to me. His is shirtless. Somehow, lately, he is more often just in his board shorts. Barefoot. He is so sexy it makes me jealous of other girls glancing at him.

"Are we going to pretend that we are strangers?" I ask.

I feel pathetic. But besides the smiles, there is no indication that we are anything but fuck buddies.

It didn't feel like that the night before or this morning.

In fact, my heart is heavy despite the smiles because I know that before, years ago, what I felt for Kai Droga was infatuation—instant, irrational, and overwhelming.

Now, there is so much more to it. Seeing him the second time, here, on the island, after years and everything that happened, feels like fate. And the last two weeks feel like magic.

Kai walks out of the deep waters toward me, bends to hook his hands under the backs of my thighs, and in seconds, lifts me up, my legs wrapping around his waist.

I smile, studying him, my arms around his neck, my heart suddenly doing a cartwheel.

"We are not," he says, studying my face. "And I am not pretending, petal." He kisses me on the lips, and I answer shyly, knowing that others further down the beach can see us. It's the first time we kiss in plain sight.

Kai pulls away, a half-smile on his face.

"I didn't want to make you uncomfortable," he says. "I don't know what you want and where you want this to go. I thought I would give you some space. But if you want"—his lips curl in a devilish smile—"I can grope and hump you in public. And I'll do it any chance I can."

I giggle, slapping him playfully on his chest and burying my face in the crook of his tattooed neck. I am so freaking happy, it's ridiculous.

He stands with his feet in the water, his arms wrapped around me, my legs around his waist, and spins slowly, making me giddy.

This is perfect.

He is perfect.

I feel tears well up in my eyes and pull away to look at him.

His dark eyes glisten mischievously when he says, "I want you to move to my bungalow."

That's fast. And exciting.

"I want to talk to you for hours," he goes on. "I want to see your pretty face when I wake up. I want you to sit next to me at meals. And I want to kiss you in front of everyone." That cocky smile is back. "And if Zach ever winks at you like he does sometimes, I'll break his face."

I chuckle, and my heart flutters at his possessiveness. I

run my forefinger down his torso all the way to where our bodies connect.

His muscles flex. He brings his lips to my ear. "You play with me like that, and I'll take you right here, in front of the entire island, baby girl."

I laugh and feel want clench inside me. I would like to have him right now.

I study his smiling face for a moment. "It's so strange that after everything that happened, we end up here. You and I."

You and I.

The words tug at my heart in the most tender way.

But his smile fades, his gaze suddenly too intense.

"Do you know what hurt the most after that night four years ago?" he asks.

I want to hear it and I don't.

Let's not do this.

Please.

Not now.

"Not everything that happened afterward," he says. "There's more than you know. Not a lost friend. Not a fire. Not the emptiness afterward."

He goes silent for a moment, and my heart starts beating fast at his words because they resonate with how I felt. I want to look away but can't, drowning in his gaze.

"I took you to my place because you were drunk and vulnerable. And because I couldn't bear the thought of Archer touching you. Or anyone else for that matter. But you never said a word afterward. No call back. No response to my texts when I asked you if you were okay. You stopped talking to me."

The silence is too heavy. The soft lapping of the waves at the shore is like an echo.

"The worst was your silence, Callie."

47

CALLIE

Kai's words flip this happy moment in a different direction.

My heart sinks. "I thought you took advantage of me, Kai. We talked about it."

Yeas, I was stupid, thinking that I was a victim.

He still holds me in his arms. It's a strange way to have a serious conversation. And it's so obvious to the others, whose voices I hear in the distance but don't look at. This is like coming out of the closet.

"And something else," I say. It has to be said. I look down, too embarrassed at the words. "I was angry. I never wanted Archer. I always wanted you, Kai. You know it, too. And I was angry that I didn't remember that night." My chest tightens. I say one phrase at a time so I can contain my nervousness. "I was angry that you did it not caring that I wouldn't remember." I take a deep breath. "I was just so angry at both of us," I finish quietly and meet his gaze.

He nods.

I can feel his arms loosening. I let my legs go, and he sets me softly down onto my feet.

The happy moment is broken, and I desperately search for words to bring it back.

He runs his tatted fingers through his hair.

"If we talked, perhaps it would have ended up differently," he says, not looking at me.

"Kai, don't."

There is never any point dwelling on past mistakes or tragedies. They told us that in communal therapy.

We stand with the waves washing over our feet and stare down as if the water holds the answers.

"Tell me something," he says. "Why did you agree to date Archer?"

"Kai…"

I exhale loudly and close my eyes. How can I explain? Being eighteen seems like an eternity from being twenty-two. The time passed. Things learned. Tragedies. War.

I open my eyes and look around. "He was so charming and swift. And you were dating Julie."

"No, I wasn't." Kai snorts.

"You were, too," I argue, looking at him, though he won't meet my eyes. "The day Archer came to invite me to the Block Party, he said that you and your new girl were coming along."

I can see Kai's jaw set, a smirk forming on his lips. He shakes his head. "Fucking asshole. She asked me out the day of the Block Party. She'd always had a thing for me. And Archer was already parading you around."

Shit.

Life is chaos. And lies. "He swept me off my feet, you know," I say as an excuse. "I went with it because I was jealous of you and Julie."

That was true. Archer Crone was the star quarterback. All the girls squealed and dropped their panties at the sight of him.

"And then he gave me those flowers, and... Gah!" I exhale. "No one had given me flowers before. It seemed so special." I smile at the memory, though for the longest time they've been the memories leading up to the Block Party. The memories laced with regret and guilt.

There is silence. It's too long. The breeze and the sun and the ocean make it too awkward. I raise my eyes at Kai, and his are blazing.

"*I* sent you those flowers, Callie," he says softly, a myriad of emotions in his eyes.

When he calls me by my name, I know he is on edge.

My heart skips a bit. "But... Archer said..."

"What, that they were from him?" Kai smirks.

"No. No." Shit, he didn't say that. He just showed up right after they were delivered. "He came over that day," I explain, "looked at the flowers, and asked me if I liked my flowers. So I said they were my favorite. He said, 'I know.'"

"I *told* him that, Callie. Peonies." He smirks with sadness, then chuckles, closing his eyes and shaking his head. "Come on, baby girl..."

My heart is too heavy to breathe properly. I bite my lower lip, trying not to cry because it's too much. The past is too much. It's fucked up and crooked and full of he-said and she-said that I hate so much.

"How did you know?" I cock my head at him.

"I saw you draw them. And heard you tell Abby that those were your favorite."

My heart tightens at the words. I lower my gaze to the tattoo of the peony on his heart. The petals falling off. It makes sense now. And, oh, does it burn me...

Why am I so stupid to realize things at the last moment?

"Then why didn't you say that you sent them, Kai?" I say it too loudly, desperately, because this guy is amazing, but, God, does he hide a lot of things inside.

He laughs through his nose, looks down at his feet, and kicks the water.

"I was twenty, Callie. I was too cool for school. I was best friends with the king of Deene, the son of the Secretary of Defense. And I sent flowers to the girl I wanted. As soon as I did, I felt stupid. Especially with Archer taking notice of you. And you know, Archer always gets what he wants. And he did. In a way."

Kai ruffles his hair as he stares down at his feet. I've never seen him like this—lost at the words. Hesitant. Awkward.

"But why didn't you admit it? If you liked me, it would be easy."

I want him to explain. Because his silence four years ago changed everything.

Kai finally raises his eyes to meet mine.

"Easy?" A nervous chuckle escapes him. "I didn't just *like* you, Callie."

He smiles, and his smile is weak. It's making *me* weak. I don't look away, though my heart is about to explode.

He takes a step toward me and cups my face, his thumbs stroking my cheeks.

He chuckles. His chuckle is so out of place in a moment like this.

My eyes burn with tears. My heart is pounding.

Say it, I beg him in my mind.

Because I feel it, too.

He leans over and presses his forehead to mine.

"You can figure it out, yeah? Why a guy sends flowers to a girl." His eyes are too close to mine, burning with emotion. His voice is soft and somehow cracked. "And he is scared shitless to admit it to anyone. *Especially* her." I swallow hard but don't look away. I won't. Not when he is confessing. "And is aware of her every time she enters a room. And wants to punch his best friend who so carelessly wraps his arms around her waist. And when the best friend kisses her in front of everyone, and she laughs so happily, he contemplates the ways to kill him. Then the ways to kidnap her. And he wants to switch schools so that the sight of them together doesn't rip his heart apart."

Oh, God.

My chest shakes as I try to suppress a sob.

"Kai…" I whisper.

I didn't know. How could I?

"This sounds so banal. Doesn't it?" He smiles but still doesn't call things what they are. I want him to. Because the only reason I was with Archer was to be closer to Kai. Because every time I looked around, I looked for him. Because I watched him with his girl and pretended it was me.

"Yo!"

The shout comes from the distance, and when we pull away from each other, it's Ty waving his arms in the air.

"Love birds! Come!" he shouts.

The moment of truth is gone.

Kai looks at me with a soft smile. "Let's talk properly later, yeah? We need to talk." He leans over to place a soft kiss on my cheek and pulls me toward the village. "C'mon, petal."

It's petal again. That defense mechanism is up.

And I can't wait for later.

Because I need this.

The words.

The closure.

The hope.

Him.

48

CALLIE

I can't wait till night falls. When it does, when the chores are done and meals are finished, I will get another chance with Kai.

When I think my feelings can't get any more overwhelming, Kai flickers here and there. His intense gaze on me makes me dreamy and useless as I fumble at every sight of him and smile like an idiot.

At dinner, we line up at the buffet, and when I sit down in my usual spot, a large form appears next to me and takes a seat.

It's Kai.

He doesn't say a word, but his inked elbow brushes against my arm, and I smile into my plate.

"Oh, the seat is taken?" Katura asks teasingly and sits on the other side of me. "Wanna take my bed, too?"

I blush. Thank God for the yellow solar lights that conceal it.

I eat without a word. The one time I raise my eyes at Ty

across from me, he glances at Kai, then at me, and winks, smiling.

Everyone is quieter than usual. The incident a day ago was a warning. There is more to come, I'm sure. The dishes are cleaned. So is the dining room.

Katura walks out onto the beach and stands in the dark, facing the Southern part of the beach.

"You alright?" I ask, joining her, looking around aimlessly as Kai and the other guys discuss something at a distance.

"I thought I just heard something," she says.

"Like what?"

"Like motors."

I frown.

"Hey!" she calls out to the guys and walks toward them, me behind her. "If there was a boat out there, behind the cliff on the south side, would you hear it?"

The guys fall into silence. Bo swipes his palm over his dreads. "Maybe. Why?"

Katura stops as she reaches the group and, hands on her waist, stares at the darkness.

I don't like this—this silence, her words.

"I swear I heard it," she says.

"No one comes here," Ty replies in a hesitant voice.

"Well, they come on foot, don't they?" Katura snaps, looking around.

Bo stirs. "Kai, Owen, Ty, grab the guns, let's take a hike."

They hesitate, but Bo is already moving. "Now!" he snaps.

His voice sends my heart pounding.

They are on the move, running too fast, too abrupt.

"Kat?" I ask quietly, suddenly trembling. It's just a drill, I'm sure. A precaution.

But a nasty feeling starts in my stomach.

Katura cocks her head like a nocturnal animal that just came out for a hunt. "Go get Maddy, babe," she says. "Tell her to stay put."

"Kat, it's nothing, yeah?"

"Go. Get. Maddy," she says, her voice low but suddenly harsh.

And I know that if anyone is ever right, it's Katura.

I walk, then trot toward the bungalows, my heart pounding.

I hear it before I see it.

A loud pop and the sound of broken glass. Then another one.

And then I see it.

A blaze, like a rocket, shoots out from the Common Lounge.

"Fire!" someone screams.

There are echoing shouts across the village, and I stare, hypnotized, at the orange blaze that, in seconds, illuminates the night.

"Get Maddy!" I hear behind me, and I stumble on the sand and run, then sprint as fast as I can toward her bungalow, the wind swishing in my ears.

I rip the door open, but it's empty.

"Maddy!"

I dart toward our hut to get Dani. I see others running toward the fire, their silhouettes orange in the glow. I hear shouts. The whole beach is illuminated by the fire, the orange glow faint but surreal like there is a party going on.

My heart pounds in my chest. I am approaching the bungalow fast when I hear the male voice, "Hey! Here!"

It's not Kai, but it's coming from behind the hut.

And I follow, on reflex.

It's one of the guys, I'm sure.

Except when I turn the corner, hands yank me into the dark so fast I don't realize what's happening until my back is pressed against someone's body, strong arm around me, almost suffocating, pulling me further back, another clamping my mouth.

And a hiss comes into my ear. "Not a fucking sound, understood?"

49

KATURA

The explosion is so sudden that it startles me for a moment. But my reflexes work faster, and I am already running toward the Common Lounge that is on fire.

Water.

Buckets.

Weapons.

The options flicker in my mind as I dart into the kitchen where several people are scrambling around.

"The fire extinguisher is in one of the cupboards!" Maddy shouts.

A bunch of people yank the cupboard doors open, pulling everything out onto the floor, tripping, scrambling, bumping into each other.

"Here!" someone shouts.

Guff yanks the extinguisher out of Mia's hands and runs toward the lounge.

Everyone follows, but I rummage through the utensils and grab a knife, then another, then follow the rest.

Guff, his body tall and strong, stands like a firefighter in front of the fire and sprays it with a stream of foam.

"Stand back!" he shouts as he does.

The fire is crackling and blazing into the night sky. The wind shoots the flames to one side, then another.

I search around.

This is not the Savages' doing—there were boats.

I step back, scanning the faces and more importantly, the dark beach.

My heart races. There is no panic. There is adrenalin shooting through my blood. So familiar. I love it. It's like a breath of fresh air. There is a tragedy happening, or one is yet to come, but my stupid-ass heart is pounding with excitement.

I am ready.

Bo and the rest come running, guns in their hands, faces illuminated by the orange glow.

And suddenly, a deafening sound rattles through the night silence around us.

Tra-ta-ta-ta-ta.

Machine guns.

I duck. The rest follow.

I won't mistake this sound for anything.

My dad used to teach me how to shoot. He had many guns. I can identify all of them—automatic, semi, pistols, rifles, shotguns.

This one.

AK-47.

There is nothing like the sound of it tr-r-r-ra-ta-tatting through the air, echoing afterward in your chest.

Only Guff is still spraying the fire like his life depends on it, the hissing of the foam over the flames subsiding.

The guys are hunching, looking around.

The girls are cowering on the ground.

Another round of gunshots slices the night air.

Closer.

Much closer.

From behind the lounge, coming from the direction of the jungles.

"Everyone down!" someone shouts. "Now!"

Another round of shots. The distinct hollow shots of a semi-automatic. Pistol shots come from another direction.

They are everywhere.

And then there is another burst of gunshots and the machine gun again as dark figures start descending into the open area where we are.

About two dozen of them.

Tall. Muscled. T-shirts and tanks. Shorts and cargo pants. Boots. Guns and rifles in their hands and across their shoulders as they step out of the darkness and circle the space around us.

Fuck...

It's an army of Commandos. Young and older ones. Most of them are not fucking spring-breakers for sure. Amateurs don't wear bullet-proof vests.

"Anyone moves, and she is dead!" one of them says and steps in front of the Common Lounge that is only four poles and the small fire still burning in the center, like a battlefield.

A guy pushes the barrel of his gun into Guff, making him retreat into the middle of the circle.

Another guy comes up next to him, holding Callie in front of him, a gun to her head.

Fuck, Callie. How does a girl get in trouble like this all the time?

And there is a distant sound of motors.

More motors?

But they are on the ground, coming from that dirt road that goes along the south shore.

ATVs.

Jesus.

I am still crouching on the ground, fists digging into the sand, knives in my hands but tucked under me as I look beyond our guys.

There is darkness behind the circle, but deep at the beach, there are more silhouettes.

More guys.

Dozens of shadows.

It's like an entire battalion here.

I turn my head to see the guys who circle us, but there are more. Many more. Invisible. In the shadows. There is no chance of escaping. Everyone is fucked.

The guy who just shouted steps out toward our cornered group.

He is tall and broad-shouldered. Dark hair, loose strands falling onto his face. Strong jaw and chiseled cheekbones. Eyes narrowed, scanning our group.

He is hot. I've seen that face on a picture before I came here.

Archer Crone.

My heart gives out an excited thud.

He is better than the picture. A muscle shirt, black jeans, and boots. A gun in his hand, but not pointing at anyone. The fucker is cocky just as they said, and fearless.

Huh.

I feel my lips stretching just slightly in a smile.

Well, hello, Chancellor.

I am hypnotized, like I just met a legend.

"Where is she?" he asks calmly as his narrowed eyes go from one face to another, all of us girls still squatting on the ground, until they stop on me.

"Ah! There..."

Our eyes meet.

I remember being tasered once. In Bangkok. For fun. The way your body jerks involuntarily. They way your heart pumps so hard that you feel like you've been lifted off the ground. The way your mind goes "bleep" for a moment.

The moment our eyes meet feels like that. It's like seeing God. Or Devil.

My heart starts pounding like crazy.

How does one get the hot looks *and* the genius brain?

The Chancellor's gorgeous lips twist into a smirk. He curls his forefinger and motions for me to stand up.

I would laugh in his face, but this is not the time. After all, I need him. I want to come with him. He pins me with his stare, like a snake charmer, and I stand up slowly and straighten, not taking my eyes off him.

Shit, what is happening to me?

My brain tries to compile every bit of info I learned about him. But my treacherous body has its own opinion—my heart pounding, shiver running down my spine.

I would fuck him. Yes. Positively. More than once, if he is any good. Especially if it gets me what I came here for.

His gaze is vicious, spiteful, and arrogant.

But also hypnotic.

Callie, babe, you might have chosen the wrong guy.

Archer Crone emanates power without visibly doing so, and it's contagious. It would be very much fitting if smoke curled around him and lightning bolts shot from the sky right now.

His eyes flicker down to my hands at my sides that hold the two knives. His eyes are cold. "Drop those," he says quietly, his eyes back on me.

Fuck you.

But I do. The knives fall into the sand with a thunk.

He motions for me to come over.

We are not enemies. We are on the same side, right? So, let's play.

I flicker my eyes at the guy next to him, who holds Callie in his grip. Her eyes are pleading. She is miserable.

You knew what you came here for, babe.

I shift my gaze to Archer again, tilt my chin up, and walk up to him slowly.

Archer Crone.

The legend.

The king of Deene.

The Chancellor.

Hello, babe.

But his gaze is suddenly indifferent as he motions for the guy next to him, and he yanks me by my hand and toward him, whipping me around, my back to him, a gun to my head.

"Don't move," he orders.

I don't. I need to play along. But this is disappointing, because Archer's attention is elsewhere.

I can see everyone in the circle now.

Most of the Outcasts.

The girls are still on the ground, looking up, scared, angry, some with their eyes down.

The guys stand tall and strong, three guns pointing at us.

Kai, Bo, Ty. Their eyes are on Archer, but they have nothing against an army of guns.

Archer slowly walks into the circle.

The fire is almost out, and several guys from Archer's crew hold flashlights that shine into the circle, blinding the cornered prey. It's darker now with the fire out. The lights in the kitchen are not nearly enough to illuminate all the faces.

"Well, well," Archer says, taking another step toward the center. His back is to me now. If I wasn't curious about how this will end, I would have elbowed the fucker who has his arm around my neck, choked him until he passed out, and then took his gun.

But this is interesting.

I expect something dark and cocky to come out of the Chancellor's mouth. But it's nothing what I expected.

"Hello, Droga. It's been a while," Archer says calmly.

Oh…

There are no theatrics, no show of power, no intentional craziness from the Chancellor.

Suddenly, I understand one simple thing.

Those two. It's never been about Callie per se. She was just a chick who came between them. Archer only dated her for a short time. As per the rumors, he never cared much for any girl, changing them like socks.

"I told you this is not over," Archer says.

The others' glances dart around.

Bo and Ty turn to look at Kai.

And Kai…

If he could kill with a stare, Archer would have decapitated, burned to ashes, and disappeared off the face of the earth.

Kai's stare is murderous. But there is a strange intensity in it.

No, this was never about a girl.

There is something much deeper than revenge.

Holy shit.

Now I see it.

Callie didn't just come between two guys. She came between best friends.

One won't forgive that a girl was more important than him. The other won't forgive that he didn't get the girl.

It's about betrayed friendship. Brotherhood. Something that men don't get over easily. Something that only a girl can ruin.

50

KAI

ANGER COILS THROUGH ME LIKE A BALL OF SNAKES BECAUSE Crone is so fucking calm, like he just came for a friendly chat.

"I told you this is not over," he says.

I want to lunge at him and break his smug face.

I did it two years ago when we had a fight on the Westside. The madman laughed. We beat each other to a pulp. But he wants more. My ruined life wasn't enough. My second-degree burns weren't. Trapping us on this island was a brutal exercise of power.

And now Callie is here. This is no fucking coincidence. Like he can't get enough of torturing me.

"I appreciate the shitty little note you sent," Archer says calmly, the gun lowered and at his side though mine points straight at his face. "You are not good at talking, Droga. Fists and punches work better with you. So then that's how it shall be."

He is so fucking diplomatic that it makes me mad.

I see Callie being held by one of his goons. The sight rips my heart. I can feel her despair which resonates with mine. But I avoid looking at her. Crone knows she is my weakness. Now more than ever. He uses it.

Fucking Crone. I haven't seen him in two years, and I wish it stayed that way.

When he stares at me like this, there is a flicker of that wildness, the bond we shared so long ago it seems like in a different life. When we used to be like brothers. When we were inseparable.

He was good. In his heart, Crone used to be the shit. A human being with trauma that always got the worst of him when it came out in public. As if he needed to make everyone pay for what happened to his mother and brother.

But in person, he was different. We used to share stories, secrets, stupid thoughts, and fucked-up moments. The craziness. The free spirit. I always admired his determination—if he wasn't filthy rich, he would have built himself from the ground up.

He was the brother I never had.

Until her…

Because she wasn't just another girl that I wanted to bang. And he saw it. And the jealousy got the worst of him.

Once thick as thieves, we became enemies. What bothers me and grinds sharp nails into my bones is that back on the mainland, I could always strike right back or walk away to the menacing sound of his laughter.

Here is a different story. It makes my blood boil in my veins.

He is a psychotic wizard who sets others on his chess

board and plays his wicked games. And he will fuck with me infinitely. Whatever it takes.

I want to say a lot of things but don't. It takes all my patience to hold back the spiteful words.

"Let them go," I say quietly and lower my gun slowly.

We used to understand each other at a half-word—a strange connection that was weird and powerful. Even now, I stare him down, trying to find that speck of compassion that even monsters possess.

For a moment, I feel like he is the same Crone I used to race on bikes with or get mindlessly drunk with in shady bars on the outskirts of the town, laugh hysterically as we smoked weed up in the hills in the condemned area, or drive exhaustedly across Mexico. That was Archer Crone stripped of his wealth and arrogance.

"Come visit us some time, Droga. You might like it," he says now with a smirk, his gaze turning spiteful again.

No, that Crone from years ago is gone.

"And that"—he waves his gun in his hand, looking around—"Danielle-what's-her-face?" His gaze stops on Ty next to me, and Ty's grip on the gun tightens.

"Easy," I whisper to him.

"Relax," Crone says with a snort. "I'm not interested in damaged goods. She is a cuckoo job. You can keep her."

He slowly blinks toward me again and takes a step back. "I'd love to talk more, Droga, but I'm not a fan of this side of the island."

Crone starts backing away slowly, his men behind him doing the same, taking the girls with them. The other minions widen the circle around us.

Wait-wait-wait.

My heart falls.

There should be a conversation. More of it. A fight. Anything to sort this out.

"Let's roll!" Archer barks, stepping back faster, his gun on us again as he backs away past the kitchen and toward the path to the jungle.

The voice is right in my ear. "Leave the girls!" Bo passes me, his gun up, aiming at them. "Archer! Leave the girls! They don't want to go!"

Everyone freezes. The synced clicking of the cocking guns echoes through the air.

It's darker behind the kitchen, and the goons shine the flashlights in our faces, blinding us.

"Bo, step back," Archer says calmly. "I respect you, man, but this is not your battle."

"Not yours either, Archer. You don't fight battles."

Crone snorts. His gaze switches to that of spite and menace again.

"Droga, it's been a while. And look at that." He motions in Callie's direction. "I delivered your favorite pussy to this island. That counts for something, doesn't it? Tell your friends to cool it. Then come visit."

I want to murder him.

He doesn't do anything for the sheer favor.

"So leave them here and go back," I say.

"Tsk-tsk. That's it?" He cocks his head and takes another step back. "You should've learned that it's an eye for an eye. A favor for a favor. So, the question is what are you willing to do for that little blonde petal of yours?" He stretches his hand toward Callie and flicks a strand of her hair with a gun.

I want to rip his arm out of its socket. I jerk toward him, but Bo's iron grip on my shoulder stops me.

There is no reasoning with Crone, I know. He wants something, and I can't figure out what it is. He got his revenge four years ago—more than he bargained for. I can never forget his mocking gaze when he first saw my tattoos on the Westside when I snuck into his party and caught him high and drunk.

"Droga, Droga. So sweet. Years later, all this"—he motions with his gun down and up my body—"and you are still playing a knight." He grins, his lips curled down. "So noble. But!"

Crone cocks his head in theatrical surprise.

"We have other plans. So if you want to find out what they are, come to the Westside. I am always willing to talk, yeah?"

He raises his gun in the air and motions in a circle.

As if on cue, his goons start backing up. Fast. Smoothly. Rifles and guns pointing at us.

How did he get so many shooters? I don't recognize any of them—they are older, not the Deene crowd or any of the spring-breakers. Secretary must have sent help.

But the thought escapes me because he has Callie, and I can't do anything. These are not the Savages, useless amateurs. This is Crone's best crew, I'm sure. And he showed up himself, which is unheard of. It's not about Callie or Katura or Dani, who he is leaving behind. It's something else. It's a mystery, even to me.

Still, I want to fucking murder him.

I shake in anger, knowing that I am no use against the AK-47s.

Bo steps forward. "Archer, let go of the girls. They are not your property."

Archer only chuckles, taking a step back, his crew sinking slowly into the darkness of the night jungle path. "Cute, Bo. Real fucking cute. But guess what? I put my time and resources into bringing them here. And I lost out quite a bit, considering the boat crash. So they have to work for it."

Bo shakes his head. "They don't. They are not slaves."

"But they are cargo, Bo." Archer smiles.

They are retreating slowly. We can barely see them but are stepping into them though we know we don't have a chance.

"There was no contract to sign, but there is always a disclaimer," Archer says calmly. And no matter what words are said, I know that he won't let go. It's in his gaze that I learned so much during the months together. He never lets go. He always gets what he wants. "Always read the small print. It says that you have to pay off the expenses. Yeah? Makes sense? So they will pay. They don't have anything, but I'll take whatever I can get."

A cold smile on his face is a confirmation.

Katura tries a move and kicks one of the guys, making him groan, but there are three of them on her at once. They twist her arms, and she is on her knees, grunting in pain.

"Fuck off," she hisses like a cat. They jerk her up and drag her further back.

Callie just walks, pulled back by one of the goons. Her eyes are on Crone. They are furious, full of hatred.

"Alright, guys!" Crone says loudly, not taking his eyes off me. "Time to move!" He swings his gun in the air like it's a lasso. And they start moving back faster, watching their step.

Crone turns away for one second.

Just this one second.

And Bo lunges at him, slamming his body into Crone's and tackling him to the ground.

The shot that follows is so sudden that I almost fire back.

"Don't shoot!" I shout and duck, my gun still pointing at the darkness where his goons are.

Everyone freezes.

There is another shout.

"Don't fucking shoot!"

It's Crone.

And he's too late.

Because Bo on top of him slumps with a growl and slowly curls into a fetal position.

Crone is up on his feet in seconds. "You fucking moron," he hisses to someone. "Don't fucking shoot! Back off! Now!"

They start backing away into the darkness, blinding us with their flashlights, dragging Katura and Callie with them, guns on us.

I stare at Bo on the ground.

My heart races.

No-no-no.

Bo's body twists slowly like burned paper.

My heart is ripping through my chest.

"Bo!" I call out.

The Westsiders are moving away. I lunge after them, but a hand grips my shirt and roughly jerks me back.

"Stop!" It's Ty. "They will fucking shoot you! Let go!"

Of course, he is fucking calm. Dani is not with them. But Callie is. And she is being dragged away.

"You follow, we shoot." The voice comes from the darkness where the flashlights flicker between the trees. There are dozens of men. Another dozen probably hiding in the bushes. More of them on the beach. We have no chance. It's fucking pathetic.

We are not following.

We can't.

We shouldn't unless we want to die.

Instead, we rush to Bo.

"Bo!" I shout, dropping down to my knees.

He grunts as we flip him onto his back.

"Bo, look at me, it will be okay."

It won't be.

For now, I push away the thoughts about Callie and Katura and Crone, and all I see is the black spot growing bigger like a halo on Bo's shirt in the faint light of someone's flashlight that flickers around like an epileptic.

"Keep that fucking light here!" I bark.

I pull my shirt up and over my head and try to wrap it around his wound, but it's too short to wrap around his torso.

"Shirts!" I shout, kneeling in front of Bo in the dark.

I crumble my shirt and press it to Bo's wound.

"Bo, stay with me. It'll be okay. Okay?"

I sound stupid, like a guy out of a movie. My hands shake.

But Bo is not responding, only grunting as his body gets lax.

Someone passes me another shirt ripped in the middle. Someone else lifts Bo to a sitting position, and I wrap the cloth around his waist, holding my shirt to his wound.

Another shirt comes.

A flashlight lights the sight.

Fuck!

"Lift him up! We have to hurry!" I bark out the orders.

And though my heart tugs in the direction where Callie disappeared, there is a life at stake.

One of us.

Another friend.

Bo.

This island is a vicious circle of hell.

51

CALLIE

THE STUPID GOONS DRAG US UP THE PATH. ONE OF THEM IS holding me by my arm, the grip so strong that I know I will have bruises.

I don't want to go to the Westside. Not like this. Not with Archer. I thought I could reason, explain. But Archer is not the guy I knew four years ago. There is something ruthless in him. Dark and cold. It's scary.

Katura tries several times to rip out of the hold of the two guys who drag her like a dog, but her hands are tied, whenever that happened. And she wanted to be on the Westside all along. So she follows, occasionally snarling at them when they handle her too roughly.

It's dark. The flashlights are not bright enough to show much of what is around. And it's much colder than on the shore. I shiver—not from the lower temperature but the realization that something is going really wrong.

"Hey!" Katura shouts after another attempt to get the guys' paws off her. "Archer!"

Archer stops, and so do the rest. He turns and points his flashlight into Katura's face, making her squint and turn away.

She lifts her tied hands toward him. "Do you mind? I am not a prisoner, am I?"

Archer sweeps an up and down look at her, accompanied by a cocked eyebrow as if he's only just noticed her now.

"Not bad." He smirks.

What a dog. Hod did I not see it before?

He pulls a cigarette out of his pocket and lights it. "It's another ten minutes to the shore further south. You can come on a boat or ATVs," he announces, stepping close to Katura. "Are you going to fight?" He exhales the smoke into her face. "Martial arts. Extensive physical training. Navy SEAL daddy. Ukrainian mommy, diseased. Home-schooled. Theft charges in Thailand. An attempted assault charge in the state of Pennsylvania. Twice."

He is reading her dossier, and man, do I find out things about Katura.

She only smiles in response. Her chin ticks up. "I chose to come to this island. And unlike other people," she pauses but doesn't look at me, "I want to be on the right side."

Good try.

"But I don't like people's fucking hands on me," she adds with a hiss that makes the corner of Archer's lips curl in what might be a tiny smile.

He nods toward her hands, and one of his minions lets her go.

Another one turns away and pisses right there, only feet away.

Gross.

Next, Archer shines the flashlight into my face, blinding me. I turn away and blink hard until the flashlight points to my feet and my vision adjusts.

The trees whisper in the wind as I take a quick look at the guys. Thy are fearless and know the way. Most of them are in their late twenties and thirties. Guns and bulletproof vests—they are trained fighters.

They shine the flashlights into the center of the circle where we stand and study me and Katura.

It's surreal. Like some bizarre night ritual. Archer's face is so familiar yet not, his eyes narrowed at me as he smokes.

"Well, well," he says slowly. "Our closer acquaintance didn't happen years ago, sweetie. But it's so much more symbolic now, isn't it?"

His smile is more of a scowl. His manner is too relaxed, considering the circumstances.

"It's not," I interject softly, trying to keep his spiteful gaze.

"Oh, I would beg different. With all that happened. You running away. Your Kai boy and the fire accident. Getting to know you closer will be even more ironic."

Closer doesn't register in my mind as much as the mention of the accident.

"What does the fire have to do with us?"

Archer's expression changes slowly. It's mostly in his eyes that narrow as if in confusion and his furrowed eyebrows.

"He didn't tell you?" he asks.

"Tell me what?"

His smile gets wider.

"My, oh, my." His chuckle is sinister. "The fucker is secretive, isn't he?"

"Tell me what, Archer?" I press on, saying his name for the first time. And the memory of how we used to be flickers for a brief moment in the back of my mind.

His grin turns into a smirk.

"That after the night that Droga took what was supposed to be mine—you—I taught him a lesson." He chuckles. "His sorry ass deserved the second-degree burns."

An icy cold feeling starts in my gut, twisting my insides. Blood rushes to my ears. But I need to hear it again. Just to make sure. Because that can't be.

"Taught him a lesson?" I murmur, frowning.

"Yeah, sweetie. Your pussy cost him his skin. And a wrestling career. I hope he thinks it was worth it."

He chuckles, and the sound of it makes my body shake. In disbelief and realization and hurt and guilt that rise in me like a powerful tide.

No-no-no-no-no.

What is he talking about?

"No." I shake my head in denial.

Can't be.

"Awe." Archer cocks his head to feign pity, tosses the cigarette away, and steps into me. He stretches his hand and strokes my cheek.

I jerk away. I want to cut his freaking hand off.

He only smiles. And I almost see a forked-tongue like that of a snake dart out of his mouth when he licks his lips.

"You didn't know. Precious," he purrs. "The day after the party, we had a giant bonfire." Archer's lips curl into a smirk as his smile fades. "After the fucking news that spread across the campus. The fucking idiots making memes of me. And your boy had the audacity to show up there to sort it out. The fucking nerve."

Archer's face is like a skull in the dim light of the flashlights. It's so close to me that I feel like he is going to swallow me. And I want to stab him in the eye.

"Yeah," he snarls. "We exchanged punches. I wanted to bury the fucker. But then he *accidentally*"—Archer chuckles as he accentuates the word—"fell into the bonfire."

The ground drops from under my feet, and I am free-falling.

I didn't know.

How could I?

All the rumors I heard afterward never mentioned that bonfire. Even Abby didn't say anything.

Kai...

His face floats across my mind, and I feel tears burn my eyes.

No-no-no.

I am begging Archer or life or whatever else there is to take those words back. To take those years back. That day. That night.

Because the knowledge is slowly ripping me into pieces.

"I'm glad we cleared this up. What a positive start."

Archer smiles, but his smile doesn't reach his eyes as he turns around and motions to his dogs.

One of them pushes me into my back, and we start walking. But I barely register anything around.

Katura pulls away from her escort and ducks her head to look me in the eyes. "Are you all right?"

I am not. I walk past her and keep walking, following the rest.

Nothing else matters—not Archer's promise to do to me whatever he wants, not the Westside, which is the last place I want to be—except for the realization that I've made a horrible mistake. That I could've fixed it all four years ago if I wasn't such a coward and so selfish.

My chest shakes as I try to suppress a sob.

But it's too late.

Tears start sliding down my cheeks. They are invisible in the dark, but they are as scorching as second-degree burns.

His burns.

I want to die right now. Fate is a bitch. Heartless. Ruthless. Unforgiving.

Dark emotions envelop me like a fog, making me dizzy as I stumble down the dark path across the hills.

Scars can be devastating. But guilt is all-consuming.

I'm sorry, Kai.

My heart clenches so tightly that it's hard to breathe.

I suppress a sob, but the tears are streaming. There is no way to stop them. There is no way to change anything or make his life better. Kai's scars are my doing.

"I'm sorry. I'm sorry. I'm sorry," I beg into darkness.

But the apology can't stitch together the years of hurting

and hating and drowning in shame with the realization that I was spared the worst at someone else's expense.

His.

The boy who once upon a time made my heart beat like nothing had done before.

Who in the last few weeks made it whole again and made me forget the awful feelings that haunted me for years.

Kai, I'm sorry.

But no amount of words can push away the sharp razors that slice my heart into pieces.

Because I can't tell him that.

He is not with me.

Because just like four years ago, he is left behind.

52

KAI

WE GRUNT AS WE CARRY BO DOWN TO THE DINING AREA. WE stumble and curse. Bo is heavy, and we are running out of time. His wound is bandaged with our shirts, but the blood is seeping through. Bo is silent, his head bobbing from side to side, and it's a bad fucking sign.

"Hold up, bro," I murmur as we approach the dining room.

The other goons are gone as quickly as they appeared. The air is bitter with the nasty smell of burned plastic and chemical from the foam.

Owen and Guff duck under our arms and help so we can carry Bo faster. They work like soldiers. We bring him to the table, other guys pick him up by his feet, and we carefully lay him down on the wooden table.

Maddy is already barking out orders, and the first-aid box is next to her.

There is a bucket of clean water.

There are bandages.

She works like a pro, the other girls setting the stuff from the medical cabinet down on the table.

I want to beat someone's face to a pulp as I stare at Bo's motionless body on that table, the girls already undoing the dirty shirts.

They talk some medical gibberish. Thank God for Maddy who is a doctor. *Was* supposed to be a doctor. She is as good at everything she does. Someone will fall in love with her one day.

I feel Ty's hand on my shoulder and clench my teeth.

"I'll fucking kill him," I hiss, thinking of the person I would like to annihilate right now.

Jeok motions for Owen to shine the flashlights onto Bo so that the girls have more light. "How is it looking?"

Maddy shakes her head. "Not good." She holds a syringe in her hand, shoots a tiny squirt of liquid into the air, and I hope for a fucking miracle. "We don't know yet," she adds. "But he might need a surgery, and I am not a surgeon."

I storm away, feeling like my heart will explode if I don't do something.

The brother that I had is fucking dying. And the girl I love has been taken away.

There is nothing I can do this very moment, and I feel so fucking helpless that I want to weep. There is a raging storm of emotions inside me. And they swirl like a tornado.

Instead, I roar as I stomp toward the beach, then whirl around, raking my hair.

I lift my head to the sky and roar again, like an angry animal.

Everyone I ever love eventually goes away.

My mother.

My father.

My sister.

Bo.

Callie.

It's like a fucking curse.

I go silent and pant, trying to calm. But the storm of emotions barrels through me again.

And then I feel it—tears running down my cheeks.

I can't help it. Because the anger is gone. And what is left is hurt. And the feeling of emptiness.

And I cry.

I am so fucking ashamed of myself, but I can't help it.

"Fuuuuuuck!" I shout to nothing in particular.

I stand in darkness for the longest time, trying to calm my breathing, when I feel a hand on my shoulder—this time it's small and soft.

The voice is as soft and almost deafening, pushing down my hurt like the sweetest fog. "It will be alright."

It's Maddy.

Fucking Maddy. There is so much compassion in her.

I rub my hands on my face to hide the tears and don't turn to look at her. But I feel so grateful there is someone in this moment of my pointless fucking life to offer the words.

I nod.

Emptiness is all around me and inside me. Suddenly, it's too quiet. Even the birds and insects went quiet at the unfolding tragedy.

Bo, don't do this to me.

We've lost our families. We've lost a few here on Zion. You think you get used to loss. Until a close friend goes, and it's devastating, rolling like a snowball with the previous losses. Until *loss* is this giant monster that sits on the edge of your bed every fucking night and stares at you with its empty eyes. And when you think you can drift to sleep, it raises its hand swiftly like an assassin and stabs you in the heart.

Again.

And again.

Maddy's hand pulls away, and I hear her footsteps disappear toward the dining room. A cigarette finds its way into my mouth. I light up and inhale so deeply that for that brief moment, there is nothing but the sensation of the smoke burning my lungs. It burns away the tears that start drying out.

Right now, I want to turn to Bo and say, "Here, bro," and pass him a joint and shoot shit about nothing.

More than anything, I want to wrap my arms around Callie and tell her that I will never let her out of my sight. That despite what happened, she's always been the one. I knew it the day she set her beautiful blue eyes on me. The day she smiled sweetly and stretched out her hand, saying, "I'm Callie."

Dwelling on the past is useless now.

The ocean waves lap softly at the shore. It's so peaceful in this fucking paradise that it's unbearable.

Everything that I've known for two years now reminds me of her though she's been here for less than two weeks. She is not here anymore, and I have to change that.

I turn around slowly.

Jeok, Ty, Owen, and others stand by the dining room and smoke, glancing in my direction.

They are my family. But they won't go with the crazy idea I have in my mind.

I meet Ty's eyes as I approach, and he looks away with guilt as if everything is his fault.

"I am going to the Westside," I blurt, walking past them and toward the workshop.

"Don't be stupid, Kai!" Ty calls behind me.

I don't stop.

He catches up, grabs me by the bicep, and whips me around.

"They have weapons. Manpower," he says.

"I have fucking weapons too," I hiss, jerking my arm out of his hold as I keep walking.

"You are not a fucking Rambo!" Ty shouts in my back.

I don't stop.

I'll be a fucking Rambo, Witcher, Deadpool, and whatever the fuck I need to be to take revenge on Crone and get my girl back.

By the time I storm into the workshop, my anger is a tamed beast, and I know exactly what I have to do.

I start opening the crates, one by one, and pulling the stash out. Knives. Handmade guns. Bullets. Tasers.

I have the inventory list, but I need a plan.

I've been here before—standing at ground zero, watching my life spiral downhill. What it taught me is that I have to get up and move my ass. And if I have to go through hell to get Callie back, I will. When I have her next to me, nothing else in this fucked-up world will matter.

I hear the door open, but I don't turn and keep setting the equipment on the floor in even rows.

The fucking Chancellor might have real guns and his goons. But nothing is like a man bound on revenge. And it will be cold by the time I get there. I knew I was on this fucking island for a reason.

The footsteps get louder and halt right behind me.

I stop what I'm doing and turn around.

Ty. Owen. Guff. Zach.

I hear more footsteps, and several other guys come in.

Fuck.

They will try to stop me, of course.

I straighten up, ready to fight if needed, ready to grab whatever I can and make my way to the other side.

The other guys cross their arms over their chests.

I meet Ty's eyes.

"We are in."

The words take me aback, and I stand frozen for a second.

"We are in, man," says Owen.

"Yeah, we are tired of this place," says Zach from the back row.

I still can't process what they mean when Ty's lips stretch in a tiny smile, but his eyes glow viciously. The fucker wants adventure.

And I want to kiss every single one of them.

On the mouth.

French kiss.

With heavy petting.

Because they are the shit.

My heart starts beating so heavily in my heart that it's hard to breathe.

I nod toward the pile of crates in the corner. "Ty, grab that crate. We need to go through it."

I turn away to face my stash on the ground, trying to hide a smile. Now with their help, we will go slowly and think everything over. We need a plan. But more than anything, I hide my eyes because they burn with tears.

God dammit. When did I get so fucking sensitive?

"I have enough guns to destroy a legion. Owen, do the ammo count."

I give orders, and they start moving. Like an army. They've been waiting for this for a long time. We are all tired of the Eastside.

"We will take revenge on Bo," Ty says from the corner of the room. "We'll show those fuckers." He brings a crate and sets it loudly on the desk next to me. "And we'll get your lady back."

I turn to meet his gaze, and the fucker winks at me, a smile tugging at the corner of his lips.

This very second, I love him so fucking much that I would blow him. I swear, that's how much his words mean to me.

And I am ready.

Ready to get the hell out of here.

Ready to meet face-to-face with the bastard who ruined my life.

But most importantly, I want Callie back.

Her face is the only one I see in my mind as I give more orders.

It's going to be a long night.

Followed by several long days.

We have to hurry.

But, goddamn, do I feel alive.

And it's her face again, smiling at me, her luminous blue eyes haunting me from across the island.

Callie Mays, it's always been you.

My heart pounds like a war drum.

Baby girl, I am coming to get you.

---

*If you enjoyed **OUTCAST** and would like to read*
Ty and Dani's love story,
please sign up to my newsletter
*to receive a FREE copy of **ANGEL, MINE**!*
www.authorlexiray.com

RUTHLESS PARADISE SERIES:

BOOK 1: **OUTCAST**

BOOK 2: **PETAL**

BOOK 3: **CHANCELLOR**

BOOK 4: **WILD THING**

BOOK 5: **RAVEN**

FROM THE AUTHOR:

Cheers to the WS where great ideas are born in amazing company.
Kisses for John and Dave for putting up with me.
Endless love to my bro, Alex, who has a brilliant mind and worked out the logistics of Ruthless Paradise.
Special shoutout to Kat who makes the strongest drinks—lady, I promised that you will be in one of my books (*wink).
And, of course, K. M.—babe, you are fire!

Printed in Great Britain
by Amazon